The
LINCOLN
Deception

Also By David O. Stewart

Nonfiction

The Summer of 1787: The Men Who Invented the Constitution

Impeached: The Trial of President Andrew Johnson and the Fight for Lincoln's Legacy

American Emperor: Aaron Burr's Challenge to Jefferson's America

The
LINCOLN
Deception

DAVID O. STEWART

KENSINGTON BOOKS
www.kensingtonbooks.com

Kensington Publishing Corp.
119 West 40th Street
New York, NY 10018

All Kensington titles, imprints, and distributed lines are available at special quantity discounts for bulk purchases for sales promotion, premiums, fund-raising, and educational or institutional use.

Special book excerpts or customized printings can also be created to fit specific needs. For details, write or phone the office of the Kensington Special Sales Manager: Kensington Publishing Corp., 119 West 40th Street, New York, NY 10018. Attn. Special Sales Department. Phone: 1-800-221-2647.

Kensington and the K logo Reg. U.S. Pat. & TM Off.

ISBN-13: 978-0-7582-9067-0
ISBN-10: 0-7582-9067-5
First Kensington Trade Paperback Printing: September 2013

ISBN-13: 978-0-7582-9068-7
ISBN-10: 0-7582-9068-3
First Kensington Electronic Edition: September 2013

10 9 8 7 6 5 4 3
Printed in the United States of America

To my father, who loved history, and a good mystery

Chapter 1

"I've been recalling Mrs. Surratt," the old man said. "A perfect she-lion, she was." His blue eyes glinted briefly, then faded to a vague, watery look.

Leaning over the bed, Dr. Jamie Fraser placed his stethoscope against the old man's narrow chest. The heartbeat was feathery. Fluid rasped in the lungs. Always slender, John Bingham seemed to have shrunk further. Nothing in particular was killing the most distinguished man ever produced by Cadiz, Ohio. After eighty-five years of life, he was wearing out. In 1900, not many in eastern Ohio lived long enough to wear out. Bingham had been tougher than he looked. Emma Bingham, who shared the big house on Main Street with her father, hovered on the other side of the bed.

"Mrs. Surratt?" the doctor ventured. "She was the one involved in killing Lincoln?"

The old man shook his head slightly. "Jamie," he breathed. "Someday you must learn about the world around you. It was the greatest crime of our age. It ranks with the murder of Julius Caesar."

"Of course you're right, sir, but as soon as I sit down with a worthy book or magazine, I inevitably receive a message that some thoughtless creature like Mrs. McDade over in Hopedale has gone into labor, and off I go."

"Or some old duffer like me takes his own sweet time about dying."

"Rest, sir," Fraser said in his warmest professional tone, "that's what you need. Spring is coming, though there's not much feel of the season out there. By the time the tulips are up, you'll be back out on your front porch, admiring the butterflies and greeting your friends."

"That's a poor lie," the old man said, "to a man who soon will meet his maker." He turned his eyes back to the doctor. "There's no risk I'll meet Mrs. Surratt."

Fraser dropped into the chair on his side of the sickbed. "They hanged her, didn't they? Was there any injustice in it?"

Bingham showed a trace of a smile. "Barely the beginning of justice." He stirred and frowned. "Can my head be higher?"

Emma stacked pillows and bolsters behind him, her narrow face yellow in the kerosene light. Fraser preferred the brightness of his new gaslights, but the old man probably couldn't afford the innovation. Mr. Bingham's treasures from Japan had long since vanished, sold to support his two daughters and grandson. When the patient leaned back on the imposing structure of supporting cushions, his head was nearly upright. He asked for a cup of broth. Expelling a quick breath that might have been exasperation, Emma left.

"There was a week that summer," he began, "a hellish one. We had in hand the verdicts for all eight of those wretches in Booth's conspiracy. But the judgments, you see, couldn't be announced until President Johnson approved them." He coughed shallowly and closed his eyes. After a small sigh, he resumed, his eyes bright again. "It was hot. Washington is the veriest inferno in summer. That prison held the heat perfectly, like sitting inside a brick oven.

"I was called to Mrs. Surratt's chamber, a complaint of her daughter. After hearing the girl out—she was rather hysterical, a pale whelp of the original she-lion—I informed her I couldn't help. It was something about food, nothing to do with me as prosecutor."

Fraser nodded, pleased by Bingham's sudden energy and the subject of his conversation. Bingham rarely talked about his public career. He preferred to inquire about other people's business or to hold forth on current affairs. Fraser knew the basics about the old gentleman that everyone in Cadiz knew. He had prosecuted the Lincoln conspirators, securing convictions of all eight and death sentences for four. He wrote the Fourteenth Amendment to the Constitution, led the effort to impeach President Andrew Johnson, and for twelve years was the U.S. Ambassador to Japan. Fraser wished he knew more about the Lincoln case.

The old man picked up his story. "Mrs. Surratt sat there, perfectly composed in that heat, monstrous in her lack of remorse. All that was missing were snakes sprouting from her head. She told the daughter to leave us. 'Mr. Bingham,' said she, 'the verdicts are in, are they not?' I assured her I could make no statement on the matter. 'We are to be hanged,' she said, 'are we not?' Again, I said I could say nothing. 'I don't think that very Christian of you,' she went on. 'I suppose we will be told soon enough.' "

Bingham paused, his eyes straying into the middle distance. He shifted toward Fraser. "Then began the most remarkable exchange." The old man shook his head. "What she told me. You must understand, I was no babe in arms. I was in Congress during vicious times before the war. As Judge Advocate General, I prosecuted our disloyal men. I knew the horrors of the bloodiest war man has fought, of the horrors of which the human spirit is capable. And yet that woman unsettled my very soul.

"Afterward, I went to Stanton." Fraser knew about Edwin Stanton, from nearby Steubenville, who had been Lincoln's rock, the redoubtable Secretary of War. "I never saw that great good man so vexed as when I related Mrs. Surratt's confession." Bingham's eyes drifted again to the far wall. The memory seemed to seize his entire attention.

"Finally, we agreed," Bingham added slowly. "Her confession was too . . . terrible. To reveal it would be to risk the survival of the republic."

Fraser wasn't sure he heard correctly. "Sir, the survival of the republic?" He used a coaxing tone. What could Bingham mean? What secret part of the assassination plot, what beyond the murder of the martyr-president had held the power to destroy the nation?

Bingham's eyelids slowly descended. His jaw went slack. He sagged back onto the massed pillows and his breath became shallow. Disappointed that the story had petered out, Fraser reminded himself that sleep was good for Mr. Bingham.

With a clatter, Emma placed a tray on a nearby table. Her father didn't stir. Fraser placed his stethoscope in his black bag and rose to leave.

The next evening, Emma met the doctor at the door with a fretful look. As Fraser peeled off his coat, damp from a punishing sleet, she explained that her father slept much of the day, taking only a piece of dry toast and some water. Reverend McGregor from United Presbyterian had stopped in, but the old man had not known him. Fraser took her hands. "Let me have a look," he said quietly. She led him into the sickroom.

The weak blue eyes opened when he called the old man's name.

"Hello, Jamie," he said. "Nice to see you." With a quick movement, Emma placed a balled-up handkerchief to her mouth. She sat again on the hard chair across the bed from the doctor. "Dear child," Bingham said to her, "our Savior will watch over me. And I have no pain."

"Will you have tea, Father? Some toast?"

"If I must."

Emma smiled and patted his arm. "I'll get them while Jamie keeps you company."

As she left, Fraser drew his stethoscope from his black bag.

"Must you?" Bingham asked.

"It is," Fraser answered, "what I am supposed to do."

"Emma's idea is better. Keep me company. How did Mrs. McDade fare?"

Fraser reported the delivery of a new daughter to the Mc-Dades of Hopedale. For the last year, births had not been entirely happy events for the doctor. His mind always returned to the death of his wife, Ginny, in their own house. Grieving for their little son, who lay cold and still in his arms, he had been slow to notice Ginny's weakening, her bleeding mostly internal. Her life slipped away while he—her physician-husband—feverishly applied packing and douches to no good end. He had sent the midwife for old Doc Marcotte, but it was too late. He lost them both. Fraser still gave thanks to God for every birth, but he could never suppress his resentment over the careless way He took Ginny and his baby.

The catastrophe strengthened Fraser's tie with Bingham. The old man took the new widower in hand. For two days, he shielded Fraser from the well-meaning people who came to call. Then Bingham made him wash and shave, dress decently, and face the world. Combining stern words with a vibrant sympathy that dwelt in those deep-set eyes, the old man brought Fraser back from the darkness.

Not all the way back, though. Part of Jamie remained in that room with Ginny and the baby—helpless, blundering, stupid, unmanned by innocent death.

After Fraser described the raw mid-March weather to Bingham, they fell into silence. The doctor could not restrain himself.

"Sir," he began, "last night you mentioned an interview you had with Mrs. Surratt, just before her hanging. I read a bit about the case this morning and remembered your description of her as so fierce. A she-lion, you said. She was portrayed far differently at the time."

"I suppose you were looking at Townsend's little volume? Ah, she fooled a great many, even old Gath." He smiled slightly. "But she knew she hadn't fooled me. So on that day she didn't even try."

"You mentioned a confession," Fraser said, "the one you discussed with Mr. Stanton. Well, sir, I was . . . I wondered if perhaps now, after so many years, it would be well to get it out? Why, after all, did she confess if not to have it known?"

"Ah, Jamie, you're exactly right. She wanted it known. Even from the grave, she meant to continue her evil mischief against our poor nation. That was why Stanton and I would never reveal it." After a pause, Bingham said, "I gave my word. Stanton took the secret to the grave. So shall I."

A few days later, to honor John Bingham's passing, a thousand people and more crushed into the Harrison County courthouse, a great stone temple that crowned the central hill of Cadiz. Businesses closed and every lawyer and Union Army veteran from three counties streamed into town. The mourners overflowed into side rooms and corridors where they could neither hear nor see.

The service was long, as befitted a man of such distinction. The condolence messages had poured in, beginning with one from President McKinley, a cousin of some description. Reverend McGregor would not be satisfied with less than an hour's oration, having delivered a speech almost as long during the family service that morning. Seated at the front as a pallbearer, Fraser found himself wondering, uncharitably, about the black-clad figures of the two Bingham daughters. Small and slim like their father, they had his haunted, sunken eye sockets. Yet they somehow had missed his spirit and grace. On him, the great eyes conveyed a depth of soul; on them, they called to mind the raccoon family.

For fifteen years, since returning from Japan, the old gentleman was a paternal presence Fraser had not known before. Bingham had been a good friend to Fraser's father, Captain Robert Fraser of the 30th Ohio, who returned from the Civil War an empty husk. He had fallen to fever in the swamps near Vicksburg and never really recovered. Recurring bouts of illness sapped his body and spirit for the few more years he had, pretending to run the family's dry goods store.

Fraser, born months after his father marched off to war, had tried to imagine his father as a vital leader of men. As a boy, he gazed at the daguerreotype of the handsome captain of the 30th Ohio. Now, Fraser resembled the man in that frame, tall and sandy haired, with broad shoulders, not at all like the distantly remembered parent with a wracking cough and no energy.

For years, Fraser's mind held only the piercing gaze of that young soldier in the gilt frame. After losing Ginny and the baby, that image faded. In its place came a long-suppressed memory of a slender man whose gentle gaze made Fraser feel awkward when it fell on him. On cold days, the man sat by a wood stove in the store, a blanket over his legs, while Jamie's mother sold sheets and towels, cloth and thread, ready-to-wear jackets and work pants, even delicate items for ladies. Sometimes an old man or two sat with his father, but the boy didn't. He ran errands for his mother or hurried off with friends, escaping the invalid who seemed to haunt the store. The revived memory hurt. Fraser had been too young to know the Union soldier, and too ashamed to know the ailing husk who came in his place.

Bingham showed a special interest in young Jamie, smoothing his way when he became Dr. James Fraser. In Cadiz, being John Bingham's doctor was a sure ticket to medical and social acceptance. Sometimes Bingham had remembered the vital Captain Fraser, who shared his passions for ending slavery, for the Republican Party, and for the novels of Sir Walter Scott. That man had driven Bingham to political meetings, sometimes using his bulk to shield the fiery young congressmen from those who feared the end of slavery would mean the end of the nation. For Fraser, it was like hearing about a stranger.

When the memorial service concluded, the crowd began to shuffle by Bingham's coffin in a ragged file. At either end of the open casket, uniformed veterans of the Grand Army of the Republic stood at attention. Fraser stepped quickly out of the building. He needed air.

Looking over the hills under a cloud-mottled sky, he felt the hint of a warmer season. The shops and houses marched downhill in each direction, fading after a few blocks into tidy farms. He thought again, with a surge of emotion, of what he had lost. First his father, later his mother, then Ginny and the baby, now Mr. Bingham. He felt empty. Yet the story of Mrs. Surratt's confession lingered in his mind. Why had the old man told him about it without revealing what her confession was?

"Care for a nip?" Charles Nugent, a fellow pallbearer, nudged him. "Still cool, ain't it?"

"That's a kindness," Fraser said, accepting a metal flask of corn whiskey. After taking a swallow, and a second one, he added, "That's got some backbone."

"John preferred it that way."

"Charles, you were as close a friend as Mr. Bingham had."

"We got on. He wasn't quite the saint that Reverend McGregor would have him, but I've never known as fine a man."

"Nor I," Fraser said quickly. "But I've wondered, in the times you were together, did he talk much about the Lincoln trial, about Mrs. Surratt?"

"Oh, now and again, when something would come out from some Democrat still angry about the war, trying to stir up the flames again. You know how they say the trial was unfair or that the Surratt woman was innocent. He might pass a remark on it."

"Did he ever say he knew something about her that these other people, these ones doing the complaining, didn't know?"

"Not that I recollect. You know, Jamie, I don't believe John lost a minute's sleep over that case. Not so I could see. He was proud of sending those villains to the gallows. I think he would've liked to hang all of them."

Fraser nodded. He hunched his shoulders against a cold gust. "I should get back inside."

To Fraser's eye, close to half the crowd had filed past the coffin, gazing respectfully at the old man in whom they took such pride. Fraser assumed a formal stance at the spot where the line turned away from the coffin, the point where some broke their silence and murmured to a neighbor. Cheeks were damp, hard features clenched against strong feelings. Mr. Bingham had touched many. Fraser was stirred by the visible grief.

A man with a café-au-lait complexion stood at the coffin. During the ceremony, the colored mourners had gathered in a side room. Bingham stood high in the area's small Negro community. His opposition to slavery before the war had propelled him into the fight for the rights of the freed slaves after it. If the colored mourners were reaching the coffin, Fraser thought, the line must be nearing its end.

The man wore a black woolen suit that would look well on any lawyer or merchant. His collar was high, starched, and a brilliant white. A silver watch chain dangled across his waist-coat. When he turned toward Fraser, his eyes were glassy, but his movements were sure. He looked familiar, but Fraser couldn't place him. His hair had early flecks of gray, as did his thick mustache. He passed close to Fraser, leading several other Negro mourners.

Turning back to the line, Fraser was surprised to find white people still inching toward the coffin. The rest of Harrison County's colored weren't even in view yet. The man in black had been far ahead of his turn.

The Union Army veterans, wearing the faded uniforms they had cherished for thirty-five years, took charge of the burial. Fraser thought of the American soldiers again fighting and dying, this time in the Philippines, halfway around the world.

The veterans bore the coffin to the hearse and escorted it to the hillside cemetery, where they fired a three-volley military salute. Fraser lingered at the graveside after the ceremony, then drove his gig to his silent, empty home.

Chapter 2

The door to the big house swung open to reveal Emma Bingham. Two days after the funeral, she still looked worn.

"Oh, Jamie," she said with a small nod. She had pinned up her dark hair, but stray tendrils hung untended. The rims of her large eyes, inflamed by weeping, glowed red. Like any doctor, Fraser saw grief on a regular basis, but he had never grown easy with it. He shifted on his feet in the front hall, wishing to comfort Emma, yet also wishing to be somewhere else.

"Will you see to your things?" Emma gestured to a coat rack mounted on the wall. Mr. Bingham's topcoat still hung there.

The married sister, Marie, waited for them in the parlor. She seemed in better spirits than Emma. Having a son and husband, even a ne'er-do-well husband, could provide emotional ballast. Also, Marie was always the bolder of the sisters.

"Dr. Fraser," Marie began after he sat. "As you might imagine, we have to deal with many realities following Father's passing. This great house, which we cannot afford—which *Father* could not afford. All these things here. Through a long life one gathers many items, but Father was the most determined pack rat. Circulars for patent medicine, absurd items torn from newspapers, invoices from haberdashers, all were for him equally deserving of preservation—"

"Marie," Emma broke in, her gaze toward the floor but her jaw set, "Father was a man of history. His papers are important." She lifted her eyes to Fraser. "Jamie, we have wondered if we could ask you to go through Father's business papers—not the family letters, of course—and help organize them. Marie may be right. Many items may be of no real interest, but others doubtless are and should be saved. You know, there was his time in Congress, his time in Japan, his time in the army, his law practice, oh, so much."

"Yes," Marie said briskly. "Emma and I are not students of history, so we would appreciate your help. Also, I must return to my family and Emma, well, dear Emma never really makes any progress through Father's papers, now, do you, dear?" Emma stared at her hands in her lap. She bit her lower lip.

"I would consider it an honor to assist you," Fraser said, surprised by how interested he was. He might have to schedule his patients around this effort, but he felt sure he could. Few presented true emergencies. "Of course, I wouldn't presume to dispose of any papers. Perhaps I could sort them into categories that we might agree on. You could determine where they should go after that."

"Oh, would you, Jamie?" Emma lifted her head. "Marie is right, of course. He retained many items of little importance, and I find it so sad to look through even them. I would feel far worse, though, if we disposed of something that might be significant."

"By any chance," Fraser tried to keep any eagerness out of his voice, "are there papers from the trial of the Lincoln conspirators?"

"Oh my, yes," Marie said, "as well as from every alderman's election in the eight counties of his congressional district, every piece of tariff legislation that was ever proposed, and every postmaster appointment in eastern Ohio since 1855. Why don't we step into the library so you can see the size of the task?"

Following the two women, Fraser paused at the threshold of Bingham's work room. It looked as though a violent tide had swept in and quickly ebbed, leaving behind it the detritus of a life. Papers piled on the desk, a small table, and several armchairs. At least a dozen wooden crates stood in the room's far corner, more papers visible through their slats.

"R-r-r-eally," he stammered out. "I had no idea . . ." He hovered at the doorway, leery of the maelstrom's residue.

"Father was a conscientious correspondent," Emma said with a mix of pride and sadness. "Perhaps if you started next week, I would be better able to assist you. We could work together in the evenings. I could prepare supper for us."

Fraser wondered for a moment whether Emma, at least fifteen years older than he and still unmarried, viewed their age differential in the same way he did. He put the thought out of his mind. The woman was over fifty.

He edged warily into the room. His hand fell on some papers on a side table and he lifted the top sheet. It was dated 1868 and was signed . . . the signature was difficult. He looked at the attached envelope.

"This is from General Grant," he said. "In his own hand?"

Emma smiled. "Oh, yes, the general and Father were quite close."

Still holding the precious letter, Fraser cast his eye around the room, feeling a thrill at what might lie buried in these paper towers. Personal notes from presidents like Lincoln and Garfield, Hayes and McKinley. The last three were Ohio Republicans like Bingham. Or from leaders like Stanton or Secretary of State William Seward or Chief Justice Salmon P. Chase, or from soldiers like Grant or Sherman. And perhaps the key to the secret told by Mrs. Surratt.

* * *

From their first sortie into Mr. Bingham's library, Fraser and Emma fell into a pattern. He arrived at five in the evening and began on papers she had arranged in rough chronological order. He sorted them by broad topics, such as family, Congress, antislavery efforts, and law practice. He kept separate piles of the correspondence with each of the great men of Mr. Bingham's time. They ate at 6:30, then continued working until 9.

Sometimes uncertain of the significance of a sheet before him, Fraser wished he had read more widely. In a pile of books he found a new volume titled "Who's Who in America," which helped with more recent letters. To interpret documents from earlier periods, Fraser scoured the library for other works that could help him. That was when he found the shelf devoted to the Lincoln assassination and those who had conspired against the president. There were books, newspaper cuttings, letters, magazine articles, and two trial transcripts, one from the trial of Mrs. Surratt and the other seven men, and one from the later, separate trial of Mrs. Surratt's son.

With Emma's permission, Fraser began to borrow books on the Booth conspiracy. He read them at home late into the night, drinking coffee at his kitchen table. Since Ginny's death, he slept in the sitting room, avoiding their bedroom and its ghosts, but the ghosts could find him in other rooms. Ginny was the sixth of eight in the hardworking Mosser clan, a farm family that spread through Harrison County. He had just delivered a crusading talk on vaccination to the local Grange. Accepting a coffee from a young woman almost his height, he was brought up short by the merry look in her eyes.

"What?" he blurted.

She cocked a hip and tilted her head to the side. "How long did you practice that speech?"

His face burned. She leaned closer, her tray between them, a curious eyebrow raised. He started to laugh despite his embarrassment. "Was it that bad?" he asked.

She turned away without answering, throwing him a grin over her shoulder. He could still see her there. How could that moment capture him so? Right then he wondered if she was the one. Now he knew there would be no other.

After only a few days with Mr. Bingham's papers, Fraser began to agree with sister Marie that most of them could be burnt without disappointing future historians. The work became drudgery, little wheat and abundant chaff. His late-night hours with the assassination volumes, however, were entirely different. He marveled at how much wasn't known about the crime, even thirty-five years later. The questions about the conspiracy ignited parts of his brain that had grown dull with the loss of Ginny and the routine of medical practice.

How did Booth find his many coconspirators? Why was Lincoln so unguarded in a public theater during a war? How had Booth found his escape route and remained free for so long after the assassination? Had Booth decided on his own to kill the president, or was he sponsored by others? Here were mysteries to solve, ones that had confounded many before him. But Fraser knew something that those earlier investigators hadn't. He knew about Mrs. Surratt's confession to Mr. Bingham. He itched to find answers to at least some of the questions.

Always an early riser, Fraser began to read about the assassination in the mornings, too. The conspiracy was never far from his mind. While driving his buggy to a patient's farm, he puzzled over Booth's escape. As thousands of Union soldiers scoured southern Maryland for him, the assassin was at large for twelve days. During solitary lunches at his kitchen table, Fraser tried to imagine Booth's character. An assassin, Fraser thought, should be anonymous and melt readily into a crowd. Yet Booth was a celebrity, handsome and flamboyant, a stage performer and a member of the nation's most famous theatrical family.

His father had been a matinee idol, as were two of his brothers. Not many Americans were as conspicuous as John Wilkes Booth was in 1865. And what of his shabby accomplices? Far from being Booth's peers, most could not have appeared in polite society.

After a week of immersion in the facts of the case, Fraser felt he was on a first-name basis with the central players in the tragedy. He resolved to organize what he knew, to shape it into a full picture of the terrible events surrounding April 14, 1865, when Booth sneaked into the theater and shot Lincoln from behind. Fraser began taking notes. He constructed a chronological list of important events, plus a separate list of each conspirator and witness, recording their qualities and histories.

Fraser learned to mistrust the yellow, brittle newspaper stories about the conspiracy. They were too often wrong or incomplete. He pored over the transcript of the first trial, held before a commission of nine army officers. The transcript should include the most complete information, incorporating evidence and argument from both sides. He took pride in reading Mr. Bingham's fiery speeches, especially his closing address. With his soaring command of the language, Mr. Bingham roasted the contemptible criminals before him. Fraser imagined his friend's eye flashing with righteous rage as he demanded the ultimate punishment.

The assassination began to take shape in his mind as a planetary system with the charismatic Booth at its center. Raised in the border state of Maryland, Booth became devoted to the cause of the South even though the rest of his family was solidly pro-Union.

In Booth's planetary system, four conspirators revolved most closely around the actor. They were the ones who were in on the dirty work of the fateful night. First came Booth's escort, the weasely Davey Herold, a hunter and outdoorsman.

Herold met Booth after the assassin slew Lincoln, then slashed an army officer sitting with the president, then leaped to the stage shouting, *"Sic semper tyrannis!"* ("Thus always to tyrants!")—Virginia's motto and Booth's rationale for his butchery. For almost two weeks, Herold shepherded the assassin through southern Maryland and Virginia, concealing him from the thousands hunting him.

Next was the furious monster who went by the name of Lewis Paine. Large and powerful, Paine was the only conspirator with battlefield experience. He tore the heart out of the family of Secretary of State Seward. Wielding a long, vicious knife, Paine ripped open Seward's face and arm, stabbed a male nurse and one of Seward's sons, and broke the skull of his other son. Leaving a home drenched with the blood of four ravaged men, Paine slid into the shadows of the Washington night, evading capture for three days.

The third was the pathetic Atzerodt, a German immigrant. Sent to kill Vice President Andrew Johnson in his hotel room, the goateed waterman tried to stoke his courage with liquor but never even confronted his target. Atzerodt slunk off to Germantown, Maryland, where he was tracked down and arrested.

The fourth conspirator close to Booth was the most unusual one, a widow fifteen years older than the others. Mrs. Mary Surratt was not part of the killing. In Andrew Johnson's words, she "kept the nest that hatched the egg" of assassination. Photographs showed her as sternly handsome, framed in dark hair. Her boarding house in Northwest Washington was the physical heart of the plot, the rendezvous site for Booth, Atzerodt, Paine, and her son, John Harrison Surratt. The facilitator's role was familiar for her. Until the autumn of 1864, her tavern in southern Maryland served as a depot for Confederate spies and blockade runners. Indeed, her son, John, though only twenty-one, was a Confederate courier for the last two years of the war, carrying messages for spymasters in Richmond. Mrs. Surratt also stashed rifles and whiskey for Booth for his flight through southern Maryland.

Those four—Herold, Paine, Atzerodt, and Mrs. Surratt—were hanged after the military commission pronounced them guilty.

Two other conspirators figured in Booth's getaway. Ned Spangler held Booth's horse at the theater while the actor shot the president. Dr. Samuel Mudd sheltered the assassin during his flight, treated his broken ankle, and lied about both when questioned.

The last two conspirators—Samuel Arnold and Michael O'Laughlen—had the least connection to the fateful night. Both were part of Booth's initial plan, hatched in the fall of 1864, to kidnap Lincoln and trade him for Confederate prisoners of war, or even to use Lincoln as a bargaining chip to end the war. When the kidnapping plot failed in mid-March 1865, it mutated into one to kill the president and other top Union officials. O'Laughlen was at the house of Secretary of War Edwin Stanton on the night before the assassination, and was with Booth the next day. The prosecutors accused him of aiming to kill General Grant but presented little evidence to support the accusation.

Samuel Arnold's connection was thinnest of all. Like O'Laughlen, he was part of the original kidnapping plot. Eighteen days before the assassination, Arnold urged Booth to abandon all plans against Lincoln. No evidence placed Arnold in Washington on April 14.

The four lesser conspirators—Arnold, O'Laughlen, Spangler, and Mudd—went to prison at the pestilential Fort Jefferson in the Dry Tortugas, a sweltering hole surrounded by the Gulf of Mexico. O'Laughlen died of fever there. In early 1869, President Johnson pardoned and released the other three.

One prominent conspirator was never convicted. Following

the assassination, young John Surratt sped to Canada, where Catholic priests hid him. With more priestly assistance, Surratt reached Vatican City in Rome where he enlisted in the Papal Zouaves, a contingent of guards. When a fellow Marylander revealed Surratt's presence to American diplomats, he fled to Egypt. He was seized on an Alexandria dock in late 1866, still wearing the baggy trousers and brocade jacket of his Zouave uniform. Tried in a Washington, DC, federal court, not before a military commission, Surratt won a hung jury and went free when the government declined to try him again. Newspaper articles attributed the jury deadlock to pro-Southern sympathies. Fraser could think of no better explanation.

The key witness at both trials was Louis Weichmann, a young friend of John Surratt's who boarded at Mrs. Surratt's house on H Street, east of Seventh Street. Weichmann described meetings among the conspirators at the house, particularly between Booth and Mrs. Surratt. The friendship between those two intrigued Fraser. What did the dashing young actor have in common with the Catholic widow in her early forties? Yet she seemed to be Booth's closest confidante among the conspirators. The others were beneath Booth. Atzerodt and Herold were no more than toadies. Lewis Paine represented brute force. Fraser imagined that Mrs. Surratt and her son dealt with Booth as equals, perhaps owing to their shared connection with the Confederate secret service.

Late one night, seated in his kitchen with a cold cup of coffee before him, reading yet another book on the conspiracy, Fraser returned to an idea that gnawed at him. During the trial, Mr. Bingham repeatedly claimed that the Confederate government was behind the assassination, but he never backed up the accusation. After the trial, critics scoffed at Mr. Bingham's claim. Fraser decided that was the most important question. Was Booth's planetary system part of an even larger system? Was Booth doing the bidding of others?

If Fraser could figure that out, he could vindicate Mr. Bingham. Fraser would like to do that, but there was more to it. Working on the assassination, he felt something he couldn't remember feeling: that he was part of the cause his father died for. Having tasted that feeling, he hungered for more of it.

Chapter 3

⁓

Careening along ten miles of bad roads from Cadiz to Adena, Fraser mused that it was too nice a day to lose a leg. Spring had finally come to eastern Ohio, but in the coal mines every season was dangerous. The telegram said: MINE ACCIDENT. LEG CRUSHED. COME SOONEST. Please, he silently asked the god of spring, make it below the knee. He shouted for the horse to pull harder up the hill. He didn't like to use the stick, but he did like to go fast, and now he had to. "Hah," he cried. "Hup! Hup!"

The mine, a new one, was east of Adena. The line of miners' shacks was uphill from the gash in the earth that swallowed the men every morning. He pulled up at a cabin where people spilled out the door and into the road, just before the mine works. A man reached for the horse's halter.

"Don't let him eat the grass," Fraser called. The soot-covered growth could foul the animal's digestion for days. He unloaded his regular bag and his surgical bag, the one with the saw and chloroform mask. His surgical tools were no better, he thought with disgust, than those used in the time of Mary Surratt and John Wilkes Booth.

At six feet tall, Fraser loomed over the miners and their families. Their clothes, all in shades of gray, hung from gaunt frames. Their skin and hair had a smudgy, subterranean look. He nodded greetings to those he passed, not pausing to shake hands. He could hardly perform surgery after shaking hands that were never clean.

"I'm Dr. Fraser from Cadiz," he said at the door, but they knew who he was.

"John Evans, Doctor." Several stepped aside for a wiry man with a thick brush of curly hair. He strode from the opening to a rear room. The air in the shack was moist, the smells sour.

"Mr. Evans." Fraser looked round for what he would need. Two chairs, a basin. The table was too small. Water was heating on a coal-fired stove. "The patient?"

"My brother Lew," the man said, leading him into the darkened room.

Fraser followed and knelt next to the bed. He reached for the arm of Lew Evans. It was cold. The man shivered and his pulse was weak. "Hello, Doc," he said. "Did it up right this time." His breath smelled of whiskey, the only painkiller at hand.

"Timber came down," his brother explained, "square on the leg."

"I'll have to pull aside the linen," Fraser said.

Lew Evans nodded. "Can you save it?"

Fraser thought a quick thanks. The timber had pulverized the left leg, but at the shinbone. "You'll have your knee, Mr. Evans, and with some practice you'll dance again. But right now"—Fraser shifted to look into the man's face—"I need to get you into the front room where I can work." He gripped the man's shoulder. "You look tough enough for this."

Fraser instructed the brother to clear the house, borrow another table for the front room so they could stretch the patient out, and start water boiling in neighbor houses. "We've done that, sir." Fraser had not noticed the woman who spoke. She had a determined look. "We have sheets to drape the table."

"Fine," he said. "You can assist me? It won't bother you?"

She nodded.

It took almost an hour. A skilled surgeon, one who had done more than the six amputations Fraser had done, might have completed it in half the time. The woman, Mrs. Llewellyn Evans, followed instructions. She didn't flinch. Though she was as thin as the rest, her hands were strong. Lew Evans, he thought, was a lucky man. In some ways.

Fraser left laudanum with her, with careful instructions about the dosage. When he stepped from the house, the tension began to fall away. He wanted to sit down but saw no seat. He leaned against the wall of the cabin. Aware of the bloodstains on his cuff, he looked at the knot of men in the road.

"Where's the company now?" one was saying. "Evans is a foreman, one of their best, and can they be bothered to see how they've maimed him?"

"Ach, they'll maim us or kill us all, then ship in a load of hunkies and niggers to do the work for less."

The group fell quiet as they noticed Fraser. John Evans detached himself from it. "Will my brother be all right?"

"I think so. It'll take some weeks to heal. He'll need crutches, and then a prosthetic leg—he should be able to tolerate one. There's a man in Akron who's good with them."

"And what does that cost?" the brother asked.

"It depends, Mr. Evans. Let me write down his name."

They walked to Fraser's gig. While Fraser wrote, Evans said in a low voice, "We can't pay today, Doc. We have only scrip on the company store. But I'll speak with them tomorrow about turning my pay over to you."

"Please, Mr. Evans," Fraser said, "please do no such thing.

You and your brother have cares enough. Please call on me if he doesn't recover well."

"God bless you," the man said. Fraser shook his hand.

The horse chose the pace going home while the Evans family inhabited Fraser's mind. Lew Evans couldn't afford the artificial leg. If he could find work on one leg, he might live longer and healthier than if he had remained a miner with two. But if he found no work, the children would have to support the family. Mrs. Evans must already take in washing or sewing or do whatever she could. He blew out a long breath. He couldn't save them from their lives.

About halfway home, Fraser's thoughts cycled back to the Lincoln case. There must have been a wider conspiracy beyond Booth's ragtag crew. Mr. Bingham prosecuted the eight conspirators on the theory that the Confederate government organized and financed the plot. Three star witnesses testified that high Confederates approved the plot. On that theory, Confederate President Jefferson Davis was arrested and imprisoned for almost two years.

Yet two of those star witnesses proved to be liars. Mr. Bingham had saved news stories about a congressional inquiry that revealed their perjury. The government, its case compromised, released Davis and never brought him to trial.

This had Fraser thinking in circles and around corners. That Mr. Bingham relied on perjured testimony was disturbing. Yet the man from Cadiz had been thoroughly unmoved by the revelations that his witnesses were liars. To his dying day, as Fraser knew, Mr. Bingham considered the conspirators incontestably guilty. The old man's conscience was easy over their fates.

After reaching home, Fraser had a supper of bread and cheese, then spread his notes across the table. He wanted to review the different conspiracy theories for the assassination. He didn't really buy any of them.

He started with the obvious question, *cui bono*—who benefits? Who benefitted from Lincoln's death? The ready answer
was Andrew Johnson, who vaulted into the presidency when
Lincoln died. So was Johnson behind Booth's plot? Booth had
called on the vice president at his hotel on the day before the assassination; Johnson was not in, so Booth left his card with the
hotel clerk. And on the fateful evening of April 14, no actual attempt was made on Johnson's life, though George Atzerodt
was assigned to kill him. Was Atzerodt acting out a ruse designed to draw attention away from Johnson's role as criminal
mastermind?

Some claimed that Johnson's performance as president rein-
forced this theory. Johnson had battled against Reconstruction,
straining to preserve the South in largely the same condition it
had been before the war except for the end of slavery. He supported new techniques for oppressing the former slaves, deny-
ing them voting rights and legal rights and land. Why not a plot
between the Confederacy and Johnson to give the South a vic-
torious peace?

A congressional committee, stuffed with Johnson's political
enemies, had inquired deeply into this theory and come up
empty-handed. No connections could be found between Johnson and the Confederacy. Although Johnson governed in a
stunningly pro-Southern fashion after the war, he fiercely op-
posed the Confederacy during the fighting. It was simply Johnson's good luck that his assigned assassin, Atzerodt, had no
stomach for the business.

Another theory proclaimed that the Roman Catholic Church
lurked behind Booth's plot. The Surratts were devout Cath-
olics, as was Dr. Mudd. When John Surratt fled after the assassination, Catholic priests concealed him in Canada and Europe.
Then he enlisted in the Papal Zouaves, a decidedly exotic desti-
nation for a young American in 1865. Yet that was all the evidence in support of the Catholic Church theory. Indeed, that

theory seemed to consist principally of a deep-seated hostility to the papacy. Those who blamed Andrew Johnson could at least point to superficially plausible motives: his own advancement and his postwar protection of the South. The Catholic Church theorists could recite no motive at all. What did the Pope or his minions stand to gain from the death of Abraham Lincoln?

The lone-madman theory, which Fraser liked no better, had been pronounced in two books by George Townsend, a writer honored by Mr. Bingham at a dinner in Cadiz only two years before. Fraser had liked Townsend well enough over dinner but found his books superficial. If Townsend was right that the assassination was the work of the mad genius Booth, then Mrs. Surratt could have made no shocking revelation to Mr. Bingham, because there was nothing to know beyond the incontestable—that Booth shot Lincoln.

Fraser resolved to apply a maxim from a Sherlock Holmes story: "When you have eliminated the impossible, whatever remains, however improbable, must be the truth." Though he loved the Holmes stories, he resented the portrayal of Dr. Watson as dim-witted. Fraser thought the habits of mind of medical men were well-matched to the disciplined investigation of a mystery. What is diagnosis but the solution of a mystery, often based on slender evidence?

He turned to the slippery question of motive. While a single assassin might be a madman, a conspiracy involves rational thought. Henchmen, even unappetizing ones, must be given reasons for joining a conspiracy, then must be coordinated intelligently.

The personal passions that can lead to murder—hate or greed—seemed not to fit the Lincoln case. Booth and his associates could have hated Lincoln, who was a hardfisted opponent dedicated to defeating the Confederacy. But surely the complex plot of April 14, with its multiple targets, embodied more than a simple act of hatred.

Fraser also doubted greed was the motive. A financial motive might grow out of the Northern blockade, which reduced Southerners to desperate schemes to smuggle cotton and tobacco past Union warships. A witness at the conspiracy trial said he spent days at the Surratt tavern in March 1865, waiting for cotton that Atzerodt was to sneak across the Potomac River. Although Fraser felt ill-equipped to evaluate such a commercial question, he did not see how material gain could justify the risks associated with killing the president. There were less dangerous ways to make money.

To Fraser, one feature of Booth's plot seemed most important: its breathtaking scope. Though Booth's coconspirators proved unequal to their tasks, the plan involved nothing less than the decapitation of the United States Government. The president was to die. So was the vice president, along with the Secretary of State and the senior general of the army. That was not the act of a deranged mind. Rather, it was a *policy.* Was the plot an act of war by the Confederate government? That had been Mr. Bingham's theory and he never abandoned it. The timing of the assassination weighed against it. The assassination occurred so late that it was hardly likely to save the Confederacy. Five days before, General Robert E. Lee surrendered the Army of Northern Virginia. Other Confederate armies were melting away, their soldiers headed home. Yet only the Confederate government had so strong an interest in striking that powerful blow against the entire United States Government.

Confederates from Jefferson Davis on down had denied any involvement in Booth's plot. For Fraser, those denials didn't butter a lot of parsnips. What else could they say? Accused of a heinous crime, denial is the only sensible response for guilty and innocent alike.

A Southern spy, Thomas Conrad, had claimed after the war that the Confederate secret service planned to kidnap Abraham Lincoln, just as Booth intended to. If Booth was acting for the Confederacy in the kidnapping, wasn't it logical that he was ordered to convert the plot to one of assassination?

Booth, of course, was the key. He wasn't just a Confederate sympathizer. He was a Confederate agent. In October 1864, he traveled to Montreal to meet with Confederates who were plotting invasions of the North. After his death, investigators found in his trunk the key to a cipher used by Confederate agents to encode secret messages. Only a Confederate agent would have that cipher. And when Samuel Arnold wrote to Booth about the assassination plot in late March 1865, he urged, "Go and see how it will be taken in R——d" —Richmond! Also, Booth traveled twice to Southern Maryland before the assassination, each time finding Confederate agents like the Surratts. After the assassination, he found more agents to aid him during his flight. Only an agent could find so many other agents.

As the conspiracy's leader, Booth would know who was pulling the strings behind it, but that trail ran cold when he died. Dead men tell no tales. The killing of Booth itself seemed suspicious. He was shot as he stood alone in a burning barn, surrounded by Union soldiers. The sergeant who pulled the trigger claimed that Booth was about to shoot at the soldiers. Yet how much risk can a man in a burning barn pose to men safely outside and able to take cover? It was certainly convenient that Booth never could tell his story.

What of the Surratts? In a lecture delivered in 1870, John Surratt described himself as a Confederate agent, carrying messages between Richmond and Washington and New York and Canada. Like other Confederate agents, he used his mother's tavern in Surrattsville as a way station. Booth stopped at that tavern as he fled Washington after the assassination. But then Surratt was spirited out of the country and later out of the hemisphere. That, too, was convenient. Had someone been tidying up loose ends?

And Mrs. Surratt? She aided Confederate agents for years, then moved to Washington in the autumn of 1864, when Booth was organizing his conspiracy to kidnap President Lincoln. Did she move to the city to establish her boarding house as the hub for Booth's scheme, much as her rural tavern was the hub for Confederate spies? She conferred with Booth frequently. Her son or Booth might have told her something about the conspiracy that Mr. Bingham, when he learned of it, thought might destroy the republic.

After two long nights of wrestling with these questions, the answers seeming to be just beyond his grasp, Fraser gave it up. He was a country doctor who happened to have access to John Bingham's library. Better-informed people had tried for decades to solve the riddle of the Lincoln conspiracy. Why should he be the one to slice the Gordian knot?

The earth was warming. The forsythia had bloomed and greened. Now the azalea was coming in. The farmers of Harrison County were plowing and planting. With a shock, Fraser realized that it was April 14, the thirty-fifth anniversary of the assassination. He left his examining room in the afternoon and slowly walked through Cadiz, enjoying the birdsong and buds on trees. When the news of Lincoln's assassination reached Cadiz in 1865, the ancestors of those birds had sung the same songs, and those same trees had brought out their leaves.

The next day was Easter, April 15, the day Lincoln died. It was time for new life. Fraser needed to slough off the past and reenter his world. He should say a prayer for Lew Evans, too.

Chapter 4

Fraser took a deep breath. By any objective standard, he wasn't that high off the ground, barely at the top of a ten-foot ladder. He reached to his right and scooped the matted leaves and seeds from the gutter. His heart raced. A drop of sweat trickled between his shoulder blades. This was ridiculous. It was mid-May, not warm enough to be sweating. His neighbors had long since cleaned out their gutters. Fraser couldn't let this foolish anxiety keep him from such a simple task. People worked on ladders every day. He reached for the leaves to the left of his ladder and dropped them to the ground.

Now he faced the devil's decision of gutter cleaning. Should he reach farther on either side, perhaps tilting the ladder and crashing earthward? Or should he, like a coward, slowly descend to the ground, move the ladder down the roof line, then carefully probe for two level spots where he could replant the ladder's legs, then rescale the heights? And again? And again?

Sighing with annoyance, Fraser let his right toe dangle until it brushed the rung below. He had at least another hour of struggling with his damnable weakness. He had no idea why he dreaded heights. He always had. But he wouldn't give in to it.

"Excuse me. Sir?" The deep voice came from his left and be-hind, from the front walk. Fraser didn't care to engage in con-versation while dangling from the ladder.

"On my way," he called, descending more quickly than he liked. His stomach muscles relaxed when his back foot touched ground.

"What can I do for you?" he asked as he turned around. His smile included a measure of relief.

He faced a light-skinned Negro of middle years, his hair and mustache shot through with gray. The man was as tall as Fraser and a trace thicker. He wore a formal black suit. He met Fraser's gaze like a white man. Stepping over to the walk where the man stood, Fraser placed the face and the suit. "You were at John Bingham's funeral," he said. "You're Speed Cook, aren't you?"

"I did attend Mr. Bingham's service," the man said, "and that's my name."

After wiping his hand on his trousers, Fraser shook the man's hand. "That was the perfect name for you. I watched you in the town games—You were fast!"

"The name ain't for being fast. It's short for Speedwell, one of the ships the pilgrims came over on." Fraser looked blankly at him so the man explained. "*Speedwell*, it was the second ship that sailed for Plymouth Rock."

"I don't remember that. So you're named for a ship took the pilgrims to freedom?"

"No, *Speedwell* turned back, never got here. It was my daddy's idea. Neither have we."

"You played for Steubenville, right? And then in college?"

Cook nodded, "At Oberlin, then for the university up to Michigan, then pro ball, too, until they run us Negroes out."

"I read about that," Fraser said. "Wasn't right." After a moment, he asked, "I can do something for you?"

"I just moved to Steubenville when my father, Isaiah Cook, took sick."

"I heard about that. I'm sorry for your loss."

"Thank you. A lady visiting from Maryland, she's related to my wife, she took a spill off our wagon this morning. Her arm's broke. Doc Marcotte's away and Doc Grimes, the new man, he doesn't treat colored. I set the arm best I could—you know my father did some of that before he took to the pulpit. She's doing poorly, running a fever. Maybe I did something wrong. I'd rather a real doctor looked at it."

"Well, let's see," Fraser said, "Steubenville's twenty miles and it's already four o'clock." Nodding up at the darkening sky, he added, "Looks like a storm, too, and I got a bad wheel on my rig."

"I know how far it is," Cook said. "I just came from there." Fraser scratched an ear and thought about his planned evening with long-neglected medical journals. Cook added, "Like I said, this lady's poorly. If the weather turns, we'll put you up, then ride you back here in the morning." After a beat he added, "They say you see colored."

" 'Course I do," Fraser said, his mind made up. "What'd you say her name is? Where's she from in Maryland?"

"She's Rachel Lemus, from right next to Washington, D.C."

"What name?"

"Rachel Lemus."

Maybe the name was common among the colored in Maryland. Fraser took a hard look at Speed Cook. Cook returned it. He seemed a prideful man. "All right, then," Fraser said. "Let me get some things together."

Fraser took his time packing an overnight bag, then checking his medical bag. He grabbed some of the aspirin powder that just came in from Boston. He wasn't sure exactly what it was good for, but the early reports were promising. Maybe it would help Rachel Lemus.

The rainy spring had left the roads soft, which made for slow going in Cook's open wagon. The horse, a sorrel mare beyond her salad days, labored up the hills and wobbled down them. "Don't know why they call these *rolling* hills," Cook said as the mare heaved up a considerable rise. "They're just damned hills."

Fraser was transfixed by Cook's hands. They were large and powerful, but the fingers were twisted and gnarled. He'd never seen hands like that, not even on the miners. He asked about them.

"You ever try to catch a professional fast ball, curve ball, with your bare hands?" Cook held up his right hand. "Did it for nine years. Most days my hands swole up twice normal size, broke every finger on both of 'em, some two or three times. Catcher ain't no little boy's job, but they paid me to do it, paid me *real* well."

"They give you much pain?"

Cook shrugged. "You get used to it."

They talked baseball for a while. Cook sputtered about Cap Anson being a race hater, how the man drove every last colored player out of professional ball. Fraser suspected that with Speed Cook a lot of conversations came back to race.

Cook said he was planning to start a newspaper for colored people, one that would explain that they had choices, they had to stand up for their rights, no matter what the cost. Fraser protested that there weren't any race haters in Harrison and Jefferson counties. It used to be so, Cook admitted, or it seemed so when he was a boy. But it didn't seem so anymore.

" 'Course, I've been baited by professionals," Cook said. "Grandstands full of white people screaming at me, calling me names, threatening me, all because my skin's darker than theirs—

and not darker than all of them, neither. Hell, they even come down out of the stands after me."

"I remember reading about that fracas, the one where the man got killed."

Cook didn't answer. Fraser looked up the hill on his side of the wagon. A few scrawny cattle cropped what looked like weeds.

"Jury said I was innocent," Cook said. "Twelve white men on that jury, they all agreed I had the right to defend myself."

"That's right."

Cook shook his head and snorted. "That's why I carry a knife, always do. And that was in the North. Don't even want to talk about down South."

Steubenville huddled on the edge of the Ohio River. Cook drove to the south side, land that was too low and too near the water. They pulled up in front of a tired two-story structure that dwarfed the shotgun shacks on either side of the street. The building expressed its ambitions through a sign that read COOK HOTEL, plus a coat of whitewash with green trim. The wind gusted in the fading light. Rain was coming, maybe a lot of rain. As they dropped off the wagon, Fraser doubted he would sleep in his own bed.

"When you said you could put me up," Fraser said, nodding at the sign, "I guess you meant it."

Cook smiled his first smile in three hours. "Rooms available." Hoisting Fraser's bag, he brushed off the road dust with his free hand.

Cook's wife, also fair-skinned but looking ten years younger than her husband, waited at the door. She led them into the parlor. Its furniture, also tired, did not quite fill the room. The woman stretched out on the divan had to be Rachel Lemus. Fraser pulled aside the window curtains to let in more light, adjusting to the way the floorboards bent to his step. Fat raindrops began to hit the window. Mrs. Cook turned up a lamp on the wall. In the light, Rachel looked to be on the far side of sixty, heavy-set, and feverish. Fraser helped her sit up and pulled a chair over. He unwound the cloth strips that held a short piece of molding to her right forearm.

"Mr. Cook's done a good job," Fraser said as he felt around the break. It wasn't puffy, didn't look infected. "I'm going to move it a bit to help it heal."

"Do it quick," she said. She grunted when he aligned the bones, sweat standing out on her forehead. He rewrapped her arm, using the same piece of molding as a splint. Then he mixed some powder in a glass of water from a side table and made her drink it. She screwed up her face. "Ee-yew. Mighty bitter. What's it called?"

"It's called aspirin. It's new. It should help you rest."

"That laudanum works good for me, you know." She gave him a hopeful look.

"Let's see how the aspirin does. I'll be here a bit longer, what with the rain." He pulled out a cloth to rig up as a sling for her arm and tied it behind her neck, then pointed to the wall behind her head. Muffled voices, sometimes shouts, were coming from the other side. "Does that racket bother you?"

Rachel eased back, supporting her slinged arm with her good hand. "That's just the dice game," she said. "Don't bother me none, not how I'm feeling."

When Fraser emerged from the parlor, the street was slick with rain. It soon would be a mass of mud. He accepted Mrs. Cook's invitation to supper, a stew featuring meat he could not quite identify. The biscuits were exceptional. Fraser praised them, probably too much. Unexpectedly, the Cooks talked of their college days. They both attended Oberlin, some years apart, though Speed admitted he'd loved baseball more than school, loved it all the way to the pros. Fraser had heard about another Negro who went to college, a lawyer in Cadiz.

After supper, Fraser found Rachel asleep on the couch. Her

fever was down. He woke her long enough to administer more dissolved aspirin.

Mrs. Cook showed him to a narrow room on the upper floor. She explained that she would ordinarily place him at the back, away from the street noise, but on Saturday night the rear of the hotel could get noisy. The bed was hard, but he saw no bugs. He was tired.

In the bright, warm morning, Fraser found the Cooks in the rear yard, seated with his patient at a table carried out from the house. There was no sign of another hotel guest.

Rachel looked clear-eyed and alert. She was feeling better, she said, the arm sore but not so bad. That aspirin, she added, tastes like the devil but works like a miracle.

The eggs were on the runny side, but the coffee was strong and the bacon thick, the way Fraser liked them. Even though Cook's hotel was empty, the man had to have income from somewhere. From his ballplaying days? The dice game? Sopping up the egg yolk with toast, Fraser spoke the question he had choked back since Cook first spoke Rachel's name.

"Rachel," he started, "I was wondering. Are you the one worked for Mary Surratt? In Surrattsville? You testified at her trial?"

Rachel drew back for a moment, then shrugged. "That I am. That trial, my Lord, I was scared to death there. How'd you know about that?"

Chapter 5

Cook broke into the conversation. "You've got no call to ask that of this woman, still with a broken arm. This some kind of a trick to catch her out?"

"*You* came to fetch *me*," Fraser answered. "Do you think I tricked you into coming to get me? Maybe I made Rachel take her fall?"

"All right, all right. It's just I don't believe in coincidences. Why're you asking Miz Lemus about the Surratts? That's all a long time ago."

Fraser put on a smile and drew a slow breath. He reminded Cook that they had both been at the funeral for Mr. Bingham. The dead man's family, he explained, had asked him to help sort through the man's papers, including some about the Lincoln case. Fraser had read about the case and recognized Rachel's name. "A coincidence," he concluded. "Really."

Rachel asked what Mr. Bingham looked like. When Fraser described him, she shook her head. "Can't say I remember him. Them generals and colonels was everywhere. I swear I was waist-deep in them." She broke into a throaty laugh. "I don't rightly remember who all was there."

"What interests me," Fraser said, "isn't the trial so much. What was it like there in Surrattsville? What was the tavern like? Were there Confederates around?"

Rachel looked at Cook first. When he shrugged, she said, "Doc, wasn't nobody there *but* Confederates, except for us colored. We was loyal to the union, loyal to Mr. Lincoln. You got to understand, 'cause we was in Maryland, people stayed slaves longer than even in the South. That emancipation didn't take effect right away in Maryland. I was free right along, though. My daddy bought his way out, then bought my momma out, too."

"What I meant was," Fraser said, "were there Confederate spies, you know, spying."

"You mean like young John?" She shook her head. "I never seen such a group of people for talking in low voices. Young John, though, he couldn't keep quiet, he'd just brag and brag on how he was meeting with the big men in Richmond and in Canada. Real proud, he was. Couldn't hardly not know what he was doing."

"What was Mrs. Surratt like?"

"Miss Mary? She was a fine woman, for a Confederate. She prayed to her savior, believed in her religion. Smart, too. Way smarter than that no-good drunk of a husband. That saloon of theirs didn't make no money till he died and Miss Mary took it over."

"Did she ever travel from Surrattsville?"

"No, someone had to run that place. Her and me, we really run it together. She said as much once."

"But you didn't move to Washington with her?"

"Me? In the city? No, I'm a country woman. I know where I belong."

Fraser shifted in his chair, choosing his words carefully. "Did you see anything, in those weeks toward the end of the war, that made you think the Surratts were planning something big? I don't mean that they said that Lincoln would be killed, but something out of the usual, something extra going on?" He hadn't chosen his words well, but the old lady nodded, raising his hopes.

"No," she said. "Nothing like that. But something unusual did happen."

"Yes?"

Rachel closed her eyes in the effort to remember. "Was this one man, named Harper, Harmon, something like that?"

"Harbin? Thomas Harbin?"

She opened her eyes. "That could be. Yeah, Harbin could be it. You been studying on this. He come in one night when young John was there; then the two of them met some rich man from New York. Seemed like they was cooking up something."

"How'd you know he was a rich man from New York?"

"They talked about New York a lot, I could hear that. And I knew he was rich from his clothes. They were beautiful. We didn't see clothes like that. I still remember that gray suit. He got off that stage from Washington, which bounced people around like popcorn, but with that gray suit he looked like he stepped out of some magazine drawing."

"What'd they talk about?"

"Lord, I don't know. By that time, white folks was careful around us colored. Everybody knew things wasn't going good for the South, and that meant the colored was going to be citizens, gonna happen sometime soon, so they got real careful 'round us."

"Did you see that New York man again?"

"No, not again. But after Mr. Lincoln was killed, that Harbin was around some. You know, we all heard that Booth was hiding somewhere near. Couldn't keep a secret like that."

* * *

The road back to Cadiz was softer after the rain, making the mare's work that much harder. Cook asked Fraser what he was after with the old lady.

"I'm not sure. You see, I don't like coincidences much myself. Mr. Bingham, you know, when he prosecuted the Lincoln case, he claimed the Confederacy was behind Booth, even had witnesses who said so. When it turned out the witnesses were liars, Mr. Bingham didn't change his tune. Ever since, people have been dreaming up all these conspiracies Booth could've been part of, but Mr. Bingham never wavered. He stuck by what he said first. Makes me curious."

"Did Rachel help?"

"I don't know. What she says jibes with what I was thinking. People don't pay much attention to how Confederate agents took care of Booth when he was trying to escape. That makes me think the assassination might have been a Confederate plan, just like Mr. Bingham said. Maybe that man Harbin was part of it. He was a Southern agent, he said so himself."

"What about that Surratt woman?"

"Some people claim she was innocent, just a weak woman, but Mr. Bingham never doubted she was guilty. Called her a she-lion. The way Rachel described her—a strong, smart woman, running her business—that sounded like the woman Mr. Bingham talked about." Fraser sighed. "I'd like to figure this out, just curious, you know."

"If you was going to try to figure it out, how would you do that?"

"Why're you so interested? What's it to you?"

Cook scowled. "What's it to me? I'm interested, that's what's it to me. Biggest crime in history, I'm interested. I'm supposed to be some ignorant coon, don't care why the sun comes up in the morning?"

Fraser wondered how this high-strung Negro had lived long enough to have gray hairs. "I've thought about writing to this newspaper man," Fraser said. "He was there back then, there in Washington when Lincoln got shot. He wrote about it then, wrote more about it since. He was a friend of Mr. Bingham's, knew everyone. Maybe he knows more."

"If he knew more, why wouldn't he write it?"

"It could be the sort of thing he's not quite sure of. Or even could be something that he doesn't really know he knows, something he doesn't see how it's important." Fraser didn't add that doctors know all about that, about missing the evidence that's right in front of your eyes and you end up diagnosing a patient wrong.

"And you'll see it, you'll see it when this writer fellow didn't?"

Fraser smiled and looked out at the road. "I suppose that's why I haven't written him. It was just a thought."

"Sounds like you're missing the big story." Cook switched the reins to his left hand, pointing in front of him with his free hand. "This woman Surratt, see, it doesn't sound like she's any big deal. Hell, they hanged her, right?"

"Right."

"But what about the men who ordered this thing? They've never been brought to account. That's the story here, that's what we need to figure out—"

"We?"

"Told you yesterday, I'm going to be a newspaper man, start a paper in that building back behind the house. Going to call it the *Ohio Eagle*. Not going to spend my life running that hotel, making sure the craps players don't cut each other up.

"This would be one hell of a story to start my newspaper with," Cook continued. "The biggest story of the old century just when we start a new one. And it should be a Negro paper breaks it. You white folks act like that war was about you, but that was *our* war. You white folks just did some of the dying"— Fraser snorted—"okay, a lot of the dying. Hey, you had the guns. But that was our war, don't make any mistake about it.

And it's not over, either. Only thing is now we're the only ones still fighting on our side. Something like this, who really killed Abraham Lincoln, this could remind people what that fighting and dying was for."

When Fraser didn't respond, Cook fell silent. The wagon lurched and rocked along. Fraser wondered about the man next to him. Baseball star, college man, hotel owner, hothead, sponsor of dice games. Not like anyone Fraser knew. He thought about what Cook said. Fraser's father did his share of dying, more than his share. It was his war, too.

"Also," Cook started again, "there's an election this year. Wouldn't that be a powerful piece of news, who killed Lincoln, keep those Southern Democrats from crawling back into power? Remind everyone this wasn't just some crazy actor did that. This was an attempt to overthrow a government. They killed Lincoln, meant to kill Seward, Johnson, even Grant."

"You know all about it," Fraser said.

"Didn't just get found in a cabbage patch. Think about it. Say they'd managed to kill everyone they meant to kill, who would've been president? Who would've run the country? Those same people, their sons anyway, who're still running the South. We can't let them fool people into voting for them anymore."

Fraser objected that the election for president was going to be about new issues—the fight against rebels in the Philippines, whether to keep the gold standard for the dollar. It wasn't about the Civil War.

Cook waved him off. "The Civil War's still going on, every day, getting worse, driving colored people out of jobs, off trains, out of restaurants, even out of the damned roller rink right there in Steubenville. It's still about that war. That war won't be over till my grandchildren are dead and gone. You and me, we figure this thing out, maybe we turn around this war we're still fighting, make sure the right side wins again. 'Cause right now, we ain't winning. Today, this ain't no country for the black man."

Fraser let some time pass. Then he said, "Okay, if I wanted to figure out what happened with the Lincoln assassination, why would I do it with you?"

"That's easy. I can go places you can't, just like you can go places I can't. You need that. Without me, you never meet Rachel Lemus. Think about it. Also, I know my way around a knife and a gun. You're serious about this business, you may need that, too."

That sounded ridiculous to Fraser, but Speed Cook had passion. That impressed him. It might help to have someone else trying to solve the puzzle of Mrs. Surratt's confession. Fraser sure hadn't solved it on his own. What could it hurt?

"Tell you what," he said. "I've got a whole shelf of Mr. Bingham's papers and books on the assassination, every sort of thing. You take some back today, look 'em over. Then we can talk about what you think."

Cook gave him a long look. "All right, Doc."

"You know, my friends call me Jamie, not Doc. Why don't you?"

"All right, then. I go by Speed."

Chapter 6

✑

Fraser tried to ignore the stares and nervous glances. He and Cook were unsettling the train's first-class car. The other passengers might have started out thinking that Cook was his servant, but they couldn't hold on to that idea very long. In his sober black suit, right leg crossed over left, and arm stretched over the back of the seat, Cook sat in first class like he was born there. When the conductor punched their tickets, Cook ignored the man's fish-eyed look.

Fraser had never traveled with a Negro before. At the Wheeling station, waiting in the honey sunshine of an early June morning, Cook grumbled about riding on the Baltimore & Ohio. During the war, he complained, Confederate sympathizers ran the B&O, and they still did. When Fraser replied that no other railroad went where they were going, Cook glared at him.

They were headed for Brunswick, Maryland, in the southwestern corner of that state. From Brunswick, they would have to get to Burkittsville and the home of the writer George Alfred Townsend, who was expecting them.

Cook had hurled himself into solving the Lincoln conspiracy with the confidence that comes when a man is good at most things he tries. Fraser had never been with someone who could be so contrary, always ready for an argument. From the start, Cook insisted that Fraser was missing important parts of the puzzle.

"So, Mr. Bingham thought the Confederates did it," Cook said early on, over Fraser's kitchen table. "So that's what you want to prove, to prove Mr. Bingham was right all along, right?"

"I just want the truth," Fraser said.

"Sure, sure," Cook said impatiently. "Mr. Bingham's truth. But the problem with that truth is that he was relying on liars, right?"

"Just because they were lying, that doesn't mean Mr. Bingham was wrong." Fraser cringed inwardly at his own words.

"Actually, I agree with that," Cook said, "especially since one of those witnesses wasn't ever shown to be a liar. He didn't ever take it back."

"Was that . . . Finnegan?"

"No, no, named Finegas, Henry Finegas. He said some Confederates up in Canada said—this was, like, in early 1865—they said that with luck Lincoln wouldn't be around any longer, and that Booth was bossing the job."

"Who was Finegas?"

"Got no idea. But Mr. Bingham put him on the stand." Cook got a far-off look and pulled his lips in tight. "What if . . . what if whoever killed Lincoln arranged for those other liars to turn up? That way, when they tell the true story, then get caught in their lies, they throw mud all over the explanation that was the *right* one. Throws everyone off the trail. D'you think about that?"

No, Fraser hadn't thought about that. It might explain Mr. Bingham's unshakeable belief in his own correctness. But maybe not. "If you're right," Fraser said, "then the people who recruited Booth and Mrs. Surratt and Lewis Paine also framed them so they would get hanged or sent to prison as traitors and assassins."

"Exactly," Cook said. "If there *were* other men arranged for Lincoln to get killed, then they *needed* those folks to get hanged and hanged fast, same as they'd want Booth out of the way. That takes away the risk that anything tracks back to them. And it wasn't any trick getting those folks convicted. They'd just helped kill Father Abraham. They'd've hung if old Bingham recited nursery rhymes at the trial."

"So, you think it was more than just Booth?"

"Had to be. Remember that thing you said from Sherlock Holmes, that you eliminate the impossible and see what's left? It's impossible that Booth did this all by himself. What's left is that someone helped him, maybe even got him to do it in the first place."

Was that what Mrs. Surratt did with Mr. Bingham, spilled secrets that might lead back to the men behind the assassination? Fraser couldn't be sure. This was *all* guessing. He didn't mind guessing. Medical diagnosis was often guessing, but that was guessing he was used to, and you found out pretty soon whether your guess was right. Patients got better or they didn't. This kind of guessing was different. Fraser didn't know how to test the ideas he and Cook were talking about. How could they evaluate their guesses? Who knew enough to tell them they were right or wrong? And if there was someone who knew, why would he talk to Fraser and Cook about it?

Fraser's mind had kept cycling back to the writer, Townsend. It seemed like that man, too, was obsessed with the Lincoln conspiracy. He wrote about it over and over, once in a novel. Could it be that Townsend didn't accept the lone-madman theory that he himself had peddled? When Mr. Bingham died,

Townsend sent a long condolence letter, so Fraser knew the writer felt something toward Mr. Bingham. Perhaps, out of loyalty to Mr. Bingham, Townsend would hear them out; maybe he could help them deduce Mr. Bingham's secret.

In May, the women of Harrison County fell into an uncharacteristically fallow period, while the rest of the populace enjoyed a spate of health. Fraser resolved to seize the moment to visit Townsend over the Memorial Day holiday. It would take most of a day to get there and another to get back, so he planned to be away for up to five days. Dr. Marcotte in Steubenville would take emergency cases while he was away. When Fraser mentioned the trip to Cook, there was no way to stop the ex-ballplayer from coming along. "You need me to figure this thing out," Cook had said. Fraser tended to agree, but he hadn't anticipated what it was like to travel with a Negro, especially one like Cook.

"You know what we've been missing?" Cook demanded, oblivious to the other passengers. Fraser said no in a soft voice. He hoped his example would lead Cook to speak quietly. It didn't. "We've been missing that whole business about shooting Booth."

Fraser raised an eyebrow.

"Didn't it strike you funny," Cook said, "Booth goes and gets himself killed before anyone can ask him a single question? And that sergeant who shot him—what's his name, Hartford?"

"Boston. Boston Corbett."

"Yeah, right. Wasn't any officer told him to go and shoot Booth. Wasn't any order to shoot. I'm telling you, Booth's standing in a barn that's on fire, soldiers all around. Man ain't going nowhere except maybe straight to hell or out of that barn with his hands up. No need to shoot. But old Boston, he just up and plugs him, does it on his own." Cook shook his head. "I tell you what, it don't add up."

"Actually," Fraser said, "that's always bothered me. That silenced Booth forever. Nothing he left behind revealed very much."

"If someone arranged for him to get shot, they surely could clean up whatever Booth left behind. What happened to that Sergeant Boston? Was he some glory-seeker, trying to do something he could cash in on?"

"Never did cash in on it. Actually, he went crazy. Mr. Bingham had a newspaper story about him years later, living in a cave out in Kansas or somewhere. Don't know what's happened with him since."

"Send a crazy man to kill an assassin. That's smart. Who's gonna believe anything the crazy man says?" Cook paused. "Another thing. Did you notice how bad that woman's lawyers were, the ones for Mrs. Surratt?" Fraser shook his head. "Well, they were. I know about that. The lawyers defending the men who went to jail—you know, the one holding Booth's horse and those boys from Baltimore—those lawyers were all right. They mostly made sense, you know, said things that helped their case. And the lawyers defending the ones who really did it, like Paine and the German guy who chickened out, what could they've done, anyway? Some cases can't nobody win.

"But those ones representing that woman, every time they stood up, they made her case worse. Didn't sit right with me. Maybe she did it and she's nothing but pure evil, but when you're sitting in a courtroom accused of a crime, you need help. Made me wonder whether they were paid to lose."

Cook had grown increasingly animated. In a low voice, Fraser said, "Speed, this is a public place here. These things, even if they happened a long time ago, they're still sensitive. Keep it down, okay?"

Cook's face registered disdain, but he answered in a lower tone, "Another thing, I'm wondering why it couldn't be someone in the *North* be behind killing Lincoln. Didn't have to be the Confederates. Plenty of crackers and nigger-haters around Ohio, all through the North."

"Quiet?"

"All right, all right," Cook said in a hoarse whisper that wasn't much softer. "But you know there's lots in Indiana, New York. Shoot, you know that Sons of Liberty group, those Northern men wanted the South to win? One of them came right from Cadiz. My daddy used to talk about it. Made him mad."

Fraser had heard enough. "There's no basis for that theory. Look at all those connections that Booth and the Surratts have with Confederates, but none with the Sons of Liberty or with Northern Copperheads."

"Have you looked?"

Fraser shooed the idea away. "There's nothing about it in anything I read. Nothing to it. Nothing at all."

"Men used to think the Sun moved around the Earth."

Fraser didn't answer. His silence accomplished what his answers had not. Cook stopped talking.

While the forests of western Maryland sped by his window, Fraser thought that even if Cook tended to overdo it, this idea might be right. Fraser had to think about it quietly, not while being hectored by Cook. Mrs. Surratt could hardly have revealed to Mr. Bingham that the Confederates were connected to Booth, since that's what Mr. Bingham had been saying all along, right through the trial—that the Confederacy sent Booth to kill Lincoln. Mrs. Surratt must have told him something else, something else that would threaten the republic in early July 1865.

And the secret was still explosive enough that in 1900, when he was dying and knew he was dying, Mr. Bingham would say only that there was a secret, not what it was. Why couldn't it be that Northerners were behind the Lincoln assassination?

It was getting awkward that Fraser hadn't told Cook about Mrs. Surratt's confession to Mr. Bingham. He never decided not to tell Cook. It just never came up, and the longer it didn't, the harder it was going to be to tell. He needed to do it soon.

They hired horses at the station and set off for Burkittsville, riding side by side through hilly country on a warm, glorious day. The farms they passed were small and neat, like those in eastern Ohio. Being close to Harpers Ferry prompted Cook to declaim on John Brown and his failed slave revolt in 1859. He quieted when they came upon a cemetery. Flowers lay on many graves. They dismounted and walked to the edge of a small crowd near a regal elm tree.

They listened to the last two speakers, a politician and a minister, for the Memorial Day observance. The minister spoke of the sacrifices of the Union dead and the Confederate dead, both of whom lay buried there. The politician talked about the Spanish-American War and the new Filipino insurrection. He said American soldiers were still making sacrifices, only now overseas. When Fraser and Cook remounted, they didn't speak.

Townsend's land was a revelation. A fifty-foot stone arch, topped with three smaller arches and a medieval tower, loomed over the entrance. They gawked at the structure, then strained to read the writings carved into its walls, along with dozens of names.

"What in blue blazes is it," Cook wondered, "out here in the middle of nowhere?"

"Beats me," Fraser said.

Townsend, a vigorous gentleman of about sixty, met them in the front drive of the stone mansion. His still-dark hair, combed straight back, gave him a sleek, aggressive look. When they reached a cavernous parlor, Townsend directed his colored servant to bring beverages. Fraser settled on a chintz-covered love seat—a feminine-looking piece in a setting that favored the gigantic—while Cook chose a straight-backed chair off to the

side. When the servant appeared with drinks, he seemed diffi-
dent about serving Cook. Fraser drank off half his lemonade in
a single swallow. Cook attacked his toddy with equal zest.

Townsend explained that the stone arch commemorated
newspaper writers who died during the Civil War. "Most were
friends of mine," he said, beginning to light a meerschaum pipe.
He spoke around deep intakes of breath as he held match to tobacco. "Everybody . . . forgets the poor . . . scribblers who
saunter out . . . on the battlefield . . . armed with but pencils."
He had ignited his tobacco. "They're there so the people know
what really happened. I'm fortunate enough to be able to make
this gesture, and proud to do so."

Townsend recalled meeting Fraser at Mr. Bingham's final
dinner. Leaning back in his large leather chair, he puffed on his
pipe, and spoke to the ceiling as though from a prepared
speech.

"Bingham, as you doubtless know, was a zealot. I will never
forget those great smoldering eyes of his. A zealot's eyes. Yet
behind those fiery windows into his soul resided a true amiabil-
ity, which was no less genuine for being entirely surprising."

"In Cadiz," Fraser broke in, "I knew him as a friend."

"Yes, yes, of course," Townsend said, seeming annoyed by
the interruption. "And your letter said you have some concern
with how he prosecuted the Lincoln conspiracy case? If you
will forgive my presumption, how could that matter to you,
gentlemen?" Townsend looked directly at Cook, who made no
answer.

"I've been close to the Bingham family for many years,"
Fraser said, "and have been assisting his daughters with his papers."

Townsend's expression showed that Fraser's remark did not
answer his question.

"I'm a newspaperman, Mr. Townsend," Cook said suddenly,
shifting on his upright chair.

"Are you, indeed?" Townsend said. "That's quite remarkable. For what organ of the press do you write?"

"My own," Cook said. "The *Ohio Eagle,* it's a colored paper."

Townsend's answering grin seemed genuine. "Good for you, young man. Good for you. I don't know the *Ohio Eagle,* I regret to admit, but I shall expect great things of it." After gazing thoughtfully at the smoke rising from his pipe, he began a critical review of Mr. Bingham's prosecution of the Lincoln conspirators. "Even a child should have known certain testimony was perjured," he sighed. "Your friend Bingham, he was too pure a sort to bring forth false evidence intentionally, but he was, as I say, a zealot. Zealots are not terribly good at winkling out the truth. Otherwise, they couldn't be zealots, could they?"

After reciting other complaints about Bingham's performance, Townsend said, "It wasn't a good effort, not at all, not what history required—nay, deserved—of that moment in time."

With an effort, Fraser ignored Townsend's aspersions against Mr. Bingham. He pressed the burning question in his mind: whether the Confederacy was behind the assassination. When Townsend rejected the idea out of hand, Fraser began to argue. "What of all the Confederate spies buzzing around Booth?" he asked. "You yourself wrote in *Leslie's Illustrated* that the Surratts were spies, and so were Thomas Harbin and Augustus Howell and Mrs. Slater. And both Booth and John Surratt went to Montreal to see the Confederates scheming up there."

Townsend admitted every fact that Fraser threw at him, but he did not budge on the basic proposition. "There was no Confederate involvement in the plot," Townsend proclaimed in a patronizing tone that rankled. "You will have to accept," Townsend said with some finality, "that the conspiracy was the spawn of one talented, charismatic, very likely insane young actor who happened to be an extraordinary athlete as well."

With that pronouncement, their host called for his man to refill their glasses. Though the evening was upon them, he said nothing of supper.

Exasperated but fortified with a fresh lemonade, Fraser deployed his most powerful weapon, Mr. Bingham's deathbed description of Mrs. Surratt's confession and how Mr. Bingham and Edwin Stanton took her secret to their graves. As he spoke, Fraser kept his eyes on Townsend, who was scraping out the bowl of his pipe. He hoped that Cook wouldn't betray that he had never heard of this episode before.

Townsend's demeanor began to change. After tapping his pipe into the ashtray, he looked up sharply. "Who else knows about this?"

"No one," Fraser said, still not looking at Cook.

"Now, if I were still working as a reporter," Townsend said, nodding over at Cook, "I might pursue that question. But as I'm a poet and a novelist now, I can only respond that, yes, I now understand your interest in this subject."

Townsend pressed for any other hint from Bingham of what Mrs. Surratt said, but Fraser could add nothing. "All right, gentlemen," Townsend said, grimacing with apparent thought, "where does this take us? What could that woman have learned in the weeks before the assassination? She ran a boarding house and regularly went to church to confess her sins. She wasn't rushing down to Richmond or up to Montreal, like Booth or her son did. So she could only know what Booth or her son told her. Or one of the priests."

"Sir," Cook said quietly, "who wanted President Lincoln dead? Who would you list?"

Townsend shook his head. "That's a fine question, but one with far too many answers. Rebels? Of course. The Copperhead Democrats in the North? Yes. Right there you've got about half the country. Crazy people? That takes you well over half."

Townsend began to pace in front of the massive stone fireplace at the end of the room. "Let's think about Mr. Bingham, shall we? After Mrs. Surratt told him this secret, he did not change how he prosecuted the case or what he thought about the conspiracy, right? He just went right on saying it was Jeff Davis and the Rebs, right?"

"So," Fraser tried, "she must have confirmed that, right?"

"Not so fast. Maybe she told him something completely opposite, and maybe he and Stanton decided to hide it so no one would know how wrong they had been. Nobody likes being wrong, least of all zealots."

"Maybe," Fraser ventured, "she confirmed that the Confederates were behind Booth, but Stanton and Bingham decided to keep it secret so they didn't stir up old wounds."

"No," Townsend said quickly. "Those wounds weren't old in July of 1865. They were quite fresh."

"They didn't want to stir up something," Fraser insisted. "Maybe people who would be angry to be investigated, people who could be dangerous."

Townsend continued to pace. The floor creaked under his tread. Fraser finally asked the question he had come to ask. "If you were going to investigate this, where would you go?"

"Ah," Townsend stopped, pointing his index finger to the ceiling. "Louis Weichmann. There's really nowhere else to start."

"He was the star witness."

"At the conspiracy trial and at John Surratt's trial. And by now he's completely loony on the subject." Townsend shrugged. "He has spent his entire life on it. Last I saw him he was assembling an archive, a veritable shrine of papers about the assassination and the conspiracy. If you're looking for a fanatic to talk to about the case, Weichmann's your man. He's in Indiana, a town called Anderson."

"Would he talk to us?"

"Who knows?" Townsend said. "It might depend on how unbalanced he has become."

"I'll send him a wire, so he'll expect us."

"No," Townsend objected, shaking his head at the floor. "I wouldn't do that. He's easy to spook. He's had a good deal of trouble because of his testimony. Threats and such. He's persuaded there are people out to do him ill. He may, of course, be right." Townsend looked up. "I'll write you a letter of introduction that you can deliver in person."

"What else," Cook asked, "what else would you do to investigate?"

"I say," Townsend mused, "perhaps we should arrange for a small repast. I will think better if my stomach is not snarling from hunger."

Over a Spartan meal of cold ham, dark bread, and pickles, Townsend regaled them with stories of the conspiracy trial, the hoods and shackles that the prisoners were forced to wear, and the degenerate quality of the prisoners themselves. "I suppose one should expect that with assassins, but we who had read our Shakespeare hoped for something finer. Compared with that fool who shot President Garfield, of course, John Wilkes Booth was a great soul."

Fraser steered the conversation back to the unanswered questions about the Lincoln conspiracy. "What parts of the conspiracy do you think were never really looked into?"

"Bessie Hale!" Townsend almost shouted the name. "That young woman was the fiancée of John Wilkes Booth. She was with him in the week before the assassination, and even on the morning of it. But she was a senator's daughter—Senator Hale was, of all things, an abolitionist from New Hampshire—so she never testified anywhere. I got run off that part of the story myself. Bessie Hale, she's always stuck in my craw. How could she not know something? She's still around, you know, in Washington." Townsend smiled. "She married a man who also became senator from New Hampshire. What, sir, are the odds on that? The daughter of a senator and the wife of another, and the former fiancée of Lincoln's assassin?"

Fraser had never read that Booth had a fiancée. He needed to learn more about her. "What else," he asked, "were you dissatisfied with?"

Townsend looked up at the ceiling and let a smile play at the corners of his mouth. "Booth and his money." The writer explained that Booth made no paid appearances as an actor for almost a full year before the assassination, yet lived in high style and supported Lewis Paine and Atzerodt, plus Arnold and O'Laughlen.

"So"—he leaned forward on his elbows—"how does this twenty-six-year-old unemployed actor, who never achieved the popularity of his brothers, have enough money to support this entire operation for months and months? Someone else was paying those bills. There was testimony that Booth boasted he would go to Richmond to get money."

"Isn't that what a Confederate agent would do?" Fraser asked. "Earlier, you were saying that Booth acted on his own, but this money question points the other way."

Waving away the question, Townsend seemed in the grip of a new thought. "Another thing," he said, "I heard talk, not right away but after a few months, that might explain what old Bingham told you. Though you didn't hear it everywhere, the smart ones, the ones who know the inside of everything, they started saying it."

"Yes?"

"The talk was that the conspiracy came from inside Mr. Lincoln's official family, that it was some of his friends who arranged the killing."

"Who?"

"Mostly the talk was about Stanton, but I never could figure that out. Why would he do it? He was closer to Lincoln than anyone, and no one except Lincoln could tolerate his company. I assumed that talk came from all the people who disliked Stanton, which was pretty much everyone except your friend Bingham."

Cook, slowly stirring his coffee, spoke for the first time since dinner had begun. "What reasons did they give for saying that it was someone in the government?"

"A lot of it was that the pursuit of Booth was so incompetent—a hundred thousand Union soldiers couldn't find the scoundrel for ten days. That made people wonder if someone in the government was protecting Booth. Stanton was in charge of that pursuit."

"What reason," Fraser asked, "would Stanton have to kill Lincoln?"

"I'm not saying it makes any sense," Townsend said quickly. "But the talk was that Lincoln wanted to go easy on the South, while Stanton, who was the most radical of Republicans, was hotted up to punish the Southerners."

Cook stopped stirring his coffee. "If Mrs. Surratt was accusing Stanton of being behind the killing, would Bingham go straight to Stanton with her story? Maybe he would naturally demand an explanation from Stanton."

"But," Fraser said, "Stanton persuaded Mr. Bingham not to reveal whatever she told him."

They fell silent for several moments. Townsend slapped the table. "God must love mysteries, my friends, since he has given us so many. I sincerely hope you boys solve this one." He looked earnestly at Fraser. "I'd be pleased to offer whatever advice and help you might need as you go along. If you want to get in touch with people from back then, I know most of the ones who aren't dead yet. I'd be glad to send a letter or wire to smooth your way."

As he showed them to the door, Townsend suggested they communicate in a confidential fashion since the subject was so delicate. Fraser should send his wires to Mr. Jenkins in Brunswick; he explained that Mrs. Surratt had been born Mary Jenkins. Fraser, he added, could sign his name Armour, which Townsend would use for his replies. Armour, they both knew, was John Bingham's middle name.

Chapter 7

The sun was down when Fraser and Cook set off for Brunswick, the closest town where they might find beds. A three-
quarters moon lit the road. They met no one else, passing
farmhouses where lights glowed softly behind white curtains.
Fraser felt like his mind was on fire.

"That financial question," he burst out when they started
out, "how Booth had so much money? That's interesting. I
haven't seen any testimony or anything else about that. Booth
had some oil investments, but they didn't seem to pay off, not
ever. We should think about how to figure that out."

For once, Cook didn't answer. Fraser kept talking. "But the
Stanton story, that he was behind the assassination? Whoo-ee,
what a humbug! Makes no sense at all. Don't you agree?"

"What do you care what I think?" Cook's voice sounded
tired.

"You heard everything I heard tonight. You've read what
I've read, most of it. If you're not going to say what you think,
why'd you come all this way?"

"I've been asking myself that question." Cook stopped his horse. His face wore an angry scowl, though his voice was steady. "To have you shush me on the train because colored men ain't supposed to talk out? To have that conductor eye me like week-old meat? To have that strange man back there not show us the courtesy you'd show a dog? He wasn't going to give us a crust of bread, after we come two hundred miles and more, until you told him about that Mrs. Surratt business. And then he don't offer a bed for the night, knowing we're riding back in the dark, him with that tremendous house echoing all around his ears?"

"Hang on just a minute."

"And then you"—Cook jabbed his finger toward Fraser, his voice increasing in volume while lowering in pitch—"you up and start talking about that secret Mr. Bingham tells when he's dying. First time *I* ever hear of it. I've been studying and talk-ing to you for weeks, but it never comes up. When were you going to get around to that? Then you spill it to that arrogant, swishy writer five minutes after we walk in the door? I do not appreciate that. I'm not just the boy along to run errands, not to be seen or heard or talked to. I ain't doing that."

"Dammit, Speed, it was a secret."

"Not for white men it wasn't a secret. That man, Townsend, didn't even ask about it. Didn't ask something *near* to it. You just told him, couldn't wait to do it. I know what that is. Don't tell me different."

"Okay, okay. I should've told you. When you started on this thing, I wasn't sure you were going to stay with it, so I didn't mention it. Then I was planning to, but I just didn't get around to it."

"Don't give it no never mind. This is good. This is real good. Now I know where I stand. Let myself get fooled. Never too old to get fooled. Now I know, and I ain't lost anything more than a day on the railroad and some time in these hills. You go ahead and try to solve this business. You just try. I got plenty of things need doing."

"Speed, what are you talking about? We need to get out to Indiana, to see this man Weichmann. You should come."

"You go on. I'm pressed for time."

Cook kicked his horse into a trot toward Brunswick. Fraser couldn't think of anything to call after him, not anything that would change his mind. It probably wasn't worth it, anyway. That man, he thought, was smart enough, but he was prickly, real prickly, which had probably got him in trouble before and it was sure going to get him in trouble again. It might be better for Fraser not to be around when it did.

Looking up at the moon, Fraser found he agreed with one of the man's points. He, too, had expected to spend the night at Townsend's house, talking through the problems of the Booth conspiracy. Townsend had been patronizing at first. Then when he heard about Mrs. Surratt and Mr. Bingham, he seemed to get friendly, even expansive. And then he showed them the door. Cold, then hot, then cold. Could Townsend still be writing about the Booth conspiracy? Townsend, though, was a minor puzzle. Right now, Fraser had to find a bed. It might be easier without Cook. He wondered how Cook would fare on his own, then remembered that the man had played baseball all over the country. He had more experience traveling than Fraser did. He'd do fine.

Fraser started toward Brunswick.

By the time he reached Brunswick, Fraser had resolved to go straight on to see Weichmann in Indiana. Townsend was right. Writing ahead would only give the man a chance to duck him. Fraser's bag held two clean collars. He wasn't due in Cadiz until Sunday night. After an extended consultation with the agent at the Brunswick train depot, Fraser charted a marathon journey that should get him to Weichmann's town in twenty-two hours. Track repairs cost him one connection, so it was midafternoon Friday when Fraser stepped onto the platform in Anderson, weary and dirty from more than a day of bouncing over a troubled track bed. Meals gobbled at depot restaurants left a haze of queasiness.

After washing up in his stuffy hotel room, Fraser set out for the Weichmann Business School, founded by the former star witness against the Booth conspirators. According to the hotel clerk, the school was less than two miles away. The walk would do him good. Fraser drew energy from the early-summer sun, from the pleasure of moving under his own musclepower. Through the endless train ride, his head had swum with facts and theories as he drifted between dozing and a dazed wakefulness. He wasn't sure what he had reasoned and what he had dreamt. He should have thought about Booth's financial situation before. Through the last months of the conspiracy, almost no one in Booth's gang had a job. Someone else was paying their bills. And then there was Booth's fiancée! Why would a man with a fiancée, on the brink of a life of marital happiness, assassinate the president, a scheme that was bound to get him killed? Unless Booth never meant to marry. Could she have been part of his plot?

Anderson was so flat that it discomfited Fraser. The expanses of level ground seemed somehow sinister, implying concealed purposes and hidden hazards. Hill country felt more honest, affording distant views. He stopped for a moment to gaze at the slow-moving White River, not much more than a stream. He shook his head. If he was finding evil in the topography, his mind must still be clouded from the train ride.

The Weichmann school was in a white clapboard house. Outcroppings from the main building reflected alterations to accommodate the instruction offered within. When he entered the front vestibule, Fraser could hear the drone of a lecture to his left. He turned the other way into an office that had been a dining room. A small, gray-bearded man sat behind a large desk. He wore a formal suit with vest. He adjusted his pince-nez to focus on Fraser.

"Mr. Weichmann?" Fraser asked.

"Who wishes to know?"

"A friend of George Townsend?" The man gave no flicker of response. "I'm terribly sorry to interrupt, but if you have a moment I can explain." The man stood and walked past Fraser, into the next room. He closed the door firmly behind him.

After standing awkwardly for a minute, Fraser remembered Townsend's warning about Weichmann's odd qualities. He knocked on the door to the next room and called, "Might we speak?" Hearing no reply, he pushed the door in on a private study. Weichmann sat in an armchair with a book open before him.

"Sir, I don't mean to be rude—"

"You're failing rather badly at that. I thought I made it clear I have no wish to speak with you."

"Sir, I've come a long way to see you."

"That's hardly any affair of mine."

"No, you're right, sir, but—"

"My time is precious to me, even if it has no value to you, and I do not wish to squander it on any associate of that charlatan Townsend, a man to whom truth and falsehood are largely indistinguishable."

"Mr. Weichmann—"

Rising to his full though modest height, the older man asked, "Must I summon my staff to expel you?"

"Sir, my mission was triggered not by Townsend but by John Bingham, who was a neighbor and patient of mine."

"Bingham? Where are you from? Who are you?"

"I am Dr. James Fraser of Cadiz, Ohio. I attended Mr. Bingham in his late illness, as I had attended him for many years before."

"Yes, I read of his death. I hope it was not a hard one."

"He was staunch in his faith and suffered relatively little."

Weichmann licked his lips. "Bingham did me a kindness when not many people would. He knew the trials to which I have been subjected. I have been shot at, dismissed from employment, chased from town to town, all for telling the truth about a terrible crime. Do you think that fair, Dr. . . ."

"Fraser. James Fraser. And, no, it's most unfair, Mr. Weichmann. And I'm sure Mr. Bingham deemed it the same."

"Indeed, he did. Indeed, he did. Are you Catholic?"

"Excuse me?

"The question's plain enough? Are you a member of a Roman Catholic congregation? Do you confess to Catholic priests? Did priests send you? Monsignors? Bishops? Archbishops? Cardinals? They're all the same to me, no matter how tall their hats or glorious their robes."

"No, sir, I was raised Presbyterian."

"Oh, dear. That must not have been any picnic." Weichmann gestured to an armchair that faced his. "Perhaps you can describe your mission, as you put it, more fully. I warn you, though, if I suspect for a moment that you are in league with Townsend, this interview will immediately end."

Despite his peculiarities, Weichmann proved a gracious host, happily detailing his travails following the conspiracy trial, and the John Surratt trial after that. When Fraser disclosed Mr. Bingham's secret, Weichmann grew thoughtful. Mrs. Surratt, he said, was an honorable and pious woman, but a bitter rebel.

"The Confederacy had no more active friend than she," he said. "She was a woman of character and sociable in the best ways of her sex. But she was devoted, body and soul, to the cause of the South." In his trial testimony, Weichmann insisted, he had said little to incriminate her. Another witness did that job. He had been surprised, he added, by her lawyers.

"She had three, you know, but at times I wondered if she would have been better off with none." Fraser recalled Cook's opinion that her lawyers made her situation worse, not better. "Senator Reverdy Johnson of Maryland appeared for her, which seemed like a great coup. He was a wonderful lawyer, respected across the country. Yet he abandoned her after one week, an act that implied he thought her guilty. That left her with two young men with little experience of the courts. They scored few hits, at least so far as I could tell. They were no match for John Bingham, that's sure."

"What happened to those lawyers?"

"The young ones? They both got patronage jobs from President Andy Johnson. Isn't *that* peculiar? Why would he hire Mrs. Surratt's lawyers, after he approved her execution?"

"Why?"

"Dr. Fraser, if you find that question interesting, then you are, as you say, no friend of the ghastly George Townsend. We should dine. Come home with me. I live with my sisters and brother-in-law, and they are forever after me to go about in society. They fear I become more strange as the years pass, while I merely fear more and more, which they do not comprehend, or claim not to. In any event, tonight you can be my rejoinder to them."

Fraser was unprepared for the theological tone of the Weichmann dinner table. Louis Weichmann, it turned out, was a seeker of a particularly persistent stripe. He trained as a Catholic seminarian but grew disenchanted with that church and sampled the doctrinal wares of the full range of Christian denominations. He was settled for the moment in an Anglican parish, to the dismay of his very Catholic sisters, each of whom cautioned him through the meal of the error of his path.

"Louis," scolded the unmarried sister, Tillie, who seemed to care more about ecclesiastical matters. "You can no longer risk your immortal soul over a bureaucratic disagreement over who manages your church."

"Tillie, that's a hideously false statement of my views," Weichmann snapped. "The day the American Catholic Church steps forward to acknowledge its involvement in the Booth conspiracy is the day I will consider rejoining that flock."

"Balderdash," Tillie answered. "You don't believe the Pope was involved in killing Lincoln any more than I do. Father Chiniqui writes utter nonsense about that."

"Ah"—her brother answered, one finger pointing portentously skyward—"perhaps not the hierarchy, the bishops and such, and I quite agree that the Pope cared little whether President Lincoln lived or died. But those priests out in southern Maryland and in Washington, those were dangerous men." He ticked off the points on his fingers: Booth met Dr. Mudd at a Catholic service in Charles County. Michael O'Laughlen was Catholic, as was John Surratt, and it was the priests who hustled Surratt out of the country, then out of Canada, and then on to the Vatican in Rome.

"What better way to conceal poisonous secrets," he asked, "than in the robes of a priest? Mrs. Surratt, you will remember, was forever at church. Where better to pass secrets than the confessional, which, after all, is designed for secrets?"

Certain priests, according to Weichmann, had sworn eternal hostility to him because of his testimony. "They have hounded me for decades, sir, and they hound me still. I will never be comfortable in a Roman Catholic congregation." He added that he faced ostracism by unnamed others sympathetic to the Booth conspirators. Fraser alternated between thinking Weichmann a lunatic or a man who was paying a high price for being in the wrong place at a very wrong time.

After the meal, Weichmann led Fraser to a small room in the back of the house. Lovingly, the small, bearded man explained the contents of each shelf and cabinet. Books and pamphlets were shelved according to the attitude of the author: Did he support the prosecution theory that the Confederacy was behind Booth, or did they portray Booth as the mad genius who was responsible for everything, or did they blame the assassination on the Pope, on Stanton, on the Sons of Liberty in the North, or the man in the moon? Weichmann had few volumes that Mr. Bingham had not collected for his own library.

The treasure trove, though, lay in thirty-five folders of newspaper and magazine articles that began on April 15, 1865. The folders, growing progressively thinner as the years stretched on, ran straight through May 1900. May 1900. Weichmann offered this archive to Fraser with only one condition: He could take notes but could not remove anything, a pledge that would be enforced by his sister Tillie, who would sit in the room while Fraser worked. Fraser agreed. Though he itched to dive into the folders right away, Weichmann said he could begin in the morning.

Chapter 8

"What about the money, Louis?" Fraser said. "What can you tell me about Booth's money?" After two days in Weichmann's meticulous archive, Fraser was on a first-name basis with the entire Weichmann family. His work was raising more questions than it answered. Weichmann had come home early so they could confer before supper. The odor of boiling cabbage assaulted the room from the kitchen. Weichmann seemed indifferent to the noxious aroma.

"Ah, the money bothers you, too?" Weichmann was stroking his beard.

"Of course, Sam Chester claimed that Booth promised him $2,000 and said there were at least fifty people in the conspiracy."

"Booth could have been lying. That would be one of his smaller sins."

"Lying about the people, sure, but not the money. He would have to pay whatever he promised. Sam Chester was his friend." Fraser leaned forward. "You know how much they were spending, how they lived. Did they have money?"

"Lots." Weichmann allowed himself a grin. "I thought John Surratt got most of the funds. He could secure any type of currency, even gold. But Booth had sources, too. Surratt promised poor Atzerodt a fortune to guide boats stuffed with cotton across the Potomac. Atzerodt would have sold his own mother for any amount. Such a low form of our species. And Surratt and Booth wore beautiful clothes. Those two"—he shook his head—"strutting like peacocks. I tell you, Jamie, they were the best-dressed killers. They were both charming, of course, that was how they made their way. With them, everything was deluxe. Fine restaurants, deluxe meals served in private rooms. Oh, they loved to spout about Southern liberty, but at bottom it was a dirty deal fired by money and greed."

"Where did the money come from?"

"There were only three places. First, of course, was Richmond. Second, there were the Confederates up in Montreal, where both of them went. But"—and here Weichmann paused, stroking his beard again—"my best guess is New York."

"Booth was there in November of 1864."

"That's right, and he went back in January. Atzerodt said Booth was going there for money. Say what you will about Atzerodt, and you can say anything you like as far as I care, he kept his eye on the dollars. If he said Booth was getting money there, then he was."

"From Booth's brothers?"

"I doubt it. They had no connection to his scheme and not much to him."

Fraser asked about Bessie Hale, Booth's fiancée, but Weichmann knew nothing about her. Booth had never mentioned her. Weichmann suspected the conspirators didn't know about his engagement. "Except, perhaps, Surratt," he added. "He and Booth were thick as thieves."

Weichmann was more helpful about another of Booth's consorts, a woman referred to in a newspaper article as residing in "one of Washington's gilded houses of pleasure." Weichmann knew her as Nelly Starr. Despite her occupation, Weichmann admired her. She was, he said, delightful, a graceful woman with a disarming manner. Weichmann saw her with Booth on several occasions.

"The newspapers," Fraser said, "claimed she tried to kill herself after his arrest. They said her name was Ella Turner."

"It was a sad story."

"She seems to have been more upset about Booth's fate than his fiancée was."

"She may have had more cause."

"What do you mean? That she was in on it?"

"No, no, no, not that. There was talk, you know. There always is."

"I see. Did she have a baby? I mean, afterward."

"Who knows? She disappeared, the way that type of woman does. John Wilkes Booth surely left babies with more women than Nelly Starr. I was sorry about her."

As Fraser raised his questions, one after the other, he found himself in surprising agreement with Weichmann. Both doubted the story of the shooting of Booth. Sergeant Boston Corbett, Weichmann insisted, had been armed with only a pistol, yet Booth was killed by a rifle bullet! Weichmann thought another shooter, one with better aim than Sergeant Corbett, had ended Booth's life in that burning barn and never came forward to take credit.

Weichmann also concurred that Booth's escape was too well organized to be the product of amateurs like Booth and his band of bunglers. Someone with brains and experience planned it. And Weichmann, too, was troubled that so many investigators had ignored the failed attempt to kill other Union leaders. Michael O'Laughlen, he insisted, trailed Ulysses Grant the night before the assassination, while Lewis Paine stalked Edwin Stanton at the same time. The wider and more ambitious the conspiracy, he argued, the less likely that it was the brainchild of a single deranged actor.

But on all of these matters, Weichmann could offer only his shared skepticism. After a lifetime of chewing on these questions, he had no definitive answers.

The married sister, who seemed to run the household, announced that dinner would be served. Fraser made his excuses. He had important business at the telegraph office, he insisted, eager to fly from the cabbage. He promised to return in the morning for a final sally into the archive.

Fraser couldn't put his finger on it. He couldn't point to a single feature of his hotel room that was obviously out of place, that proved someone had been there. His dirty clothes were still in his valise. His remaining clean collar still sat in a bureau drawer. His shaving brush and razor lay next to the pitcher and bowl. His book sat on the bed table, roughly where he left it. Yet someone had rifled through his belongings; he felt it. There had been nothing to find, of course. Fraser kept his notes with him. He must be imagining it. He was thinking too much about conspiracies hatched in hotel rooms. He was spending too much time with Weichmann, a man who suspected his enemies of poisoning the air he breathed.

Dinner in the hotel dining room was blissfully free of cabbage. The cook produced a tolerable pork chop with mashed potatoes. The shortcake featured the first strawberries of the season, which might have benefitted from a few more days in the garden. The dish nonetheless signaled warm summer days to come. Fraser rose from the table in a benign humor that flowed from having eaten his fill, plus a bit more. He resolved to deal with the latter sensation by taking a stroll around town before turning in.

Not far from the hotel, he paused to admire an auto that stood idle on the side of the street. Its high leather seat, open to the weather, would comfortably seat two people. A steering shaft rose through the center of the floor.

"She's a beauty, ain't she?" The voice came from the far side of the contraption, where a man was reaching under the vehicle's frame. "Brand-new design. Eight-horsepower engine. Gas tank's in back."

"It's handsome," Fraser allowed. "What's it called?"

"A Lambert, after me. I'm John Lambert." The man straightened. He grabbed a cloth from the floor of the auto and wiped his hands. "I'd offer my hand, but it's greasy." He walked around the front of the auto with a proprietary air. "Pneumatic tires, top speed of fifteen so far. I'm working on a new transmission that will make Lamberts the most popular autos on the road."

"They're not for sale?"

"Not yet. The transmission can be a bit balky, also the brakes."

"The brakes?"

"Yes, the transmission doubles as a braking mechanism. If the transmission seizes up, well, things can go poorly."

"We don't have too many autos where I live. Really, we don't have any."

"These don't really crash. More like unplanned stops. You get bounced around and might end up on the ground. Nothing to bother a true motorist, but I want the Lambert to appeal to more than just enthusiasts. It'll be for everyone. We make the parts right here. It'll be a corker when it's right."

Fraser watched the man light the kerosene lamps at the front of the auto and fire the engine, then rattle down the main street, waving to a passing couple.

Fraser pondered the wonder of automobiles as he turned down a side street toward the river. The machines were smelly and dirty, of course, but so were horses. An auto might make his life easier. Then he thought of the roads of Harrison

County. He could not imagine an auto strong enough to pull through the mud at the bottom of those hills after a downpour. No, not in Harrison County, not yet.

The river was still a hundred yards before him when a wide figure stepped out and blocked his way. A gruff voice said, "Dr. Fraser?"

Distracted by movement in a grove of trees to his right, Fraser did not see the blow coming, a powerful fist driven into his midsection. Someone small jumped on his back as he doubled over, then was yanked upright in time to catch a second punch next to where the first one landed. Lacking the breath to cry out, Fraser tried to crouch and turn from his attacker. The next blow landed on his elbow, which shielded his throbbing ribs. The force of that punch, combined with Fraser's weight, wrenched him from the grip of the man behind him. He fell to the ground and tried to crawl away.

A rough hand grabbed Fraser's shoulder and his attacker leaned close, his face inches away. Beery breath, combined with the evening's pork chops and the beating, made Fraser's insides heave. He gasped from the pain, his ribs on fire, and couldn't stop the flow that surged up and out of his stomach. It hurt. Then it stank.

His attacker pulled back. "Just look at him," he snorted. "Sort of a delicate type, ain't he?" The other man didn't comment. Fraser couldn't.

"That's just a taste," the attacker hissed at him. The man's feet straddled him. Fraser was completely exposed. Able to draw some breath now, he tried to rise on an elbow.

"Don't be a hero, Doc." The voice was still close, pitched low. "Just remember that we stopped. This time, we stopped. And we didn't have to. And also, remember that the Sons of Liberty are watching you."

Fraser saw the next punch coming but was powerless to stop

it. The fist smashed into the side of his head, driving the other side into the dirt and gravel of the road.

He didn't remember the men leaving, nor did he know how long he lay there. The clammy feel and sour stench of vomit brought him back. He thought a rib or two might be broken. Gingerly, he rose onto all fours. Stable in that ignoble position, he experimented with ways to breathe that caused the least pain. Shallow panting hurt. Slow breaths also were bad. He came upright by small stages, each triggering knife blades of pain. His balance gone, he used a tree trunk as an anchor as he lurched to his feet. His head felt wrong.

Looking around, Fraser wondered about the people of Anderson. It wasn't late, maybe 9:30. Light shone in the windows of a few houses. Did no one hear anything? Was no one aware of what happened in front of their homes? Perhaps, he wondered, they were all in on it, or were too cowed by the Sons of Liberty to step forward.

That was crazy thinking, the product of a beating and too much time with Louis Weichmann. He shuffled slowly back the way he had come.

"Good evening, Dr. Fraser." The desk clerk handed over his room key but said nothing of Fraser's battered appearance. Without looking in a mirror, Fraser knew the side of his head was bruised, his face scraped by the gravel on the street, his clothes dirty and askew, his gait wobbly. Were such traits unremarkable in this town? Was the desk clerk in on it, too?

He held the banister with both hands as he climbed to his second-floor room.

"Oh, dear, Dr. Fraser, what has happened to you?" Tillie Weichmann still wore her church finery, a wide-brimmed hat tilted at a rakish angle to show off a bold flower of yellow ribbon. She placed her small hand on his forearm as he stood on their front step. Her eyes were large with sympathy. He had spent much of that Sunday morning trying to improve his appearance, starting with a hot bath. He brushed his suit vigorously, donned his last clean collar, and carefully tied his cravat. He could not conceal, however, the scratches on one side of his face or the swelling on the other. His expression probably reflected his injuries. If he sat quietly, he had a lot of pain. Movement was much worse. He had aimed to arrive at the Weichmanns' in the early afternoon, just before they sat down to dinner.

He tried to smile and adopt a cheery tone. "Tillie, I was hoping to visit Louis's library today. And to speak with him, if he's available?"

"You must come in and let me see to those wounds."

When Fraser followed her into the front hall, Weichmann looked up from the dining room table. His mouth fell open. He threw his newspaper down. "No, no, no, no, no, no," he cried. "He must go. He must go this minute." Weichmann strode past Fraser toward the archive. He slammed the door behind him.

"Oh, dear," Tillie said. "You know how Louis can be. I'm sure we can see to your injuries before you go."

"That's all right. I'm a doctor. Maybe I should return this evening."

She shook her head. "No, he doesn't want you here, and I don't blame him. He has had bad experiences from all the Lincoln business. You must understand, Doctor. We grow less brave as we grow older, and you've just given him quite a fright. He won't see you. You may be sure of that."

"Forgive me," he said, lowering his voice. "Perhaps you could take him a note with one simple question." When she made to object, he raised his hand. "He need not speak with me, but if he would look at my inquiry and make any response he thinks appropriate, I would take it as a kindness."

She agreed.

Drawing a pencil and paper from his case, Fraser wrote:

> *Mr. Weichmann:*
> *I was waylaid last evening by men who called*
> *themselves the Sons of Liberty, and who may*
> *have been concerned by my inquiries here. I am*
> *nevertheless resolved to continue those inquiries.*
> *Where should I look next?*
> *James Fraser, M.D.*

He folded the note and handed it to her. With a careful dignity, Tillie took it and passed back toward her brother's library.

She returned with the folded note in one hand, her hat now in the other. "Doctor," she said in a peremptory manner, "you should leave."

When he reached the street, Fraser crumpled the note and was about to throw it in the gutter. When he opened it he found a single word under his question: *"Barstow."*

Chapter 9

❧

Cadiz looked good to Fraser when he arrived home, though his all-too-visible injuries drew concerned questions from his patients and neighbors. Fraser insisted he had fallen from a horse, though he never detailed which horse, or where, or how. Let them talk, he thought. The real story would not improve his standing as a citizen or a physician. No one wants a doctor who runs off to investigate an assassination thought to have been solved long ago, and then gets himself thrashed by strangers.

Fraser resolved to abandon his grandiose effort to solve the Booth conspiracy. He had patients to care for, medical journals to catch up on, and a hundred chores he had neglected, beginning with the loose doorknob at the entrance to his examining room. That wobble conveyed to patients an unfortunate message of carelessness. It was intolerable. The tongue-and-groove mechanism had to be replaced. The task consumed an entire evening.

But it was no use. After a week of healing, while lurid shades of purple and black bloomed between his left ear and cheekbone, the itch came back. He couldn't keep his mind from the Lincoln case. What happened to Booth and Bingham and Lincoln was so much more interesting than Mr. Van Dusen's dyspepsia or Mrs. Markham's gravel or stitching up another farmer kicked by an ill-tempered cow. Sitting in that empty house, which for him always would be Ginny's house, Fraser needed something more to care about.

Another force drove him. He was angry now. He had always been slow to anger and much slower to cool off. He wasn't going to cool off anytime soon. He was an American, with the right to know his own history. Who were those Sons of Liberty to stop him? His father gave his life for the ideals of the nation. Fraser would not dishonor that sacrifice by being scared into silence by street thugs.

Fraser pulled out his notes and chronology, then inserted what he learned from Weichmann. He didn't have much about the Sons of Liberty. With the itch still prickling his brain, he stood on Emma Bingham's front porch on a close afternoon that badly needed a thunderstorm.

She wore a sun bonnet and apron, and apologized for her appearance. Though they would be selling the house, she explained, she was hoping to get a crop of vegetables from the garden that summer. He asked to look in the library for a few additional items. After a slight hesitation, she led him there. He noted with satisfaction that their earlier efforts had quelled some of the room's chaos, though districts of disorder persisted.

"Jamie," she said, turning to look up at him, "I fear I've caused you trouble by burdening you with my father's papers."

"Emma, it's been my great privilege to work on these. It's been a chance to repay the kindnesses I've received from you and your father."

"Oh, Jamie, just look at you! I know you're involved in

something terrible and it's my fault." She reached a hand toward his bruised face.

"Sheer clumsiness," Jamie said, trying a grin intended to be rakish. "Better men grow out of it."

"I'm not so stupid, Jamie. It's not a compliment to act as though I am. I'm sure it's something to do with Father, perhaps something he asked you to do. Really, Jamie, you never leave Cadiz for years and suddenly you're gone for almost a week and come back looking like . . . that!"

Fraser was not sure what bothered him more—that Emma was tracking him, that she thought he never left Cadiz, or that she thought he would leave only if Mr. Bingham sent him on a posthumous errand. Suppressing his annoyance, he took her hands.

"Emma, dear Emma. It's a fine thing to be worried about, especially by a friend as good as you. But I assure you, I left Cadiz for business, and your father made no request that triggered the journey. I have my own concerns, and they can take me away."

Had her sallow complexion permitted it, she would have blushed. "Of course, I was being foolish." He held on to her hands as she tried to pull back.

"Not foolish at all. Your heart is one of the best, but there's no cause for concern over anything other than my sorry lack of coordination." He released her hands and nodded toward the shelves around them. "I will return everything where I find it."

"Of course. You're always welcome. I'll be out back if you need anything."

Three hours of reading brought precious little information about the Sons of Liberty. The group had roots in the Knights of the Golden Circle, which dated to before the Civil War and aimed to expand the nation into Mexico and Canada. He thought one of Booth's gang had been a Knight of the Golden

Circle, but was disappointed to discover it was Michael O'Laughlen, one of the least important.

During the war, the Sons of Liberty were active in Ohio and Indiana, planning uprisings by Confederate soldiers held in Union prison camps. Their plans dissolved with the arrest of their leaders in mid-1864. As Cook had said, one of them was from Cadiz, a man named Lambdin Milligan. It was Milligan who challenged the way they were prosecuted, in front of military commissions. After the war, the Supreme Court ruled that he was right, that a regular court should have held the trial. The decision came too late to help the Lincoln conspirators, who also were tried before a military commission.

But Fraser found no evidence that the Sons of Liberty or the Knights of the Golden Circle survived the war. Then again, they were secret organizations. The whole point was for no one to know they existed. Could the Sons of Liberty still be around, out of sight, thirty years later? Could they be big enough to track someone as inconsequential as Jamie Fraser?

Fraser never much liked the Fourth of July. He remembered, as a boy, feeling sticky most of the holiday, sweat mingling with watermelon juice and slopped-over lemonade, coated with a light layer of dust. Always big for his age, he was expected to excel in the town's athletic competitions. Being slow afoot, he rarely did. His size would have helped in the wrestling, but he never entered. He couldn't see the point in fighting someone who had done nothing to make him angry.

He did enjoy the morning baseball game between Cadiz and Steubenville. He watched it every year until he was old enough to play, a lumbering first baseman who could hit the ball a long way if only he could make contact. This year he was the umpire, which not only testified to his reputation for fairness but also would protect his still-tender ribs. Yet, he resented the assignment, a clear message that his best days on the diamond were behind him, even though his best days had been on the pallid side.

Still, he smiled at the shiny morning at McGregor's field, a corner of a local farm long devoted to the needs of Cadiz's ballplayers. Nervous energy charged the air as the players warmed up, calling out greetings and insults, trying to identify the field's more pronounced dips, rills, and half-buried rocks. Steubenville usually won, a tradition since Speed Cook anchored their nine twenty-five years ago. He was the umpire, Fraser reminded himself. No choosing sides.

He didn't notice Cook until the bottom of the sixth inning, the second time he called Joe Mooney out on strikes. Joe, a rugged teamster for an express company, took exception. Fraser waved the next man into the batter's box, but Mooney didn't move, loudly describing Fraser's visual limitations. Fraser turned his back so Mooney's teammates could haul the young man out of reach. As the disappointed batter's harangue faded, Fraser saw Cook on the Steubenville side, past first base. The old ballplayer's posture carried the controlled eagerness of a hunting dog alerting to nearby prey. Fraser wished Cook were playing. Even at his age, he would be the best player on the field. Fraser raised a hand in greeting. Cook didn't respond.

After Cadiz submitted, 18-10, the combatants and spectators repaired to the nearby picnic. Fraser joined a group in a shady spot and soon was licking fried chicken batter and watermelon juice from his fingers. The conversation was politics. The Republicans had re-nominated McKinley for president, adding a combative young New Yorker named Roosevelt as his running mate. Fraser didn't join in. His politics were instinctive and he articulated them poorly. Being Republican was bred into his bones. He knew the Frasers were Republican before he knew they were Christian. Yet the prospect of reelecting McKinley depressed him. More war in the Philippines, more of the same. He decided to walk around.

He greeted friends, admired babies, turned down more food, and found a place to hose off his hands. The sun grew warmer. Fraser wiped his face with a handkerchief already soggy with sweat. Then he decided. He left to find Speed Cook.

Fraser took the path down to Liming Creek, where the colored families gathered for their picnic. He entered the cool of the woods and followed the cries of children. As he neared the tumult, he thought through what he wanted to say. It had been simmering inside him for days.

Cook crouched in the middle of a bright clearing, fifty yards from the larger gathering at the creek. A dozen children circled him, whooping and laughing and leaping, bouncing off his hard muscles and sliding down his arms and legs. He twisted and dodged, darted away from them, then slowed enough for them to dive at him again. He caught the reckless ones with his powerful hands, keeping them from collisions that might have meant catastrophe, or at least an extended bout of bawling. "Come on, come on," he taunted, flashing a grin Fraser had never seen. "Where's the strong ones here? Can't catch up to an old man? Come on, come on!"

Four of the larger children grabbed him, two at the waist and two at the knees. Cook gave a great roar and bellowed, "Are the strong ones here? Where'd they come from?"

The younger ones shrieked and jumped as he sank slowly under the weight of the squirming bodies, crying, "Oh, no! Oh, no!" The laughter became riotous and the joyful shouts proclaimed, "We got him! We got him!"

After more minutes of mad wrestling, the quarry finally fell still, which cast the children into a state of instant boredom. A few younger ones nudged Cook, sprawled on his back. They begged him to do something, to play some more.

"You all go on now," he said as he sat up, brushing grass from his hair. He stroked a small boy's cheek with the side of his finger. "Wash your hands in the creek before your mama sees you. She'll skin us both." The boy followed the others toward the stream.

When Cook caught sight of Fraser at the edge of the clearing, his nod was neither friendly nor hostile.

"You're a popular man," Fraser said.

"They're easy to please." Cook stood with impressive quickness for a man who had recently been buried under several hundred pounds of howling boys and girls. "You're looking all right. I heard someone was dancing on your face. Heard it was bad."

"I'm fine. Took a spill off a horse."

"Uh-huh." Cook smiled. "Most folks around here know what it looks like when you've been slugged." Fraser looked at the ground. Cook turned to go.

"Wait." Fraser walked toward him. "I wanted to talk, about the trip we took. Some of the things you said that night, you were right. I can't fix everything for you colored in this country, but I didn't act as a friend should, and I regret that."

"That an apology?"

"Yes."

"Not always easy to tell with you white folks."

Fraser stuck out his hand. Cook took it without enthusiasm. "If you've got a minute," Fraser said, "I'd like to tell you about that trip I took to Indiana."

Chapter 10

They walked down the creek away from the colored picnic. The words tumbled out of Fraser, telling what he learned from Louis Weichmann and his archive. He talked about Nelly Starr and her baby, about Bessie Hale, and about all the money Booth spread around the conspiracy. He mentioned his unhappy encounter with the Sons of Liberty, but didn't linger on the subject.

"So?" Cook asked.

"So what?"

"So why you telling me this?"

Fraser stopped and faced Cook. "It may be crazy, I know, but I can't let this go. I came back busted up, angry with myself, ashamed to be running around the countryside like a damned fool. I figured I'd learned my lesson. A stupid escapade by a man feeling bored with his life, who once dreamed of doing great things and was starting to realize he wouldn't ever."

Fraser had never spoken like this with anyone, not even Ginny, but he rushed on. "But this *is* important. The whole Booth business is fishy. How it was investigated, how it was prosecuted, how it was wrapped up and tied with a bow with answers that don't hold up. Mr. Bingham knew that, and I believe he knew the right answers, but he didn't trust me enough to tell me. Maybe he was right not to trust me. Maybe I'm not the one to do it, but I need to try."

Cook stared at him without any expression.

"And," Fraser started again, "well, I'd just like . . . I think we, you and I, could maybe get back to working on this, put together a real investigation of the Booth conspiracy. You—"

"That's it!" Cook cried out. "You're looking to get you a bodyguard, right? Figure I'll take care of all the bad men for you, that right?"

"No, that's not right." Fraser could not keep the annoyance out of his voice. "What's right is that you can figure things out, sometimes you see things I don't. You were right about what we need to look for. It has to be something in the North, that has to be why Mr. Bingham never would say what it was. And I may see things that you don't. We match up together. We can each do different things. Together we're a lot more likely to get to the bottom of this."

Cook looked thoughtful. "Then again, you could've used me that night you got jumped in Indiana."

Fraser shrugged. "I could've used a small dog or a crippled nun." He stopped. "Look, Speed, I've never taken a lot of chances. This business may involve some chances. Sure, we'd have to look out for each other."

Cook looked at him through flat eyes. "No white man's ever looked out for me."

"That jury in Syracuse didn't hurt you. That was white men."

"Not what I meant."

"Okay. You don't have to trust me. But you can."

They started walking back the way they came. Cook asked how Fraser figured to pay for this investigation. There was a piece of land from his mother's family, Fraser said, it had been a farm. He always figured he'd sell it to pay for his old age. But he could sell it now, close his practice for a few months, and use the money to pay their expenses.

"I know this matters to you," Fraser said. "It's part of that war you talked about, the one you said you're losing. Since we traveled together, I've been noticing things in the paper. Just last month, Negroes were lynched over in West Virginia, in Colorado, in Mississippi. North Carolina's talking about taking the vote away from them. Maybe this is a chance to turn that back, to expose the people who set all that hate and violence in motion. When will you have another chance like this?"

"That sounds nice," Cook said, "but I'm a family man. I'd have to ask my brother to watch over my businesses. And he's still learning about business."

Fraser drew a breath. He had planned this part of the conversation, too. "You're still serious about that newspaper?"

Cook nodded.

"Could you use an investor? Someone to help pay for getting started?"

"Sure."

"What would you need?"

"What've you got?"

"Five hundred dollars. After I sell the land."

"That'd help."

"We'd have to work out my share of the business."

"You wouldn't control what went into the paper. That's what the editor does. And this editor is going to use that newspaper to fight our war."

"Fine."

They sat on a log next to the creek. Fraser had to talk about the ideas and questions that he had been chewing on for the last month.

He started with Townsend, ignoring the frown that crossed

Cook's face at the mention of the writer's name. Yes, Fraser said, the man was rude, but he asked a good question: How would Mary Surratt know this great secret she told Mr. Bingham? She moved between her boarding house on H Street, her tavern in Surrattsville, and her church. It had to be something she learned from Booth or her son.

So, Fraser went on, that meant the answers might be where Booth and Surratt had been—Montreal, New York City, and Richmond. The Confederate agents in Montreal were long gone, as was the Confederate government in Richmond. But New York was still there, especially the same money interests that existed back in 1865.

The small boy who had been the last to leave now strolled back toward them, tapping a stick on the ground. He ran over to Cook and climbed up on his lap. His shirt bore fresh food stains. "Joshua," Cook said to him, "this here's Dr. Fraser. Shake the man's hand and say your how-dos."

The boy held out a small hand and said softly, "How you do?" Fraser smiled and shook it. Cook turned back to Fraser.

"Motive," Fraser said, "that's the big question. It wasn't an act of vengeance against a single man by a single man. It was a coup d'état, an attempt to destroy the Union government. Have you ever thought who would have inherited the government if Lincoln, Johnson, Seward, and Grant had been eliminated?"

He didn't wait for an answer. With a look of triumph, Fraser announced, "Lafayette S. Foster."

Cook's face turned to bemusement. "Say again?"

"Lafayette S. Foster. He was president pro tem of the Senate, next in line to be president. There was some provision that the Secretary of State was supposed to call a new election for president, but Foster would have been president, Lincoln and Johnson and Seward would have been dead, so I figure Foster would've held the job easily."

"So who was Lafayette Foster?"

"Exactly." Fraser felt a rush of excitement. "He was a Republican from Connecticut, not a real strong Republican. He came from the eastern part of the state, where the textile mills were. During the war, those mills lived on cotton smuggled from the South. Foster understood that, even sponsored legislation about how to manage cotton lands the Union Army took from rebels. But that's not all." Fraser made an effort to slow himself down. "Okay, so, if Booth and his gang kill everyone, who would've run the army?"

"I don't know. Sherman, I guess. He was the next biggest general after Grant."

"Right," Fraser said. "And not many Union generals were more pro-South than William T. Sherman."

"A whole lot of Southerners'd disagree. I've heard them. They spit when they hear his name. The man burned down near half the South."

"Who said those people ever knew who their real friends were? Sherman was a tough fighter, sure, but he was against abolition. He sided with Andy Johnson after the war. He was one of your race-haters, much more than Grant. Before the war he ran a school in Louisiana and he *liked* it down there. When Joe Johnston surrendered to him in April 1865, Sherman gave away everything, left the Confederate state governments in power, gave them control over all their army's weapons. Their weapons! Grant had to rush down on the double-quick to reverse the whole business."

"Where you going with this?"

Fraser shook his head. "I don't know, but I've got to stay at it. I've got to get to the end of this trail."

"Daddy." Joshua was holding up the index finger on Cook's left hand. "Tell me again how that happened?" The finger bent sharply to the right at the first knuckle, then straightened out at the second.

"That one?" Cook looked at it thoughtfully. "That happened so I can tickle around corners." He demonstrated by reducing Joshua to a squirming mass of giggles. The boy slid off his lap and sat on the ground between Cook's feet. He resumed tapping his stick.

"Okay," Cook said, "let's say there's a new government after Lincoln's killed. Foster's president. Sherman's running the army. What happens different? The South's been beat."

"Maybe two things. First, we know Sherman wanted the easiest possible peace terms. Maybe that's what they wanted from Foster and Sherman. Also, Foster ran for reelection as a Democrat after the war, so like I said, he wasn't much of a Republican. For someone who wanted to get rid of Lincoln, Foster may have been the perfect successor."

"What's the second thing?"

"Second, it could have been about getting that Southern cotton and tobacco up to the North, something that involved making a lot of money."

"Come on now, the war was ending. The cotton and tobacco was coming up anyway."

"That's right. But maybe it was *how* it came up, who was going to make the money."

"Killing Lincoln and those others seems like a lot of trouble to go to just to get some money."

"That may depend on how much money, and how bad you need it." When Cook shook his head, Fraser played his strongest card. He had researched Barstow, the name Weichmann gave him. When he found no Barstow in the Lincoln conspiracy materials, he mentioned the name to a friend who was a banker in Columbus. His friend had laughed. Samuel Barstow, a former Confederate officer, was the wizard behind the Cotton Trust in New York City. That trust had a stranglehold over the worldwide cotton trade. From Calcutta to Cairo,

Barstow's name reverberated for growers, shippers, and mill owners.

"Don't you see?" Fraser said. "He may be the connection between all of it—the Confederacy, the cotton smuggling then, the Sons of Liberty now."

They sat silent. Cook straightened and cleared his throat. "It sounds a bit too Southern to me," Cook said.

"What do you mean?"

"Remember, Mr. Bingham said it was something that could destroy the Union. I still think that means Northerners. Where are they in what you're talking about?" Fraser stayed quiet, listening. "What about politics? The Democrats had just lost the election in 1864 and Lincoln was just sworn in, so they were stuck with him for four more years. It feels like that might figure in this somewhere. Then there's those Sons of Liberty."

Joshua stood up. "Mama said she was going to bring out her cobbler. I want some."

"Count me in, little man." Cook said to Fraser, "You don't want to miss that woman's cobbler." They followed Joshua at sashay pace. "What're you thinking about doing?" Cook asked.

"I want to start at the source. The Booths. You know, there's still Booths around. We can wire Townsend for help tracking them down."

"That shouldn't take long. Can't imagine any of them'd care to have a long sit-down about the Lincoln assassination."

"And we've got to go to New York. Booth went there, Surratt went there. That's where the money was, that's where the rich Democrats were, the ones backing George McClellan against Lincoln in the 1864 election. And that's where the cotton trade was. There's the Cotton Exchange there now, even the Cotton Trust. And that's where Barstow is."

"New York's a rough town for colored. Those Irish boys don't mess around."

"If you're afraid, I can go by myself."

"I ain't afraid, but I ain't stupid."

The cobbler was as good as advertised. While Fraser was eating, an older woman wearing a patchwork skirt approached him. She asked what she should do about her back pains. Another brought her little girl over so he could look at her eye, which seemed infected. It took close to thirty minutes for Fraser to work through the picnickers' ailments.

Cook rejoined him as the last patient limped away. "No way to make a living, Doc," he said. "Shouldn't be giving it away."

"Never got the knack of turning sick people away." He put his hand on Cook's arm. "Speed, we've got more to talk about. I think we should go to Maryland and Washington City, too. That's where it all happened, and people there know more than they've ever said. John Surratt's in Baltimore, and so's his sister. In Washington, you've got Bessie Hale, Booth's fiancée. And there must be more."

"All these people, you really think they're just aching to spill their guts to John Bingham's doctor and a colored ex-ballplayer?"

"Not everyone can keep a secret like Mr. Bingham could. Maybe we can figure out some reasons for them to talk to us. I keep thinking about this, too. We may be the last people who can figure this out. The people who know things, people like Weichmann and the Surratts, they're getting on in years. They're not going to live forever. We need to do this now."

Chapter 11

Cook's father had always marveled at how his neighbors talked about the weather. "Gets hot in the summer," he liked to say. "Gets cold in the winter. The wind blows, and sometimes it rains. So why we got to talk like the Lord's brought us some curse, never been heard nor seen nor even suspicioned before?"

For Jamie Fraser, Cook realized as they rode along the edge of Lake Erie, the weather was a daily revelation.

It *was* hot, even for early August, and it had been hot for weeks. The farms they saw from their train window, and now from their buggy, were dappled with brown, not the rich green they should be showing. Truth was, the sun and the drought were burning up the crops. That phenomenon, which could be crisply described in a single sentence, had occupied Fraser's conversation for the last day and half, slackening slightly now that they were approaching Fairview, a dozen miles west of Erie.

Their departure from Cadiz took longer than they intended. Fraser couldn't sell his land right off, so he had to borrow against it. The bankers kept asking what he wanted the money for, and Fraser chose not to say he was investigating the Lincoln assassination. Cook agreed that damned few bankers would consider that a sound purpose for a loan. Finally, Fraser borrowed the money from a farmer whose fields butted up against Fraser's land. The farmer probably figured he'd get his hooks into Fraser, then grab the land for less than it was worth. Cook wasn't impressed with Fraser's business sense, but that wasn't his lookout. Fraser said he'd come up with the money for their trip and he did it. That was all Cook needed to know.

A hot wind was blowing waves onto the pebbled shore. Cook had low expectations for this leg of the trip. Through Townsend, that slippery writer, they had located the summer home of John Wilkes Booth's nephew, Creston Clarke, who was a big-shot actor himself. Cook couldn't think of a reason why someone who was kin to Booth would help them out, but Fraser insisted. The man had an optimistic streak that could prove dangerous. Cook went along with him this time. What could it hurt? He'd been thrown out of lots better places than the home of John Wilkes Booth's nephew.

"Will you look at that," Fraser said, pulling up the horses. "A castle fit for young Lochinvar, out of the West." Before them loomed a three-story stone mansion that bristled with turrets, roof gables, and a widow's walk at its peak. The effect was monumental and ugly.

"Some folks don't deserve to have money," Cook said, "the stupid things they do with it."

"Must be chilly in the winter, with the wind coming off the lake."

Yup, Cook thought. Cold in the winter.

Fraser climbed down to approach the entrance. When a colored servant answered, Fraser said he represented an Ohio theater chain and asked for Clarke. The servant said Mr. Clarke was away and wasn't expected that day. Fraser left no message.

They drove past a grove of majestic sycamores and stopped

at the side of the road. Fraser pulled out a volume of Shakespeare's plays. He had said he was reading them to understand John Wilkes Booth, who portrayed most of the murderers and assassins in Shakespearean tragedy.

"Which is this one?" Cook asked.

"*King Lear.*"

"They kill the king there, too?"

Fraser shook his head. "I'll let you know." Fraser opened the book while Cook set off on foot toward the back of the mansion. When Cook returned ninety minutes later, Fraser was asleep.

"Well?" Cook asked as he climbed into the buggy.

Shrugging off his nap, Fraser said, "Didn't kill him off, just made him old and crazy."

Cook nodded back at the mansion. "First-class grub there. I got to say, having your uncle shoot the president don't seem to hold a body back much."

"What'd you find out?"

"The man's fishing, way out in the middle of the lake. S'posed to be back by end of the day."

"So he is expected."

Cook smiled. "The answer you get depends on who's doing the asking."

They returned as the fiery afternoon faded into evening. This time both men climbed the four stone steps to the front door. Fraser presented his card as an officer of the Chillicothe Theater Company, along with a letter of introduction from Townsend. The entrance hall was at least fifteen degrees cooler than the front stoop. Those stone walls might be cold in the winter, Fraser whispered, but they were a blessing in early August.

The servant gestured for Cook to wait while he showed Fraser to the parlor. "Mr. Cook is with me," Fraser said. They both followed the servant.

A booming voice, more like a shout, bounced around the im-

mense room as they entered. "Creston Clarke here." The echo
seemed to exaggerate the man's British accent. Cook wondered
if it was genuine. A handsome man of middle size and middle
years greeted Fraser with a firm handshake. He nodded at
Cook. Sunburned cheeks confirmed his time on the lake. His
long hair, cunningly shaped to curl over his collar, announced
his high opinion of himself.

Clarke presented his dark-haired wife, though she went by
another last name, Adelaide Prince. She was not a pretty woman
to Cook's eye, but she radiated energy. Then Clarke introduced
his business manager, a Miss Eliza, no last name provided. Now
she was a looker, with thick brown hair and large hazel eyes.
Her blue dress was not as stylish as Miss Prince's lavender, but
it suited her better. Clarke offered brandy and they accepted,
dropping into massive leather chairs that were arranged in a
semicircle before a baronial hearth.

Fraser began with the contrived explanation for their visit.
He was the agent for three theaters that would like to book
Clarke's company when it next toured Ohio. He placed the
imaginary theaters in small towns, hoping that Clarke wouldn't
know they didn't exist.

As Fraser spoke, Cook's attention strayed to the mementoes
in the chamber. Posters from Shakespearean tragedies and
comedies lined the walls. A brooding portrait of Edwin Booth,
the most successful brother of John Wilkes, hung over the fireplace. Instruments of mayhem, enough to arm a platoon, clut-
tered the room. Daggers sat on the mantel near a skull. Swords
spilled out of a marble umbrella stand. With an effort, Cook focused on Fraser's words.

"Mr. Clarke," Fraser was saying, "I can understand that performers of your distinction can command such terms, but
we're just a couple of Buckeyes, and I fear we couldn't meet
them."

As Clarke leaned forward to stand, ready to put a speedy

end to the encounter, Fraser raised a hand and plunged on. He had received a new play, he said, from a playwright who claimed that the truth never came out about the Booth conspiracy, that John Wilkes Booth was the fall guy for other men who planned the assassination. As Clarke's sunburn seemed to glow more brightly, Fraser added that Clarke's company could make a pretty penny with the drama.

"Are we to have no rest from you bone-pickers?" Leaping to his feet, Clarke advanced on Fraser. "Do you not realize how my mother's life was blighted by the association with Wilkes Booth, as mine has been? Have you no shame? If dueling were still legal, I would insist on immediate satisfaction, and you may be sure that I am skilled with all personal weapons!"

Fraser attempted to calm the man, explaining again that the play contended that Booth was not the villain of myth, but rather was the dupe of others.

Clarke's indignation only grew. The business manager, Miss Eliza, intervened. They should go, she said in an unruffled manner, herding Cook and Fraser out of the room while Clarke continued to spout outrage. In the vestibule, she spoke softly to Fraser. He should return at eleven in the morning and ask for her.

"That was about what I expected," Cook said as he took the reins of their buggy, "until that last bit."

"Let's see what she says in the morning."

"Oh, no, not *we*. You keep that appointment by yourself. That particular filly, you may have noticed, is one fine piece of horseflesh." Cook took Fraser's silence for agreement. "And she might just have eyes for a fine strapping white man like yourself."

Fraser continued his silence. He might not pick things up right off, but he could learn.

*　　*　　*

The morning was growing warm when Eliza Scott met Fraser at the front door. He was glad to step into the cool of the mansion and equally glad to view her in a pale green dress. A businesslike flutter of white at her throat was contradicted by the snug bodice and flare of the skirt. Fraser, he reminded himself, was there for information.

She led him to a patio overlooking a lawn that sloped to the water's edge. A trellis of grape vines shielded them from the sun, but the heat still pressed down.

After offering lemonade, which he accepted, Miss Eliza apologized for Clarke's outburst the night before. "He is in an ill humor from some recent reverses," she explained, "though they have nothing to do with his connection with Wilkes Booth. Indeed"—she flashed a mischievous smile—"the association with Wilkes is the pillar of Mr. Clarke's theatrical career."

"I understood that Creston Clarke was much acclaimed," Fraser said. "That was the basis for our approach on behalf of my theater chain."

"Mr. Fraser, if you will stop pretending that you represent a nonexistent theater chain, I will share with you perhaps the most telling review Mr. Clarke received in his recent tour out West, a tour that can only be described as calamitous."

Though her smile was several degrees beyond winsome, Fraser felt a hot shame that she penetrated his ruse so easily. He decided that a silent nod was the safest course.

She leaned forward. "A critic in Denver—in Denver, mind you!—wrote that in *King Lear,* Mr. Clarke played the king as though in the immediate apprehension that someone else was about to play the ace!"

Fraser chuckled at the bon mot, though he found it obscure. Did it mean that Mr. Clarke had been tentative in his portrayal? Never adept at repartee, Fraser feared that this fetching woman could lead him far beyond his depth. He was undecided whether it was her eyes, which had glints of yellow and brown and green, or that sweet yet daring smile. The smile disappeared as she seemed resolved to raise a more serious matter.

Describing herself as a member of Mr. Clarke's household and friend of the Booth family, she said she must ask his true reason for coming there, since it was not to book theatrical performances. When she added that even an Ohio theater agent would not have dressed as he had the night before, Fraser thought she might have a tendency to the waspish.

He saw no course but to tell the truth, or some of it. Fraser explained that he and his colleague were pursuing a historical inquiry concerning the Lincoln assassination. They believed that the accepted version of events was substantially untrue and assigned to Booth an unfair share of the opprobrium for the crime. Other forces, he added, may have been behind the assassination, forces that hatched the plan and pulled the strings.

Her mischievous look returned. "The Pope?"

"Alas, no. But we had hoped, perhaps presumptuously, that the Booth family would consider cooperating with us. I am sure it's a painful subject for them, and for you, but it will not go away. Not ever."

"Forgive me, Mr. Fraser. When you speak of an investigation or inquiry, I grow confused. Are you and your colleague part of some official body?"

He shook his head, trying to look pleasant.

"Or perhaps you are scholars?"

Another shake of the head, his cheery expression weakening.

"Who, exactly, are you?"

He drummed the fingers of his right hand on the table at which they sat. "We are, I admit, the rankest amateurs. I am a physician from Cadiz, Ohio. My associate is a . . . a journalist of a sort. Through our association in Cadiz with John Bingham, who prosecuted the conspirators"—Miss Eliza tilted her head in recognition of the name—"we have reviewed archival material about that conspiracy and have devoted ourselves to unraveling this devilish knot. Now, I apologize for our presumption in coming here and—"

She held out a hand to stop Fraser.

"Your actual identity, then, is Dr. Fraser of Cadiz?" she inquired.

"Yes." The day had grown very warm.

"That, at least, matches your costume." This time she drummed the fingers of one hand, first in one direction, then in the other. "What, exactly, did you imagine you could learn here? Mr. Clarke was barely born at the time of the assassination."

"We thought there might be family papers, particularly financial records of Booth's activities. It's a painstaking process, putting together something like this, and you never know what might turn out to be helpful."

"I am afraid that cupboard is bare," she said. "The government seized all of the family's papers relating to Wilkes and did so with considerable violence. We have not a scrap left that would be of any use to you."

"Perhaps family stories have been handed down that might shed some light on what Booth did in the weeks and months before the assassination? For example, about his engagement to marry Miss Hale, or of other . . . liaisons?"

She stared off at the lake, then spoke. "Dr. Fraser, you must understand that I am not an official part of the Booth family, but only a paid retainer, though our families have enjoyed a sentimental attachment through the years."

He nodded.

"So whatever I say comes not from the Booths, but rather from one devoted to their success and happiness. As you heard last night, Mr. Clarke would not be disposed to speak with you, nor would others of the family."

He nodded again, surprised that she seemed on the verge of telling him something interesting.

"I have heard," she said, "several remarks concerning Wilkes's connection to cotton brokers during the final months of the war and the smuggling of cotton into the North. You know, of course, that fortunes were made in that trade, and that even Mrs. Lincoln's family was active in it, with the connivance of Mr. Lincoln, of course."

Fraser found his voice. "What sort of connection?"

"I cannot help you there, but it was focused on New York City. The cotton trade still flows through New York, and the Cotton Exchange there is dominated by Southern men."

"Were there specific men whom he did business with?"

"I cannot say. I have on occasion wondered on it myself. It's impossible to be engaged with this family and not think of the darkness that overtook it in 1865."

Fraser said he was traveling to New York and would explore any connection between Booth and the cotton trade. Expressing his gratitude for her assistance, he reached for his hat. She placed her hand on his. "The Clarke company will be in New York in a week," she said, "to begin rehearsal of our plays for the new season. We use one of the theaters that's dark for the summer. We'll be preparing *The Lady of Lyons,* and *The Bells. Richelieu,* too, which Mr. Clarke loves beyond all others, and the usual Shakespeares." Turning on him the shifting colors of her bewitching eyes, she added, "Perhaps we will see you there? We stay at the Waldorf-Astoria."

With great sincerity, Fraser said he hoped to call on her there.

When Fraser reached his hotel room, he could think only of how hot he was. He shed his coat and shirt. The water in the pitcher was tepid as he poured it into the basin, but still cooler than his skin. He splashed it on his face and shoulders, then cupped his hand to pour some on his scalp. He grunted with pleasure. Cook had planned to find a place on the lakeshore for a swim. That sounded good to Fraser, though they might have rules about Negroes on the beaches.

Wiping off with the rough hotel towel, Fraser noticed the envelope on the floor near the door. It wasn't sealed. A note from Cook?

The handwriting was unfamiliar, a poor scrawl, though the message was succinct:

> *Dear nigger-lover,*
> *We are watching you. You cannot change*
> *history. It will not be allowed.*
> *More Sons of Liberty*

Fraser felt his temperature begin to soar again. Who were these sons of—? Where were they? And where do they get off threatening him?

He tore down to the hotel lobby, buttoning his shirt as he walked. Cook was at the bell desk, his jacket slung over his shoulder. Fraser thrust the note in front of him. The hinges of Cook's jaw bulged as he read it, then nodded toward the front door. Outside, he wheeled on Fraser.

"Did you see anyone follow you?" Cook looked down at the note again. "Of course you didn't."

"No, did you?"

Cook kept staring at the note. "You need to start carrying a gun," he said.

Fraser didn't argue.

Chapter 12

New York was colossal, dazzling, thrilling. Also nightmarish. Fraser had never seen so many people. They boiled out of buildings and jammed the streets. A single block of Broadway might hold the entire population of Cadiz, with dozens more blocks just as dense stretching in either direction. Jostled, ignored, then berated for his country ways and indecisive stride, Fraser struggled to follow the rapid New York speech, delivered in a multitude of accents. Was there oxygen enough for all these people, especially on sweltering August days? The stench of horse manure, which Fraser knew well, was overpowering. Between street railways and careening autos, danger loomed at every turn. He ventured cautiously from his hotel in the mornings, disbelieving where he was, unsure of almost everything.

Their lodging arrangements heightened his disorientation. Cook insisted that they change hotels every day. Surely, Fraser objected, they could spend two nights in the same rooms. Who could track them down in this gigantic metropolis? Cook ignored his protest. Every day, they moved. Cook insisted on inconspicuous quarters, rooming houses and fleabag hotels. They were easy on the budget but hard on the backbone. Fraser also suspected that such places were less fussy about accommodating Negroes, which simplified arrangements.

Today's hostelry, their third, was on Avenue A below Tompkins Park, an address with the empty sound of anonymity. Descending the half-flight of steps in front of the building, Fraser and Cook plunged into a welter of swarthy, jabbering people. Russian? Italian? Hungarian? Harrison County held some immigrants, but not like this.

They were headed for the Cotton Exchange on Hanover Square. Cook, more experienced with New York's ways, found the downtown omnibus line and they climbed aboard. Fraser wore a new linen suit, beige, suitable for business meetings with financiers. Miss Eliza's remarks about his clothes had nettled. He was the best-dressed man on the omnibus, including Cook. Cook would not be meeting financiers.

They got off at Exchange Place and separated with only a nod between them. After two wrong turns, Fraser stood before a three-story structure at the end of Hanover Square. Covered with rich brown stone, the Cotton Exchange housed the principal American traders in cotton in all its forms and permutations. As the clock atop the Exchange rang twelve, a man in uniform opened the heavy front door for Fraser. Once inside, hushed elegance and marble opulence reflected the fortunes made and lost within those walls. The stony corridors calmed him.

Fraser asked an attendant in a cutaway coat for the offices of Lehman Brothers. After gazing at Fraser long enough to be rude, the man pointed up. "Third floor, north side." He left Fraser to sort out the points of the compass.

At the door to the Lehman Brothers' office, Fraser presented a letter of introduction from his banker-friend in Columbus. The letter described Dr. John McIntire as a man who was liquidating his real-estate holdings in Ohio and needed investment opportunities. Cook, always cautious, had insisted on the false name. A short, stout man with a gleaming bald head appeared before Fraser.

"Dr. McIntire," he said in a rhythmic Southern accent, pumping Fraser's hand. "Ned Rosenstein. Been expecting you. Perhaps you'd like to look at the exchange before our meal?"

The trading floor occupied one end of the building's first level, but Fraser could detect precious little business being transacted. Several groups spoke in subdued tones in the large room, which featured leather chairs and a plush carpet of blood red. Far from the bargaining or haggling that Fraser associated with a market, no one seemed to have a care in world. No pencil or paper was visible.

Rosenstein pointed out cotton-related objects that members had donated. Framed bills of lading recalled the ports of the world. An early cotton gin produced by Eli Whitney's works filled a corner. Everything except the whips used on the slaves who harvested the crop. While admiring the artifacts, Fraser kept an eye on the desultory traders.

A faint stir rose when a silver-haired gentleman entered. He stopped for a word with the more senior traders. He was a fleshy sort, but fluid in his movements. "That's Barstow," Rosenstein confided in a low voice. "Something must be up if he's on the floor. You don't see him here very often. See how they watch him? They're trying to read his mood, his gestures. Millions turn on whether he frowns or smiles."

"I've heard of Barstow," Fraser returned. "A successful man?"

Rosenstein rolled his eyes in merriment, placing an index finger by the side of his nose.

Rosenstein had booked a table at the famous Delmonico's, a few steps from the exchange. Moving from a high temple of finance to the great shrine of food, Fraser felt a bit giddy. At

Rosenstein's urging, he ordered the renowned Lobster à la Newburg.

Fraser slid easily into his role as a naïve potential investor, and Rosenstein was happy to share his knowledge of the cotton business. The exchange, he explained, was formed after the war to revive trade in the essential fiber. Many of the founders were Southerners, both planters and cotton brokers like the Lehmans.

"And which side of the business do you come from?" Fraser asked.

"Not the cotton-growing side. My daddy started out trading in New Orleans. When business dried up during the war, he followed it to Texas, down near the Mexican border. He came back to New Orleans after the war and did well, but I wanted to come up here and play at the high-dollar tables."

"Is the cotton business such a gamble?"

"Not when you have the best information about crops, weather, and demand all over the world. Only New York gives you that type of information. That's why I came here, and that's what we at Lehman Brothers can share with you."

"I'm curious," Fraser said, "about that Mr. Barstow back there." He nodded toward the semiprivate table where the great man dined with another solid-looking gentleman.

"Sam Barstow?" Rosenstein's round face was lit with amusement. "Hardly anyone gets into bed with that old fox who wasn't in the Confederate Commissary Corps with him. Does business only with men he's known a long, long time. They say he's never lost on a cotton deal."

"Confederate Commissary? Was that their quartermaster service?"

Rosenstein nodded. "The finest thieves and scavengers we had to offer. They spent four years getting cotton and tobacco through the blockade. Those New England mills didn't ask where the cotton came from, nor how it got there. Friendships formed in perilous times, those have a tendency to last."

"So this Barstow, he was a blockade runner?"

"They say he was the best, fiendish clever. Of course, the best way to run the blockade wasn't by taking a lot of damned fool chances. The smart ones went into business with men on the other side of the lines, with Union Army officers. They say Barstow's deals went right to the top of that army."

The lobster smelled wonderful, but Fraser started to have second thoughts about warm cream sauce on a hot day. The lobster meat was tender, though, and the flavor sweet and rich. Mopping his forehead on occasion, Fraser tried to ignore the sweat trickling down his spine. Rosenstein continued his salesman's patter, emphasizing that his firm made money in fat markets and thin ones. And if the weather didn't shift soon, he emphasized, this year's crop would be very thin.

As they leaned back in their seats at the end of the meal, Fraser noticed that Barstow's dining companion had departed, leaving the great man alone. The opportunity was too good to miss.

"I wonder"—he said, nodding over to Barstow's corner—"if you might introduce me to him? It would be quite a treat!"

"Well," Rosenstein began, "I don't know . . ."

But Fraser was already out of his seat. "Shall we?" he asked. With a sigh, Rosenstein stood.

After the introductions, Barstow turned to Fraser. "Did I see you on our trading floor, Dr., uh, McIntire?" He had only a trace of Southern speech.

"Indeed, sir. Actually, a banker-friend has recommended cotton for investment, which is why I'm in New York. He specifically mentioned your firm."

"It's a tricky market, but we limp along—following, in so many ways, Mr. Rosenstein's excellent firm."

"Mr. Barstow is far too modest," Rosenstein said, a slight edge in his tone. "Spencer, Barstow leads the cotton business."

Barstow turned back to Fraser. "I hope you're not allowing business to occupy your entire visit to our great city."

"Oh, dear. I'm still finding it a challenge to avoid being run down in the street." Barstow issued a polite chuckle, leading to an awkward silence. Casting about for some non-business topic, Fraser added, "Actually, I'm hoping to see Mr. Creston Clarke, the actor, to look in on their new touring repertoire. It's in rehearsal here."

"You know Mr. Clarke?"

"Indeed, I was a guest at his rather remarkable castle on the shores of Lake Erie."

"I've not had the privilege," Barstow said in a warm voice. "Creston speaks of it with real enthusiasm."

"Marvelous views there, and splendid fishing—lake trout."

"Have you seen Mr. Clarke's King Lear?"

"Indeed not, sir."

"Well, Dr. McIntire, you must. It contains all of life in a single evening."

"As to the play, I couldn't agree more, sir."

"It includes the finest advice a businessman could receive. Do you know the passage I mean, sir?"

"In *King Lear*? Nothing comes to mind. It's not a commercial setting, by any means."

"Ah, Shakespeare's wisdom was never confined by his settings." Barstow threw his head back, preparing to orate:

Have more than thou showest,
Speak less than thou knowest,
Lend less than thou owest.

"Of course," Fraser said. "Scarcely the words of a fool, to be sure."

"Why, you do know your *Lear*, bravo! Rosenstein, you have been hoarding the doctor's company."

As they bade their farewells, Rosenstein went to see the room captain to resolve the bill. Alone with Barstow, Fraser seized the moment. "This doubtless seems sudden, sir, but would you be free this evening to join me at that new musical piece from London, *Floradora*? It's not the sublime Bard, of course, but the *Floradora* girls are supposed to be charming."

Barstow smiled slyly. "As Mrs. Barstow has left for the seashore, I would be able to join you. Shall we meet at the theater?"

Scarcely believing his good fortune, Fraser agreed.

After four omnibus rides across a fair swath of Manhattan island, Fraser managed to buy the necessary theater tickets and return to their sad little hotel on Avenue A.

Cook sat at the top of the stairs to the lobby, elbows on his knees and his head sagging between those large, twisted hands. When Fraser paused at the bottom of the stairs, Cook raised his glassy eyes.

"Hot enough for you?" Fraser asked.

Cook closed his eyes. He then brought forth a belch of real dimension.

"Speed? You all right?"

He moaned softly. "That man," he started, then took a breath. "That man, works for Barstow, at the cotton building? He knows how to drink."

Fraser smiled. "A rugged athlete getting outdrunk by a porter?"

"He went back to work when we were done." He belched again, this time more gently. "He has a gift."

"So?"

Cook smiled. " 'S'all set. Eight tonight, in I go."

"So, you've got four hours to sober up."

Cook shook his head and straightened. "I'll make it. Before I go, tell me again: Why would Barstow keep something around about killing Abe Lincoln? Smart guy like him, why keep it?"

Taking Cook's elbow, Fraser shrugged. "I don't know. Maybe he's sentimental. Why did Creston Clarke's business manager talk with us? Why is Townsend helping? We won't know what's in that office until you look. And since I'm going out with Barstow tonight, his office will definitely be empty."

Cook stopped short. "You're going out with Barstow? That was fast."

"Yes, sir," Fraser said. "Real fast."

Cook resumed his unsteady entry into the hotel. "Real fast," he said.

Chapter 13

Sweat ran down Cook's face as he stood before the back entrance to the Cotton Exchange. The light was softening at eight p.m., though the air was still dense with heat. He had two keys, both from the porter with the hollow leg. Cook had to return them in two hours. No time to waste.

Hinges protested as he eased the door open, the sound magnified by his nerves. His lunchtime beers were barely a memory. He always enjoyed the tense moments during ballgames, when his senses were charged and his concentration sharpest. He often felt most calm in those moments.

He took his time climbing the three-and-a-half flights of darkened stairs, up on his toes, carrying his canvas bag out to the side so it didn't bang into anything. He stopped every few steps to listen. He heard only a faint scrabbling, probably rodents in the cellar.

The offices for the Spencer, Barstow firm were on the top floor. Windows at either end of the corridor yielded dusky light. Though he stayed on his toes, the wood floor underneath the carpet complained quietly.

He fitted the second key into the door lock. The door handle yielded easily. A small screech from the frame made his fingers tingle. The door swung open. Cook stepped in and closed the door behind him.

After pausing to settle himself, he pulled a small lantern from the canvas bag. He lit it at a low setting and shielded it with the canvas bag. A door to his left led into a corner office, which would be Barstow's. If the man had confidential records here, that's where they should be.

Cook walked behind Barstow's desk, which faced the room's entrance. Sweat beaded on his forehead and ran down an arm, but he still felt solid, contained. Keeping the lantern low, he began his search. He passed on the desk drawers. Desk drawers should contain current items about current business. He was looking for something thirty-five years old. It would be concealed.

He approached a locked file cabinet in a far corner. The lock looked simple and he had his old picks with him. He was clumsy at first, out of practice or more nervous than he thought. The lock clicked. He worked the drawer open, unable to avoid the scrape of metal on metal. It held only documents of recent vintage. A waste of time. He locked the cabinet with the same low click.

He had to work faster. It was near dark outside, which would amplify the lantern's glow through the window. He redraped the canvas bag over the light.

He noticed a door tucked into the room's interior corner. A closet. Kneeling at its entrance, he felt along its floor. In the back, his left hand hit a metal box. He placed it next to the lantern. The padlock was a pin-and-tumbler design. He used a wrench to steady it while he worked the pick. It was a five-pin lock, so he had to be patient, take one at a time. It must have been ten minutes before the final pin yielded. Relief flooded through him.

The lid stuck. When he yanked, it gave way with a loud rasp. Cook froze. He slowed his breathing. He heard nothing.

Inside was a stack of Confederate currency, worthless for anything but starting a fire. He unfolded a document declaring Samuel Justice Barstow a major in the Commissary Corps of the Confederate States of America. A daguerreotype depicted a slender young man in a uniform with proud epaulets. He wore a drooping mustache and side whiskers. It had to be Barstow.

Cook pulled out a leather-covered book that fit in his hand. Its opening page had an ink sketch of a frog with sleepy eyes and a bow tie, every bump and wart lovingly noted. Several more pages were covered with columns of numbers. Cook put the book in his jacket pocket.

And then there it was, a tattered memo book, tied to a small dictionary with a piece of string. The pages were stiff with age, filled with notations that had to be in code or cipher. He turned the pages quietly, trying to pick up a pattern in the markings.

There. He stopped his breath. Steps? Two people. Maybe three. Cook slipped the memo book and dictionary into his other jacket pocket and snuffed the lantern. He heard the door to the suite swing open. He took a long breath. No time to put the box back. Clutching the canvas bag, he moved across the room to keep Barstow's big desk between him and the intruders. Crouching behind it, he had to hope whoever was out there wouldn't find him. Almost immediately, he realized his mistake. Whoever it was had no light. That meant they knew he was here. He was trapped. His heart began to race. He worked to calm his mind.

Two figures came through the doorway, their features dark. One was tall, Cook's size. The other seemed thicker. Cook tensed. The power of his first move would determine whether he left under his own steam.

The intruders paused, side by side, just inside the door. Cook sprang, stepping on the desk and vaulting over it. He aimed between the men, splitting them and bursting through the doorway. In the anteroom, Cook brushed aside a third man like some flyweight second baseman.

In a few strides, Cook was leaping down the stairs, taking three at a time in the near darkness. Halfway down, he heard steps above him. That didn't bother him. He was faster than they were, as long as he didn't miss a step.

He burst out the building's rear door, his heart hammering. He ducked behind a colony of dustbins to the side. Better to lie low than be chased. A black man running down a street could draw the wrong type of attention.

When the three men broke through the rear door, Cook's hand went to the knife in his waistband. It would be better not to use it. He pulled it out of its sheath and held it to his side.

His pursuers looked in all directions. A voice spoke. "Damned coon is fast." Another chimed in, "Not fast enough. We'll get him." Two headed up Pearl Street and the third set off west on William.

Cook waited ten full minutes, long enough to start to resent his partner, the upright Dr. Fraser. You didn't see him sneaking into buildings, risking arrest, then fleeing from a gang of toughs who no doubt were well-armed. You didn't see him crouched among the trash cans. Oh, no, Dr. Fraser enters by the front door in the daylight, shakes hands with powerful men, and eats off fine china.

Cook brushed off his clothes and walked to the saloon on Beaver Street. His lunchtime companion was there, deep in communion with a schooner of beer. Cook could not imagine how much the man had absorbed that day. A gift. Cook handed over the office keys along with a five-dollar gold piece. That would keep the beer flowing.

Back on the street, Cook took no time to look at the books in his pockets. He needed to get out of that neighborhood. The light in Barstow's office had been too dim for the men to tell anything about Cook except his size, yet they knew he was colored. Either they watched him enter the building or they knew who he was. Cook was inclined to believe the second explanation. Either way, he didn't like it. They could recognize him. A colored man his size was easy to recognize.

He walked up Broadway, moving fast but not so fast as to stand out. After twenty blocks, he hopped on a northbound stage.

Chapter 14

It was near midnight when Fraser left the uptown Delmonico's, the one at Fifth Avenue and Forty-Fourth Street. This was rich living. On a single day, he had eaten at both branches of the famed restaurant. With a firm grip on Samuel Barstow's upper arm, Fraser steered the cotton tycoon across the sidewalk to his waiting carriage.

Floradora had been an inspired choice. For all of Barstow's highfalutin' talk about Shakespeare, he loved the show's sweet ditties and pretty chorines. Over dinner, the older man proclaimed his passion for the theater, trumpeting his charter membership in The Players Club, which Edwin Booth had founded. Barstow boasted that he had been a pallbearer at Edwin's funeral. Creston Clarke, he confided, could not hold a candle to The Great Edwin, but then no one could. "An actor of force and subtlety," Barstow said. "It's rare enough to find either quality, but to find them together!"

Between the heat and the tobacco haze, the dining room had been oppressive. Bending its rules, the restaurant allowed gentlemen to peel off their suit coats and dine in vests and shirtsleeves. Fraser had ordered the porterhouse. It proved just as inappropriate as the lunchtime lobster. Nevertheless, its herculean proportion was a virtue in itself. The steak was as thick as a medical text and considerably tastier.

On his fourth brandy and third cigar, Barstow yielded to Fraser's prompting and began recounting tales of running the blockade from the Virginia coast. Fraser asked, perhaps too pointedly, how he coordinated those efforts with the rebel government. Barstow smiled knowingly in response. He even might have winked. But he never answered the question. When Fraser said he had heard that some Northerners aided the cotton smuggling, Barstow grinned affably. "We certainly wouldn't have gone to such lengths to get the cotton out," he said, "unless we knew men who were prepared to buy it."

Both men sweated clear through their vests. Then the talk reached the last months of the war.

"That must have been a terrible time," Fraser said, "with the Union armies rampaging through the South."

"Ah, Dr. McIntire," Barstow said with a mournful look. Fraser enjoyed being addressed by his new name. It was like being a new person. "If ever there was a time for inspired leadership. It was not too late, mind you. The South had great strengths yet. A lasting peace was possible, as were ways to finance it. Do you know that a single pit in the Virginia woods held 200,000 bales of cotton? All that wealth, just sitting there rotting."

Barstow blew his nose noisily. He pointed at Fraser with the hand that clutched the handkerchief. "Instead of inspired leadership, what did we have? A prissy old lady in Jeff Davis. On the other side, human battering rams like Abraham Lincoln and Ulysses Grant! Perhaps the nation's greatest tragedy was forged in those months. Reconstruction didn't have to be, this lingering ill will between North and South didn't have to be, nor this endless cosseting of the Negroes."

"How should peace have been achieved," Fraser asked, actually curious, "after all the bloodshed and slaughter?"

"Dr. McIntire, is Ohio such an Eden of nigger loving that these thoughts have never penetrated there?"

"I can't speak for others, but this is an object of some wonderment for me."

"You know your Shakespeare—remember the dying king's advice to Prince Hal?"

Fraser struggled to focus. The brandy was making him immune to the room's sodden heat, but it also obstructed thought. He read that one, *Henry IV*, on the train to New York. The phrase was close, floating nearby. Something about foreigners. He looked up triumphantly. "He should 'busy giddy minds with foreign quarrels'!"

"Bravo, Doctor, bravo! What a perfect opportunity it was for North and South to join together, to merge their armies. Why, between us we had over a million men under arms. It was the largest military force in the world. We could have seized Canada with its broad lands and Mexico with its glittering silver. Who, sir, could have stopped us? We could have created a great bounty for every American. Surely even an Ohio man can see the truth in that." Barstow's eyes glistened with excitement.

Fraser could not stifle the objection that formed in his mind. "But after all the fighting the people had been through, how could anyone have persuaded them to start two new wars?"

Barstow snorted with derision. "Who would you rather fight—some Mexican peasants and some Canadian fancy boys, or the battle-hardened legions of the Union and Confederate armies? Imagine George McClellan, Robert E. Lee, and William T. Sherman leading armies into Montreal and Mexico City.

What glorious days we were cheated of! It would have required little more than a few long marches, the easiest assignment our soldiers would have had for four years. And, my good sir, it would have enriched the nation. All that stood between us and that stupendous destiny was a few lily-livered men in Richmond and a few stubborn ones in Washington."

The tycoon finished his brandy. "Some very powerful men," he said, "on both sides, endorsed that course. A terrible missed opportunity. You do see that?"

"Of . . . of course," Fraser stammered. "I suppose, with some luck, and some—well, wait, Mr. Barstow. Would President Lincoln have considered such a course?"

Barstow's eyes flashed a malevolence that shattered the brandy haze. In an instant, his expression returned to that of the genial fellow with friendly white mustaches. He stood to greet another aging gent who approached their table.

"Why, Jimmie Smith, as I live and breathe," he cried, extending the hand that did not hold his handkerchief. A slim, stooped man in a white linen suit shouted with hilarity at the sight of Barstow. After the two men finished family inquiries, Barstow introduced "a scoundrel and a gentleman, Senator James Smith of the great state of Arkansas."

Barstow summoned a chair from a passing waiter. Three brandies appeared. Smith had recently been at the Democratic National Convention in Kansas City. He regaled them with tales of William Jennings Bryan, who had been nominated for a rematch against President McKinley in the fall. Senator Smith asked what Barstow thought of Bryan's prospects.

"You know," Smith addressed Fraser while patting Barstow's forearm fondly, "Major Barstow has been the leading strategist for every Democratic candidate since the war—hell, even *during* the war. A veritable Warwick." An impish smile creased the old man's face.

Barstow grinned even more broadly. "Didn't I tell you about this rascal? You can't believe anything he says."

"And I offer the same advice about your companion," the senator said to Fraser. "He hails from the great state of cotton, which is on nobody's side and everybody's side."

"Cotton's done well for you, Senator," Barstow said, "once you started trading it and gave up trying to grow it."

Fraser took this turn in the conversation as his cue to repeat his interest in a cotton investment. At the prospect of business talk, Senator Smith excused himself.

In response to Fraser's inquiries, Barstow explained with a patronizing gentleness that the cotton market was unsettled. Opportunities were scarce. Were Dr. McIntire willing to look beyond cotton, the old man added, one very interesting prospect had just emerged.

With careful courtesy, Fraser explained that his partners in Ohio were dead set on cotton. He would have to consult with them by telegraph to see if they would consider anything else. He, of course, would greatly value the chance to invest with the legendary Mr. Barstow. Barstow replied that McIntire could review this investment prospect firsthand if he came to Barstow's office that Saturday at 5 p.m. Fraser agreed.

When Fraser attempted to acquire the bill from the waiter, he found that Barstow had already settled it.

After depositing the tycoon in his carriage, Fraser paused to admire his surroundings. Despite the late hour, most of the people of New York seemed to be out on Fifth Avenue, enjoying the slightly fresher night air. For a moment, he missed the sweet vapors of Cadiz, the breezes that curled on a summer night. A small Oriental man jostled him from his reverie, reminding Fraser of the range of human sizes, shapes, and colors that occupied that single street corner. What were all these people like? Where did they live and how did they pay for themselves? What did they do all day in that overwhelming city? Where were they going at that hour, especially those who stepped with such purpose? What could possibly be that important so late at night?

Fraser decided to proceed on foot to where he thought the omnibus line ran down to Avenue A. He was in no rush to reach tonight's hotel, which was even more disreputable than its predecessors. Yes, a walk, he decided. It would clear his mind and allow him to reflect on some of the astonishing things Barstow had said.

Embarking west across Fifth Avenue, Fraser marveled at Barstow's notion that North and South should have joined to invade Mexico and Canada. Could any sane human being have entertained that view in early 1865?

Fraser decided to take the proposition seriously. Barstow admitted that Lincoln would never have pursued that plan. Was that why Booth and his gang were sent to remove Lincoln, Grant, Johnson, and Seward from the United States Government? Would a Union led by Lafayette Foster and an army led by William Sherman have undertaken that audacious foreign adventure? But the theory didn't match the facts. Lee had surrendered by the time of the assassination. The soldiers of his Army of Northern Virginia had started their long walk home.

Perhaps Barstow was leading Fraser on, intentionally misleading him with a fantastic story of continental conquest. For that to be true, though, Barstow would have to know a great deal about Fraser. He would have to have pierced Fraser's false identity as Dr. John McIntire. Fraser believed that Barstow was connected to the Sons of Liberty; after all, Weichmann gave him Barstow's name on that last day in Indiana. It was true that the Sons of Liberty had tracked Fraser's visit to Weichmann, but Fraser was using his own name then, and wasn't changing hotels every day. Fraser doubted that Barstow knew his real identity.

Oblivious to the river of bodies passing on either side of him, Fraser reached Broadway. Shouts drew his eye to a ruckus across the street. Screaming men ran through pools of light from streetlamps. Shifting for a better view, Fraser could make out a man on the ground, surrounded by others. Then he made out flailing fists and legs swinging into vicious kicks. Fraser ran to a policeman and asked why he wasn't doing anything. "Ah, don't fash yourself," the cop answered. "It's just the boys blowing off some steam with a few niggers. Nothing to get in a state over."

More men ran down Broadway from uptown. An elemental timbre in their shouts made Fraser afraid. People hurried past, looking away from the street. Some of the rampaging men stopped an omnibus and circled it. They pounded on the sides with pieces of wood, then began to smash windows. The horses, screaming in terror, tore loose from their harnesses and galloped uptown, scattering people before them. Fraser saw astonished black faces in the passenger compartment as white-shirted men piled in after them. Was that Cook? The one crouched near the back? The shouting men were dragging passengers off the omnibus.

Fraser rushed to the edge of the melee and then was swept into it. It took all his strength to remain upright. He pushed through surging bodies, driving with his legs, using his weight to force people aside, moving toward the focus of the crowd, the black men. When he burst through, he could see Cook at the center of an open space, fending off a half-dozen white men. They ran at him from alternating directions, often absorbing a fist or a kick or a knee from the grim-looking Negro. It was a vile mockery of the Cooks' Fourth of July romp with the colored children by the side of the stream.

Cook's face was bloody, his clothes torn, one eye swollen. Fraser called to him, but Cook didn't hear. If the attackers could corner him, he'd be done for. Then the other whites, the ones who were wary of Cook's powerful blows, would pile on. A short man stepped out from the crowd and smashed a board against Cook's side. Cook's knees buckled.

Fraser pulled his pistol from his coat jacket and fired into the air. The rioters halted for a moment, looking for the source of the shot. Fraser pointed the gun at Cook. He screamed at the top of his lungs: "This man is my prisoner, and I'll shoot any man who stands between us." Addressing Cook, he added, "Come quietly, you black bastard, or I'll shoot you down like the dog you are." Cook, hunched over, arms clasped around his chest, stared at the pistol. Fraser quickly crossed to him, grabbed an elbow, and began to haul him through the startled crowd. Miraculously, the people parted for them. Fraser kept his pistol at shoulder height, pointing upward, conspicuous.

With the riot stretching north, Fraser dragged Cook downtown, ignoring his groans. There was no time to attend to any wounds. They had to get away. Looking back over his shoulder, Fraser could see flames, carriages on fire. Men were building bonfires in the street. More white men ran by. For the first time Fraser could make out their yells. "Get the niggers!" echoed down Broadway.

They had gone two blocks when Cook doubled over and started to cough blood. Fraser propped him against a building. They were in a darker patch between streetlights. Cook slid down to a seated position. They had to get off the street, away from the whites, but Cook couldn't keep walking. Fraser had to leave him and find a hack, hoping that no rioters happened upon Cook.

At the curb, Fraser waved madly, but no cab ventured so close to the riot. Acrid smoke from the fires mingled with the heat. The scene was infernal, the marauding men like imps from hell, delirious with their ability to damage and hurt. Should he try a cross street? Fraser looked back at Cook. He hadn't moved. No one was molesting him.

A carriage stopped in front of Fraser, blocking his view. He turned away impatiently and craned his neck to peer down Broadway. A hand grabbed his arm from behind and a woman's voice cried out. "Dr. Fraser? What on earth is happening?" A face leaned from the carriage. It was Eliza, Miss Eliza, Clarke's business manager.

"It's a riot," he said. "They're beating the colored. My friend is hurt." He pointed toward Cook. "I must get him to safety." She insisted they enter her carriage and come to her hotel suite. It wasn't far.

With one of them on either side of Cook, they wrestled him into the carriage. When they were moving, Fraser thought of the reception they would face at the hotel.

"Does the Waldorf allow colored?" he asked in a sharp voice.

Cook was slumping onto Eliza, since she was the smaller of his supports. With a grunt, she pushed him upright. "I don't know. Staff, I suppose."

"Well, even if they do, they won't welcome one who looks like this."

For an extra dollar, the driver took them into the alley behind the hotel. They found the staff entrance. As several hotel workers watched, Fraser and Miss Eliza helped Cook stagger inside. An older colored man pointed them to the service elevator.

In Miss Eliza's suite, they deposited Cook on the sofa, but when he lay back, his legs overlapped the end. She agreed he should be on the bed.

Fraser asked for water, soap, and a cloth to clean Cook's wounds. When he despaired that his medical bag was back at their hotel, Eliza offered to go to the hotel's drug store, which was open all night. This seemed one more wonder of the metropolis. Fraser wrote a list of items to buy—carbolic, aspirin, laudanum. Cook seemed to have no broken ribs. His bones must be made of granite. But his torso had absorbed powerful blows. Fraser could not gauge the damage. The blood Cook spat came from a cut where his own teeth tore his cheek. Fraser considered trying to close the wound with stitches but decided against it. It was too difficult to get to, and the blood flow was slow.

Cook winced while Fraser handled him, but said nothing. Fraser gave him a strong dose of laudanum, one calibrated for a man of his size and constitution. Eliza turned down the light. Within a few minutes, Cook was asleep, breathing evenly.

Clammy with sweat, Fraser followed Eliza into the dark sitting room. They sat in overstuffed chairs that flanked a row of windows. No shouts came from the street. Either the riot had subsided or the hotel was too far away for its noise to reach them. Fraser thought the air carried a whiff of smoke, but it might have been on his clothes. They sat quietly for several minutes. He was grateful for the silence. Fatigue crept into his arms and legs.

"You're a caring doctor," Eliza said, "and a good friend."

"What comes over men?" he said. "Attacking strangers! I don't know what we would've done if you hadn't come along."

"It was a lucky chance."

"Lucky for us, yes, ma'am. I will arrange to move him tomorrow."

"I think not, Dr. Fraser. That's the last thing that poor man needs."

Fraser was too tired to argue. He was pleased to feel safe in a room that—it had to be acknowledged—was acres more pleasant than any he had occupied since leaving Cadiz.

He sat up with a start. Spending the night here was not a proper arrangement. "I must find somewhere to sleep," he said. "I'll return in the morning."

"I won't hear of it," she said. "If Mr. Cook should need aid in the night, I would have no idea what to do. I would count it a kindness if you would remain here. I can find accommodations with one of the ladies of our company."

He meant to shrug and express his gratitude, but instead he slid into sleep.

Chapter 15

"You look very nice." Eliza reached to flatten Fraser's cravat. "Not at all like a theatrical manager from Ohio."

His cheeks warm with embarrassment, he turned to Cook, who was showing improvement. After two days of soup, Cook had eaten bread for his evening meal. His eyes were clearing. Fraser had stopped the laudanum. "Rest easy this evening," he told his patient. "We'll just be downstairs." Cook grunted his understanding. Talking still hurt his mouth.

After moving in with one of the actresses, Eliza had spoken with the hotel maids and bellmen to explain the presence of Cook and Fraser. She probably added gratuities to smooth the business. The Clarke company's rehearsals began early and ran late. From Eliza's offhand remarks, they weren't going especially well, which didn't seem to trouble her. Other than retrieving luggage from their wreck of a hotel, Fraser had done little for two days but watch over Cook and plow into the more obscure tragedies. *Timon of Athens* bored him, while *Coriolanus* lacked the magic of Shakespeare's other dramas.

When Eliza invited Fraser to dine with the Clarke family at

the hotel restaurant, he worried that they might resent Fraser's visit to the Lake Erie mansion under false pretenses. Eliza smiled.

"You've not dealt much with actors," she said. "They memorize hundreds of lines but are oblivious to the world around them. You may revive your pretense of managing Chillicothe Theaters"—he winced at the phrase—"or you may affect your true identity. Creston and Adelaide will notice neither, as you are much less interesting than themselves. And because you've not heard Creston's stories before, your presence will be invaluable."

She had dressed plainly. Her high-throated white blouse had frills and ruffles, but struck a severe note. Her straight black skirt accentuated her figure. She had pinned up her hair, probably due to the heat, creating a luxurious wave above her brow. Fraser found her such a pleasant sight that he schooled himself to look away at intervals, for fear of being rude.

When he and Eliza joined the Clarkes in the dining room, he was delighted to meet Dr. Joseph Booth, the brother closest in age to the notorious John Wilkes. Dr. Booth, slight and reserved, lived in Baltimore and was addressed by all as Uncle Joseph.

They were six of them, counting Clarke and his wife, Adelaide, Dr. Booth and his wife, and Fraser and Eliza. But they might as well have been one, as Creston Clarke's conversational style involved lengthy proclamations punctuated by longer anecdotes.

"Wilkes," said Clarke halfway through his second glass of wine, "now there was a man with talent and courage. Eh, Uncle Joseph?"

Dr. Booth nodded.

"Did you know," Clarke asked Fraser across the table, "that Wilkes performed the most outrageously dangerous swordplay during his performances? No pantomime of conflict for Wilkes.

No, sir. If you were Laertes to his Hamlet, you had better brush up on your fencing or you wouldn't survive the rehearsals."

He drained his glass and held it out for refilling. "One night in Albany, that benighted city, he tripped and fell on a knife he was wielding. He missed ending it all by a whisker—a whisker, I tell you!" After assuring himself that the new wine in his glass was acceptable, Clarke added loudly, "And that wasn't the only time he was stabbed in Albany!"

"Creston," his wife said.

"What, my dear? Must we conceal the truth about such a banal matter?"

"I'm sure Dr. Fraser would like to hear of something other than your illustrious forebears." The woman's tone could have scratched glass. It did not deter Creston Clarke.

"So, some young girl, some *Albanian*"—he grinned over the term for residents of that upstate city—"took a knife to Wilkes in a hotel room, eh? No doubt Dr. Fraser has experienced similar conflicts with the fair sex. Who hasn't? More to the point, when has the fair sex ever treated us fairly?" He beamed happily at his thrust, one that seemed familiar to all at the table.

"Creston," Eliza hazarded. "I've been wondering about Richelieu's final soliloquy. Are you quite comfortable with King Louis's position downstage during it?"

Clarke waved his hand. "No, no, no, you clever girl. I shall finish the story. So this young strumpet, who had doubtless been in Wilkes's room before—she had a key, mind you—she hides in a corner and springs at him with a knife when he enters the room. The wound she delivered was only superficial, isn't that right, Uncle Joseph?"

Dr. Booth nodded.

"And Wilkes sweetly talked to her until she relinquished the knife and fell into his arms. What a moment! The curtain falls. The audience rises with a shout. Magnificent!" Extending his glass for another refill, Clarke added with practiced rhythm,

"And that, dear friends, is why the Creston Clarke company will never play Albany."

Fraser longed for a quiet exchange with Uncle Joseph, one physician to another. He imagined that talking about shared experiences might lay the basis for a further interview about more sensitive matters, about the notorious brother. Alas, it was not to be, though the long-dead assassin remained their constant guest at the meal. For a quarter of an hour, Clarke described how Wilkes joined the pursuers of John Brown when the abolitionist made his doomed attempt to lead a slave rebellion in 1859. Above all objects, according to Clarke, Wilkes cherished the spear carried by one of Brown's insurrectionary legionnaires, which Wilkes retrieved after the old man and his followers were overwhelmed at Harpers Ferry.

When dinner was done, Eliza agreed to join Fraser on a tour of Fifth Avenue. After looking in on Cook and finding him asleep, Fraser met her in the sparkling hotel lobby and walked out into the night. They fell in step to the south.

"You and Mr. Cook are an unusual pair," she said. "Are you an athlete as well? Is that how you met?"

Fraser smiled. "I'm large, but no athlete. Speed is much more than an athlete, though. He's very smart."

"Yes, they can be."

"No, that's not what I mean. Not smart for a colored man. I mean, he's smart. He attended two colleges, you know."

"Dr. Fraser"—she stopped to turn toward him. Other strollers had to veer around them. "I hope I've given no offense. I'm sure I don't know Mr. Cook. He sounds a remarkable person, as you describe him, and as he works for you, I am sure he is an entirely reliable man."

"He doesn't work for me. He's my friend." With a slight bow and a gesture, he suggested they resume their walk.

"You took grave chances on his behalf the other night," she said. "You have been a good friend to him."

"I have, I suppose, learned to be."

"How did you come to know him?"

"By accident, really, but it was a lucky one." He could no longer suppress the thought. "Does it make you uncomfortable to have a colored man in your suite? We have been a terrible burden."

"Not at all, Dr. Fraser, certainly not as he's a friend of yours." At an intersection, she proposed that they seek cooler breezes by the river. They turned west.

"Your Mr. Clarke," Fraser ventured, "seems always to be on stage."

"I hope you don't find him too appalling. He is appalling, of course, but never mean-spirited. He has been generous with me, and I am fond of him."

"Heavens, I meant nothing of the sort. He is an object of the frankest amazement. He has the energy of ten! It's exhausting simply to listen to him."

"It's rather sad, the way he keeps telling those same stories. I cannot calculate how many times I've heard them. But there is no firmer friend when times are difficult."

"And Uncle Joseph?"

"Dear Uncle Joseph. In his whole life, no one in the family has allowed him to get a word in edgewise." She gave a short laugh. "I believe he prefers it that way. He must by now."

"He must have fascinating stories of John Wilkes Booth."

"That is a peculiar thing," she said. "I have never heard him speak of his brother. I have always supposed it's too painful. When Uncle Joseph sits quietly through Creston's endless stories about Wilkes this and Wilkes that, I feel as though Uncle Joseph is using Creston's words to salve a wound that will not heal."

"You know the family well."

She said nothing, casting a glance at him as they approached the intersection with Broadway. "Look," she said, pointing up the wide street. "Where is the evidence of the riot?"

She was right. Traffic, both on foot and in carriages, proceeded as though nothing unusual had happened there for decades. Whatever had burned was gone. The people on the street looked no more threatening than those anywhere else in that swelling city. No Negroes walked the street, but Fraser could not judge whether that was a change from the ordinary.

"Tell me," she said after they crossed the avenue, "about your researches. How do they progress?"

"Haltingly, I fear. Just as I think we're on the verge of resolving some piece of the problem, some new complexity arises."

"Do you still think Wilkes was the pawn in some larger game?"

"More than ever. Demonstrating that, of course, is where the difficulty arises."

"And the cotton business that I mentioned in Fairview—has that proved of any help?"

Though he had not intended to, Fraser began to tell her his theories of the conspiracy and the role of cotton smuggling in it. With Cook in no condition to hear about his dinner with Barstow and the outlandish ideas the tycoon had spouted, Fraser described them to Eliza. She listened attentively, interposing a question here and a comment there. When they reached the Hudson, they walked along the trading ships that loomed on the waterfront, slowing their pace to absorb the breeze.

When he came to the end of his speculations, she paused to gaze at an old steamer with rust trailing from its portholes. He had not been so comfortable talking with a woman since Ginny died. He could complain to Ginny about the ignorance of his patients, share with her his hopes for a Harrison County hospital, or at least a clinic, though she didn't always take his side. She knew their neighbors, too, sometimes better than he did. He had missed her so.

Eliza turned her hazel eyes to him. "You will continue with your researches?"

It took him a moment to focus. "As soon as Cook is fit, we'll head south, to Maryland and Washington. I'm never free from the fear that we won't be successful, but we must try. We've come this far."

"That's fine," she said. "You should. I believe the Booths would be grateful for it."

"If it's not too bold, you seem on such intimate terms with the family. How did that come to pass?"

"It's rather an involved story. I have known the Clarkes for much of my life. Creston's mother, who was a wonderful woman, I knew as my Aunt Asia. She provided me a home and a family after my mother died."

"Very kind, indeed."

"And when my husband died three years ago—he was a playwright, Edward Scott, though his works never became popular—Creston made room for me in his company. He gave me a life. We grew up together, along with his brother. Both boys, I'm afraid, were always performers. Their father was an actor, too, so they inherited it from both sides of the family. We lived in England some of the time, so Creston's accent is not entirely artificial."

"How old were you when your mother died?"

"Twelve."

"And your father?"

"My mother never married." She said this simply, looking directly at him. Fraser was surprised that he was not shocked. Spoken calmly by this ineffably lovely woman, it seemed not scandalous at all.

On their way back to the hotel, he asked about life in England, feeling keenly his own dull history. She had lived in London, had traveled all over America with the Clarke company. Fraser had barely left Ohio before this year.

As they recrossed Broadway, he felt her hand on the crook of his arm. He placed his hand over hers. Their fingers intertwined. Long-dormant feelings surfaced as she looked into his eyes. Something clenched inside him. Was he being disloyal? Eliza was so different from Ginny, but his longing was the same, the ache for warmth and absolution that only a lover can grant. Could he find that with this poised and worldly woman? Could he give the same back to her?

"Oh, but you are a good friend, Dr. Fraser."

"Good enough," he said, "to be Jamie to you?"

A playful look passed over her face. "I suppose we could try that, Jamie."

His heart performed somersaults like a schoolboy's.

Chapter 16

The next morning, Cook was hungry. His head still felt like a mule had kicked him. His back felt like it got the mule's second kick. He had dreamt about the riot, the angry faces in the night, the screaming of "nigger nigger nigger." He remembered fighting, though not how it started. It was strangers, not the men from Barstow's office. His muscles tensed at the memory—ducking, circling, lashing out, feeling cornered. He remembered Fraser making him walk when he needed to lie down. And here he was in this fine hotel room.

He had little strength, but his mind was clearing. According to Fraser, he had lingered in a twilight consciousness for more than a day. He was through with that, through with lying there in bed.

After Fraser finished examining him, Cook levered himself upright, then stood. A wave of dizziness sent him stumbling to a straight-backed chair. Hanging his head in his hands, he breathed carefully. He gathered himself.

"Easy stages," Fraser said.

"S'pose I should be thanking you," Cook said, "taking care of me."

"It's what doctors do."

"Also, for getting me out of there."

"I've never seen anything like that. Those men were crazed."

"Nothing new, Doc, though I've never seen that many at once." He sighed deeply. "You came out okay?"

"I'm fine. Miss Eliza saved us both."

"Thought I saw her. This is her room, right?" Fraser nodded. "Yeah, that's a lady's hair brush." Cook rubbed his eyes, then each arm and each leg. The pain in his back was less. Not the pain in his head. He leaned forward and looked straight at Fraser. "I remember hearing something about a black bastard?"

A knock on the door brought a waiter with a breakfast tray. He set it on a table next to Cook. The smell was unwelcome. "Is that oatmeal?"

"Cream of wheat, sir," the waiter answered.

"I'm hungry. How about steak and eggs?"

"You haven't been able to handle much in the way of food," Fraser said.

"That's why I'm hungry." Cook turned to the waiter. "Steak and eggs. Four eggs. And biscuits. My friend here will eat this." As the waiter left, Cook poured himself some water from the pitcher on the tray. He spread butter and jam on a thick slice of toast. After a second slice of toast, he sat back. The headache was relenting. Coffee? No, coffee would make the headache worse. It was warm for coffee, anyway.

"So what happened at Barstow's office?" Fraser asked.

"Hold up. When you saw him at the downtown Delmonico's, or before or after that, or really anytime, did you notice anyone watching you? Is there anyone you've seen more than once? Have you noticed anything unusual?"

"No, nothing I can think of."

Here he looked straight at Fraser. "Three of them came after me in his office. They either followed me there or were expecting me."

When Cook was done describing the encounter, Fraser let out a low whistle of admiration. "You had quite a night. Sorry I wasn't there to help."

Cook let the remark pass. No reason to point out that Fraser would have been a hindrance, not a help. He remembered something. "You never looked in my jacket, did you?" Fraser shook his head. "Bring it here." Cook patted the garment, relieved to find everything there—the memorandum book and dictionary, and the book with the frog drawing. "See here," he said, "we may have ourselves some clues."

Setting the volumes on the table before him, Cook explained where he found them. Fraser pulled up a chair. They decided that the frog book looked too new to have anything to do with the Booth conspiracy. Its columns of numbers ranged between three and five digits. There were no headings or markings other than numbers.

"Must involve money," Cook said.

"Why?"

"What else do you write down in numbers and hide in a steel box?"

"Money that Barstow got or money that he paid?"

Cook shook his head. "One or the other. Must be some sequence in time here, too, but I can't pick it up. What's the pattern?"

After a few more minutes they put the frog book aside and turned to the worn volumes. Fraser leaned over the memo book's entries. They were numbers and letters, strung in rows. That was a cipher, Fraser said, presumably the code that the Confederate secret service used. He had that cipher key, which came from Booth's own papers. It was in his luggage, which was at the new hotel he had checked them into the day before, while Cook was lying dazed in bed.

"You didn't register under our names, did you?" Cook asked.

"Of course not," Fraser answered, "I signed the book as John Bingham and friend."

Cook was irritated by the man's smile. "Don't be so damned clever. You need to move us to a new hotel this afternoon under some other names, and we might just think about leaving this town. I'm not enjoying myself here like I'd hoped."

Fraser started to tell Cook about his conversation with Barstow. He stopped when the waiter returned with Cook's second breakfast. Cook pitched into the food but soon slowed his pace. The steak felt greasy; the eggs were more than he wanted. As Fraser finished the tale, Cook was picking at a biscuit, most of the food untouched.

"That's the biggest cock-and-bull story I've ever heard," Cook said. "Those armies, after massacring each other for four years, they're going to trot off together and invade Canada and Mexico? Answer me this. What were they going to do with the 200,000 colored troops in the Union Army? Those were black men with guns and army training. They weren't about to lock arms with those Confederates and go off and conquer some foreign countries. Nor the other way around, either. Those rebels going to fight side by side with the sons of Africa? That's all just crazy. You know what that would have brought on? A real race war. He's trying to fool us."

"But he thinks I'm Dr. John McIntire, not Jamie Fraser."

"You sure about that?"

"Of course, I'm sure."

Cook's mind wasn't all the way clear yet, but he didn't like this Barstow situation. Fraser agreed that the tycoon was probably connected to the Sons of Liberty. Weichmann as much as said so when he wrote out Barstow's name for Fraser. Maybe the frog book included something about the finances of that group.

Figuring out Barstow's books would have to wait. Now they had to protect themselves. Barstow knew by now that Cook had taken his secret records. He must suspect that Dr. John McIntire was connected to it. So they should be wary of anything coming from Barstow.

Eliza stopped in on her way to the theater and expressed pleasure at Cook's improvement. Fraser explained that they would be moving to their own hotel. He would let her know where they settled.

"What's this?" she said, picking up Barstow's memorandum book. She riffled the pages with an air of curiosity.

"Nothing, really," Fraser said, holding his hand out for the book. "Something we've been working on."

Eliza looked up to him with an open countenance. "Oh, I see." She handed him the book, which he slipped into his jacket pocket. She explained that the Clarke company would pack up in two days. Their first stop would be Trenton, then Philadelphia. "We'll be in Washington in ten days." She sat at the writing desk and jotted a note. "We're playing at the Columbia Theatre there, and, of course, we'll stay at the Willard. These are the addresses. Perhaps if you're in town, you might care to see our show?"

"I was hoping we might see each other again before we leave New York," Fraser said. He accepted the note, holding her hand for an extra moment.

Eliza smiled. "You know where I'll be. Getting ready for the road is always a hubbub, but I'd be glad to see you."

After she left, Cook gave Fraser an appraising stare. "I see."

"What do you see?"

"I see that you and she have traveled a ways while I lay here in cloud cuckoo land. Not that I'm criticizing. She's a fine-looking woman."

Fraser didn't answer. He moved around the room, ineffectually collecting their things. Cook added, "But can we trust her?"

"Of course, we can trust her. If she hadn't helped us, you might not be alive right now."

Cook nodded. Fraser went into the next room.

After Fraser transferred their luggage to the Miller Hotel on Madison Avenue, the two men slipped out the back of the Waldorf and into a hack. At Cook's insistence, they registered as Mr. Smith and Mr. Jones. The new hotel's nondescript front pleased Cook, and it matched the forlorn atmosphere inside. In the lobby, no piece of furniture matched any other. The water pitcher in their room was chipped. The beds sagged. Cook collapsed on his bed with a grunt of satisfaction. This place, he declared, was perfect. Soon he was snoring.

Fraser dug out his cipher key and set to work on the memo book. There were variations between Barstow's code and the official Confederate cipher, which probably involved a book code keyed to the dictionary that Cook also took from Barstow. It was tedious work, particularly the book code entries. Three consecutive numbers would refer to the page, line, and word in the dictionary.

Many of Barstow's entries recorded ships and dates, time and tides, presumably the arrangements for running the Union blockade. The references to Spencer must mean Julius Spencer, a New York cotton trader who partnered with Barstow after the war, creating Spencer, Barstow & Company. From Mr. Bingham's library, Fraser knew that Spencer was a leading New York Democrat, deeply involved in George McClellan's campaign for president in 1864. Had Confederate cotton financed McClellan's campaign?

When Cook snorted awake, Fraser showed him some of the late pages in the memo book. Barstow's notes stated that "au"—the chemical symbol for gold—went to New York on three occasions in February and March of 1865. Each transfer was for $3,000. The final entry on each line was "JH." John Surratt, whose full name was John Harrison Surratt, often went by the alias "John Harrison."

"So," Fraser said, "the question is why the Confederates were sending gold to New York so near the end of the war? And having John Surratt carry it?"

"You think it was getting to Booth?"

"Don't you?"

Cook made a face. "This could be Confederate money, but it could be Barstow's money. Maybe he was just getting his own money someplace safe."

"But he's using a Confederate courier, John Surratt, to do it."

"Barstow may not have been too fussy about who he used to run his errands, not at that point in the war. And his business and Confederate business may not have been entirely separate." Cook shook his head. "Something else doesn't add up for me. Why does Barstow still have this book? Can't help him any, not thirty-five years later. Actually, it can only hurt him. I thought he was so smart."

"It could be he needed this record to get his share from his partners in the cotton smuggling. The man from Lehman Brothers said that Barstow's partners today are the men he went through the war with. Maybe he kept it as a sort of insurance, to keep them under his control, so he could prove something against them if he had to."

Cook pursed his lips. "Maybe. I don't like it when really smart people do things that seem dumb. Makes me think I'm figuring something wrong."

They agreed to go to Baltimore next. Many of the story's strands led to that city. Anna Surratt, the conspirator's daughter, lived there still, as did her brother John. Sam Arnold, one of the conspirators, lived in a town to the south. Fraser proposed to wire Townsend, the writer in western Maryland, for advice on how to track them down. Cook assumed he would wire Eliza as well, but didn't say anything about it.

When Fraser returned from the telegraph office, he had bread and liverwurst for their midday meal. As they ate, Cook grumbled that the trip to Baltimore wasn't worth it. "Those Surratts and Samuel Arnold won't ever talk to us."

"Maybe they're ready after all these years. Maybe we can find something like this memo book so they won't actually have to talk. Anna Surratt might be a good bet. Weichmann said she's a sensitive person. She may be less devoted to the Lost Cause of the Confederacy than her brother is. And Sam Arnold may be angry about what happened to him, since he actually tried to pull out of Booth's conspiracy. He might blame the people who got him into it. We'll never know if we don't try."

"What about Barstow?" Cook asked. "He could start trailing us again."

"He doesn't have to trail us, actually. I have a meeting with him at five this afternoon. Or, rather, Dr. McIntire has a meeting with him. And he'd better get a move on."

Despite the heat of the afternoon, which crowded into their small room, Fraser began to don his cravat. As he peered into the cracked mirror that hung askew on the wall, he explained the special investment opportunity that Barstow had mentioned at their dinner.

"So what is it?" Cook asked.

"I don't know. That's why I'm going to meet him."

Cook shook his head. "You don't see what a bad idea that is? Whatever the truth is about Barstow, he's not trying to find you a good investment. And it ain't like you're looking for one."

"Every time I talk to him, we learn something. We even learn from how he lies."

"That's either the dumbest thing I ever heard or it's just way over the head of this poor colored man. You say he's the one who wanted to talk to you in that restaurant, right? Why's such a rich man want to talk to some hayseed from Ohio dressed up in his best suit?"

When Fraser didn't say anything, Cook added, "So what's this going to prove? You figure it's your turn for the next beating?"

Fraser clenched his jaw but remained silent. He had made up his mind to go.

"I can't be there to protect you," Cook said. "I ain't up to it. You'll be on your own."

"Speed, the man's seventy-five years old if he's a day, I'm meeting him in an office, and he doesn't even know my real name. He thinks I'm Dr. John McIntire. What can happen?"

It was like, Cook thought, nothing bad had ever happened to the man. He always thinks things are going to be fine. Must be nice.

Chapter 17

Fraser wore his other new suit, pearl gray, to Barstow's office, arriving promptly at five. The tycoon met him in the anteroom, a cadaverous-looking attendant at his elbow. "Dr. McIntire, we must fly." Shaking hands, he pulled Fraser closer and confided in a low voice. "It's the Williamsburg Bridge to Brooklyn. A few friends and I have a large position in the company building it, and there's a splendid opportunity with the bridge bonds. News of faulty cable from the Roebling company is driving the bonds down, quite erroneously. They will recover handsomely. We can talk on the way. It's a magnificent sight."

On the street, Fraser tried to appear decisive as he stepped into Barstow's carriage, but Cook's cautions ran through his mind. He gauged that he could climb over the carriage side in the event of some ill-seeming development. Barstow certainly couldn't restrain him, while the gaunt attendant was seated next to the driver, on the front bench. In any event, they were in the middle of the city on a late afternoon in August. What could happen? He began to relax when the carriage rolled in an unremarkable fashion to the north, toward the East River crossings.

Barstow pointed out the lines of wagons, carts, and carriages snaking onto the Brooklyn Bridge next to City Hall. "Ever since they brought Brooklyn into the city two years ago, the demand for this second bridge has increased daily. It's desperately needed. It will prove, I'm quite sure, a brilliant investment."

When Fraser reminded Barstow that his partners in Ohio would have to review any venture that did not involve cotton, the other man was unconcerned. "They cannot fail to appreciate this opportunity. They are men of business, are they not?"

"Of course."

Barstow shifted the conversation to politics, inquiring whether Ohio would vote for McKinley. Fraser used the opening to ask about Barstow's suppertime banter with Senator Smith—specifically about being involved in the McClellan presidential campaign of 1864, at a time when he wore a Confederate uniform.

"Sir," the tycoon said amiably, "don't be misled by a joke between two former rebels. Of course, General McClellan's loss was a matter of regret to us. He could have made a peace that brought the nation together. If the Southern states had been able to vote, McClellan would have won in a landslide!"

"It was the choice of the Southern states not to vote that year."

Barstow allowed a silence to collect. Looking out his side of the carriage, he said, "I suppose I should expect no less from the son of a Union Army captain."

The hair on Fraser's neck prickled. Was Barstow referring to the father of Dr. John McIntire? Or was he showing that he knew that Dr. McIntire was a phantasm? Barstow was trying to put him on edge. He was succeeding.

At the bridge construction site, a watchman waved them through the gate. Huge girders and spools of cable, the playthings of titans, lay on either side of the passageway, but the site was quiet. The crews were gone for the evening. Since it was Saturday, they would not return until Monday morning.

The breeze on the riverbank was welcome. The carriage drove directly to the bridge's steel tower, which loomed 300 feet above them. Fraser stared up.

"Extraordinary, is it not?" Barstow waved toward the monster. The daring of it flooded Fraser's mind. It was the work of puny men, thousands of them, abetted by the skill of the few who could imagine and design it. He loved its presumption, extending the land from one shore to the next.

"I must speak with a man for a moment." Barstow alighted from the carriage. "Mr. Brown, can you point out the finer points until my return?"

The skeletal Mr. Brown stood by the side of the carriage. "Sir," he said, in a surprisingly deep voice, indicating the few steps to the tower.

Fraser stepped down warily, stealing glances at the peak of the bridge tower. "It's a suspension design, of course," Mr. Brown said, pointing to a companion tower rising from the Brooklyn shore. "The road and railroad tracks will hang from cables strung between the two towers." The project's immensity dazzled Fraser. Mr. Brown pointed to a massive spool of cable that sat on a barge, ready to be lifted to the top of the tower. Steel bars and wood lay in heaps.

"Two thousand men work here," Mr. Brown continued. "Only four deaths so far. See here"—Brown pointed to the tower's base—"the riveting is essential. If we step over here, you can see the engine they use to drive the cable across the river."

"I'm not a great one for heights," Fraser said.

"Oh, just see this engine housing here, shipped all the way from Scotland." Mr. Brown held up a bar to a platform and Fraser stepped onto it. The other man flipped a switch and the platform began to rise. The motor accelerated. Fraser looked around. Mr. Brown was not on the platform. Fraser looked down. He was already fifteen feet off the ground. His heart raced. He couldn't jump. He reached for the lift switch and flipped it down. Nothing. He flipped it up and down. Still nothing. He turned it up and down, over and over. He gripped the railing with both hands, squeezing it until his fingers ached.

Too late, Fraser thought to call for help. He was a hundred feet up the tower. When he shouted, the breeze swallowed his voice. As the platform rose, the breeze became a low roar in his ears. He forced himself to look down at the work site, though the view made his stomach flutter. Barstow's carriage was moving toward the gate. He had brought Fraser here to be abandoned. A guard might stay at the yard through the night, but that promised no relief. Even if the guard could hear Fraser's voice, he would be part of Barstow's plan to strand Fraser.

The lift continued to rise. Every twenty feet, its wheels ground noisily, setting off shudders on the platform. Fraser forced himself to look at the vertical rails where the wheels turned. The shaking came from the joints between rails, as the wheels bumped from one rail to the next.

Helpless, hopeless, Fraser rode this open contraption into the sky. He fought off waves of panic that locked his muscles. All that stood between him and plunging to his death was a simple iron bar about three feet high on each side of the platform. What was most terrifying was the perverse pull he felt to the edge of the platform, the fantasy of stepping into thin air, if only to end the anxiety that screamed in his head.

The lift stopped just below the top of the tower. He could see a wooden platform at the top of the tower, beyond his reach. The wind was strong, gusting and blowing.

Fraser was ashamed at what a fool he'd been. Barstow knew far more about Fraser than Fraser ever would know about him—not only knew about Dr. John McIntire and about

Fraser's father's military service, but also that Fraser was terrified of heights.

Unsteadily, Fraser sat down Indian style, as close to the center of the platform as he could calculate. He had to control his mind, to still the fear echoing inside. If he could get his mind to work, perhaps he could gain control over his arms and legs.

Was there anyone who might help him? The construction site was deserted. He peered over the platform edge to confirm it. Yes, deserted. He could not expect anyone to notice that the lift was out of place, frozen almost 300 feet above the ground. For the next thirty-six hours, until Monday morning, no one other than a watchman or two would be on the construction site. It was hard to believe that Barstow arranged to leave Fraser at the top of this tower without making sure no workman would rescue him.

In fact, Fraser could think of only two people in New York who might want to help him. Cook was in no condition to be useful, and had no reason to look for Fraser at the bridge site. Nor would Eliza think Fraser was anywhere but the Miller Hotel on Madison Avenue. The thought of that decrepit lodging triggered a powerful longing for its shabby safety. He would never again complain about their hotel rooms.

If he was going to get down, he had to do it himself. Fraser realized his panic had slackened a notch. He had passed several minutes without falling off the platform. The wind still blew, but it was becoming familiar. The platform was holding in its place. Presumably it was used to transport large work crews, not to mention equipment and tools, so it should be solid. Fraser resolved to make a more active review of his situation.

He looked around the platform, moving only his eyes, then rose to his knees and pivoted in place. He examined every part. It was larger than it seemed at first, perhaps fifteen feet deep by twenty feet across.

Fraser found it more difficult to think while up on his knees. He felt exposed. He resumed a cross-legged position. The wind, he told himself, could not sweep him off his perch. The day had at least two more hours of light.

He could stay where he was. That would mean thirty-six hours without food or water. He had trouble imagining going to sleep up there, what with the distressing prospect of groggily rolling over and tumbling off. If he did not go insane, he might make it through thirty-six hours at the top of New York City.

Could he get down on his own? He stretched out on his belly and wriggled to the edge nearest the tower. He kept his eyes on the solid tower and away from the void that yawned on the other three sides.

The gap between the platform and the tower was narrow, no more than six inches. He couldn't fit between the two. To get off the platform, he would have to . . . he felt dizzy to think of stretching an unsupported leg off the side of the platform.

The tower consisted of two steel beam structures, each built with girders in an "X" design and leaning into each other. A horizontal girder about three feet below the platform crossed from one of the steel beam structures to the other, joining them. That cross girder was about ten inches wide.

Fraser would have to drop to the cross girder and slide along it for fifteen feet to the corner of one of the steel beam structures. Each structure seemed to have hand and footholds affixed to its outer edge. He could try to swing his legs around to the handholds and footholds, then climb down hand-over-hand. A confident, agile man could do it.

A spell of vertigo made him tremble. Fraser closed his eyes, took a breath, and looked at the situation again. That settled it. He could last thirty-six hours atop the tower.

As the panic receded, he slid back toward the center, staying on his belly. He remembered something he needed to look at. The world had darkened. The sunlight was gone. Lifting his head, he looked to the west, over Manhattan. There they were. Black clouds piled up at the horizon. They were taking over more and more of the sky, racing toward him. At the leading edge, lightning flashed.

Fraser's stomach churned. Could he sit out a thunderstorm in this eagle's nest, when the winds would howl? Or did he have to get down now, right now? If he was going to beat the storm down, he had to move. Clenching his jaws, squinting at clouds that seemed larger every second, Fraser decided. He didn't want to be there through the storm, a human lightning rod.

He slid on his front until he was next to the tower. A steel upright at each corner of the platform supported the rail that ringed his little world. He could hold on to the upright as he reached for the cross girder. Grabbing the upright, he turned backward on his knees. The black cloud bank was speeding across the sky. He forced himself not to look.

Slowly, he pushed his left leg back into space, angling it down. First the foot, then the knee. His toe strained for contact with the crossbeam. Where was it? Had he stretched it too far back? He tried a little lower. There. Firm against his foot. He put weight on it, then a little more. Dropping to his belly, he did the same with his right leg, this time knowing how far down to reach. The platform lurched from the tower with a sickening jolt. It was his weight shifting off. With both hands, he clung to the upright, then lowered to his knees on the crossbeam. He was going to have to let go with one hand, then reach down and grip the crossbeam. He would bear-hug the crossbeam and do the inchworm to the corner of the tower. To his dismay, he couldn't touch the crossbeam with his free hand while holding on to the upright.

With a lunge, he let go of the upright and fell down to the crossbeam. He gripped it with knees and feet and arms. His momentum swung to the far side of the beam, but he righted himself. He realized his eyes were squeezed shut. He opened them and began to inch. No time to lose. He kept his focus on the tower, looking neither left nor right, neither up nor down. The wind blew harder, roaring into his ears in bursts.

When he reached the edge of the steel structure, the panic stirred again. His muscles froze. He wanted to cry. He could let go and end this torture. How bad could it be?

He pushed up as close to the structure as he could get. He would have to reach out for the first hand grip. Then he would have to swing over empty space until he found a foothold to steady himself. He couldn't do it. He cursed himself. Why had he left the safety of the platform? What was he thinking, taking this kind of risk? Then he cursed himself as a coward, frozen with fear when he needed to act. A sharp gust broke into his terror. To his left, the cloud bank had advanced to the middle of Manhattan. Thunder growled. He could see rain pelting down. No time. He had to go.

He could reach a grip with his right hand. He would hug the cross girder with his left and bring his legs over with one movement. He could not afford to swing. He had to control his momentum, not allow it to strain his grip. And he had to do it before the steel became slick with rain.

For a moment, he felt calm. He moved. His right foot pawed the upright, desperately seeking purchase. It was smooth, nothing to wedge his foot against. He would slide all the way to the ground. His right arm, clinging to the hand grip, began to ache. Where was the next grip? He pulled his leg back and squeezed the girder with his knees.

He extended his foot again. Nothing. A hole of dread opened inside. Wait, there it was. The slant of the beam structure meant the grips were slightly to the side, not straight vertical. He had no time to think. He dropped his left foot for the next step. He stared straight ahead at the gray steel, reached his left hand to a second hand grip, and let himself down. He was descending.

The grips were at a uniform distance. He learned how far to drop each foot, at what angle, and how far to reach down the next hand. He couldn't hurry. He couldn't look down. One grip. The next grip. And the next. After what seemed like several hours, the rain arrived. It swept across his face. His suit became heavy with water. The grips felt slicker under his hands. He worried about his toes slipping. The wind dug at him. One gust seemed to push him sideways. When it stopped abruptly, his weight lurched back. His clothes were heavy with water, his shoes threatened to slip off his feet.

He didn't look down. One foot, then the next. One hand, then the next. After another eternity, his peripheral vision picked up images of piled lumber, spools of cable. He was close. With each step down, he longed for the ground. When his left foot touched a new surface, he toed it gingerly, then flattened his foot against it. With a gasp, he slid down the girder and collapsed. Tears came, unbidden. He was down.

Drenched by the rain and shaken by his escape, Fraser mounted the stairs of the Miller Hotel. He dreaded Cook's reaction. He had been a fool. Stepping into their darkened room, Fraser said nothing. He dripped on the floor and shivered in a woeful fashion. Cook threw him a towel, told him to get his clothes off, then wrapped him in a blanket. When Fraser's shaking stopped, Cook listened to his tale with a steady expression. At the end, he showed neither scorn, though Fraser had earned it, nor sympathy.

"See?" he said. "It's like I been telling you. These folks ain't playing. You need to start being smart, stop thinking like you're white, you're going to live forever."

Fraser agreed, but he said one thing more. "We're on to something, Speed. He wouldn't go to all this trouble if we weren't."

"Wish I knew what it is we're on to. We sure know he's on to you, maybe on to me, too. Dr. McIntire just left town for good."

Both fell asleep without any supper. The next morning, they moved to another hotel, another day of laying low and healing, deciphering Barstow's memo book, thinking about Booth's conspiracy. They had to leave New York. It was dangerous being near Barstow. Fraser traded wires with Townsend in Maryland, getting leads on the people to see in Maryland. Neither man said anything about turning back.

Chapter 18

Sitting on a bench in the Newark train depot, Fraser tapped his foot impatiently. The Chesapeake Limited was delayed. Theodore Roosevelt, the Republican candidate for vice president, was leaving for the West that morning. His supporters, taking advantage of the break in the heat wave, had swamped the station, snarling trains all morning. Cook sat reading a newspaper.

Their misadventures in New York seemed to have reconciled them to each other. Fraser appreciated that Cook was capable, smart about the world, smart about people. And he was steadfast. After being manhandled by the rioters, he could have chosen to pack it in. Fraser's escapade on the bridge might have persuaded him that Fraser was too rash and foolish, and Barstow too dangerous, to keep going. But here he was.

As for Fraser, he was angry and getting angrier. He didn't like being pushed around. He meant to do some pushing back.

Looking down the train platform, Cook folded his paper and stretched. "Let's go take a look," he said. "Not going anywhere till this man's done inspiring the nation."

They walked outside to where the honored speaker stood in a vested suit on an overturned crate. They circled the crowd until they could see him. Roosevelt's high-pitched voice, bursting with fury, was clear when he rotated toward them, muted when he turned away.

His movements were violent, left fist pounding into the palm of his right to punctuate his points. Even at a distance, his large teeth looked wolfish. His eyeglasses, far from making him seem like a sissy, flashed with menace when they caught the light. They gave Roosevelt a supernatural air, a man able to see into the brains and hearts of his listeners.

He was laying into the Democrats and their demand for self-government in the Philippines. Roosevelt dismissed the natives as "Malay bandits." Yet, he bellowed, those same Democrats schemed to deny the voting rights of "Americans of dusky color" in North Carolina.

Roosevelt's fearsome intensity grew as he spoke of the Filipino war. War was necessary, he shouted, to avoid chaos and anarchy. Americans had a duty to put down the armed resistance without pussyfooting, parleying, or faltering. "All the great masterful races," he called out, "have been fighting races. The minute that a race loses the hard fighting virtues, then, no matter what else it may retain, it has lost its proud right to stand as the equal of the best. Cowardice in a race, as in an individual, is the unpardonable sin."

The crowd roared its approval. Roosevelt clasped his hands together in victory.

Cook shook his head as they stepped back toward their idle train. "What a load of bunk. That man ought to be ashamed of himself."

"Truly?" Fraser said. "I thought you'd like the way he spoke for Americans of a dusky color."

Cook waved the comment away. "He don't mean anything by it. He says just enough to get the votes of the few colored who still can vote. He won't do anything for us, like stop the lynching. You notice he didn't mention that riot in his own city, New York, where he was police commissioner? Or that it was his police joined in the rioting, busting colored men's heads?"

Fraser said nothing, but Cook kept on. "Makes me sick, all that stuff about the glorious war in the Philippines. He wants to get everybody on the same side, North and South, black and white, by shouting out, 'Let's go kill us some yellow men!' "

"He wants to 'busy giddy minds with foreign quarrels.' "

Cook looked at him sidewise. "I suppose you could say that."

When the Chesapeake Limited began to board, Fraser put a question to Cook that had been bothering him. "Do you still think it might make a difference in the election year if we prove that Democrats were involved in killing Lincoln?"

Cook smiled. "Can't do them any good. But even if it killed them off as a party, it wouldn't change the race hate. The haters'd start up another party, call it something else."

As soon as they were seated, Cook whispered in Fraser's ear. When the train pulled out, he hissed, they should get off. Fraser raised an eyebrow. "We ain't alone," Cook added, "must be Barstow's men. You go first. Stroll toward the next car like you're stretching your legs. From between cars, you jump off. We meet up at the next station."

"What about our things?"

"I'll take care of them."

Fraser scanned the car for the men Cook had spotted. The one in a straw boater? Too old. The bowler? Too fat. Barstow would send only the fittest on his dirty errands.

The train jerked. Its wheels screeched and their car vibrated with the throaty rumble of the engine. Fraser remembered the two thugs in Indiana, the note in his hotel room in Fairview, the Williamsburg Bridge. He had no wish to meet up with Barstow's toadies.

He walked to the rear door and out between cars. Another man was there, leaning against the doorframe, smoking a thin cheroot. He nodded at Fraser, who swung a leg over the gate between the cars, scissored the other one over, and dropped to the ground. He executed the maneuver with complete nonchalance until the landing. He fell heavily on his left leg, twisting it, then rolled down a slope not quite dry from a recent rain.

Limping alongside the tracks to the next station, Fraser regretted that he had jumped so soon. He might safely have ridden several more miles before jumping. After more than an hour, he reached the Elizabeth depot, mostly deserted in the midmorning lull.

Cook was sitting on his trunk to the side of the platform. Fraser's trunk stood next to him, supporting a medium-sized white man in a dusty gray jacket. Cook nodded and said, "Say hello to John Buckner. If that's his real name."

Fraser stared at Cook. Cook shrugged. "While I was arranging for the baggage, I run into this man and I realized I know him. So we decided to get off here for some talk." Cook clapped a heavy hand on Buckner's shoulder, then nodded down to his other hand in his jacket pocket, which might well hold a weapon.

"So far," Cook continued, "Mr. Buckner's been quiet. I thought maybe he'd feel better spilling his guts to a white man. That way he gets a choice. Spill his guts to you or have this colored man spill his guts for him." As he stood up, Cook gave the man's shoulder a last squeeze. Buckner made a face. "I won't be far."

Fraser moaned as he sat on the trunk Cook had just vacated. His feet hurt. He pointed to Cook's receding figure. "I hope you didn't rile him up. Once he gets hot, he's hard to settle down." Cook stopped about thirty feet away. He leaned against the depot wall and stared back.

"Honest, mister, I don't know what that crazy nigger's going on about. I was just riding the train, minding my own business, when up he comes—"

Fraser held up his hand. "Mr. Buckner, if you want to tell me my friend has a bad temper, I won't argue. You want to criticize his manners, I'll let it go. He *can* be a little rough-edged. But you shouldn't start telling me he's wrong about you and what you're up to. He doesn't make that kind of mistake."

Buckner protested his innocence again. This time Fraser sat through it, eyes cast down at the planking on the depot platform. When the man grew quiet, Fraser asked, "You're done?"

The man nodded.

"You still see my friend there?" Cook hadn't moved. "Now listen close this time. I would describe my friend as, well, moody. You might call him crazy. Different words, but the same point. You know he's carved up white men before, don't you? They should've told you that. I don't know how many he's done. What I know, and maybe they didn't tell you, is that he doesn't mind it. I don't know, maybe he likes it." Buckner shifted his weight.

"You can see he's close to losing his temper, and that'll be worse for you than for me," Fraser said. "You're the only one can keep that from happening. Now why not say who sent you?"

The gray man looked across the tracks.

"Somebody hired you." The man remained silent. Fraser sighed and stood. "That's too bad. You give me a name and address, I can send word where your people can find you. You know, after."

Cook started walking toward them.

"Stoneman," the man blurted.

Fraser signaled Cook to stop. "Okay."

"I didn't sign up for no rough stuff. Not my line. It was this Stoneman, though, I done some jobs for him before, following guys, you know."

"Tell me about Stoneman."

"He's a big fellow, works for some shipping company. You know, private police. Out of Baltimore. He was a cop there, a rough one. Proud of it."

"What company?"

"Don't know."

"Has he got a first name?"

"Jed, I think. Least that's what they call him."

Fraser pressed him for a description. Stoneman was of medium height, broad across and without much hair. He favored a wide-brimmed hat. Buckner claimed not to know any others or to be able to describe them.

"What'd he hire you to do?"

The man looked over at Cook, who was about fifteen feet away, looking full of energy. "Does he have to stand so close?"

"What were you supposed to do?"

"I started about three weeks ago. Stoneman hired me and three others, three that I knew about. Told us to be watching for you two—a big yellow nigger with graying hair and a large white man, sandy haired."

"Why did he say you were watching for us?"

"Didn't say." The man looked up at Fraser. "What do I care? I watch at train stations, ferry slips. When you two are together, you stand out a mile."

"So what're you supposed to do when you find us?"

The man shrugged. "Find out where you're staying, where you're going. Tell Stoneman. After that, I don't know. Stoneman handles that. I'm just a guy who watches." He looked over at Fraser. "You ought to know, it changed a few days back."

"What changed?"

"Stoneman hired more guys. Said we weren't going to let you leave New York. Said you stole some things."

"What?"

"Books. He said one's got a picture of a frog. I didn't ask about it. Like I said, I'm purely a watcher."

Fraser tried more questions, but the man offered nothing more. Then Fraser had a thought. "When you saw us, did you send any kind of message about it, before you got on the train?"

The man denied it, but Fraser didn't believe him. They needed to get off this train platform. He waved Cook over. "Mr. Buckner here's been talking."

Cook gave the man a hard look. Fraser added, "We're at the part where he agrees to stop following us. Keeping after us would be a real mistake."

The man agreed emphatically.

"You want to let him go?" Cook said. "Just like that?" Disappointment suffused his tone.

"Unless you've got a better idea."

Cook shook his head and cocked a hip. "All right. Not as messy, I guess." Lifting his chin, he said directly to the man, "Don't let me see you again."

The man nodded and stood. Fraser shooed him with the back of his hand and Buckner scampered away.

Cook began to smile. "Damn, Doctor, I'm thinking maybe you missed your calling, you should've signed up for something a bit rougher, collecting gambling debts and such."

Fraser smiled. "It wasn't me he was afraid of. What'd you say to him?"

They sat down on their trunks. "Nothin'." Cook smiled again. "Saying nothin', that can be real powerful. Also, showing a knife."

After Fraser related what the man had said, Cook puffed out his cheeks and let out a long breath. "Okay. We're riding the tiger here. Stoneman, Barstow, they aren't fooling around. They want those books back. Funny that he mentioned the frog book."

"Don't you see? That means we're getting closer."

"Yeah, closer to getting killed."

They agreed on a radical change in their travel. Stoneman was watching train stations and piers, but he couldn't cover every country road in New Jersey and Maryland. They would ship their luggage to Baltimore, buy a couple of horses, and ride there.

Fraser made a face. "That's a long ride. Why not just build a hot-air balloon and fly there?"

"Balloons are damned easy to follow." Cook grinned. "Come on, it'll toughen up your backside." As his grin faded, he added, "I don't have a good feeling about Baltimore. That's a Southern town, and it's Stoneman's hometown. We're walking right onto his home field."

"You want to go back to Ohio?"

"Just letting you know how I feel."

Chapter 19

Cook didn't mind hanging back while Fraser asked the farmers if they could sleep in the barn or shed. They never talked about doing it that way, having Fraser do the asking. First time they did it, Cook just let Fraser ride into the farmyard ahead of him. With his gentle manners, Fraser looked as harmless as the straw he was asking to sleep on. Farmers naturally liked blond, shambling Jamie Fraser. They wanted to help him get out of the weather. They trusted him not to burn the place down. So Cook stayed out of the way.

The journey was proving more difficult than it sounded. Neither of them had spent much time in the saddle. They tried to buy horses in Elizabeth, but the ones they found were either half-dead or high-spirited—real high-spirited. When a stableman watched them spook their mounts into near hysteria, he spat tobacco juice and held out the money Fraser had just paid him.

"Come on, come on," the man called. "Get down off those things before you kill yourselves."

He told them to try mules. When Cook objected that mules would be slow, the stableman spat again. Drops of brown juice spackled his chin. "I got a conscience, you know, but you two are fully growed. You can choose. Slow or dead."

Fraser bought the mules, Annie and Dusty. Not that the mules knew their names or cared who was trying to ride them. In the man-mule relationship, Annie and Dusty took the leadership role. They set their own pace, a deliberate one. They stopped when they wished to graze and stayed until they were done. When an automobile roared up behind them, they trotted off in whatever direction promised the quickest relief from the machine's thunder and smoke. After one encounter with an auto, Annie didn't stop for more than a mile, leaving Fraser red-faced and even more saddle-sore. He and Cook learned to bend every effort to avoid motorized vehicles, which suited Annie and Dusty just fine. On the plus side, the mules didn't mind the rain on the second day, though the riders found it dispiriting.

Indeed, so long as their terms were honored—and the men had little choice in that matter—the mules proved willing partners. They walked steadily for up to ten hours a day, submitting without complaint to ferry rides over rivers. Crossing into northern Maryland on the third day, the men expected to reach Baltimore the next afternoon.

They didn't talk much on the road. The mules walked single file, which discouraged conversation. Fraser called out remarks on the breeze, the sun, the clouds, but Cook mostly didn't respond, neglecting Fraser into silence.

In the evenings, they pulled out Barstow's books and stared at them until fatigue got the upper hand. They made no headway with the frog book. Cook still insisted that some of the numbers stood for dates and others for dollar values, but they could pick out no patterns. They did better with the book in Confederate cipher. They puzzled out a flurry of references in early 1865 to Julius Spencer, who would become Barstow's partner. They looked for a connection between Spencer and John Wilkes Booth, but found none.

On the third night, Cook had some things on his mind. He waited until they finished their canned soup and loaf of bread. Neither of them was much for cooking.

Staring into the dwindling fire, Cook started talking about the men who were chasing them. They were serious about this business, he said, serious enough to set traps for them. What did Fraser and Cook know about them? Did they know enough to figure out how to avoid them, or even stop them?

"Well," Fraser started, "we know Barstow's in the middle of it—"

"More like at the top."

"—and we know something about Stoneman. And we know they call themselves the Sons of Liberty."

"They could call themselves the Knights of the Second Coming," Cook said. "The name don't mean anything. That's just how they fancy themselves."

"I think it matters. The Sons of Liberty means something to them. They think they're defending a cause, liberty."

"Brother, all it means is they're defending themselves. From us. This has to be about assassinating Lincoln, right? They're making sure to keep that covered up, making sure the trail always ends at Booth, the mad killer. If you were involved in killing Lincoln, thirty-five years don't make you any safer than you were the day he died. Someone finds out you did it, you're going to hang."

"Okay, fair enough. How does that help us find them?"

"Can't think of anything helps us find them. They don't always wear red shirts or blue hats, or work in a building with a sign saying 'Sons of Liberty' out front. The ones we've seen have just been regular-looking white men, right? Could be anyone on the street."

Fraser smiled. "That one back at the train station. You scared the willies out of him."

"He should've been scared."

"It isn't like we were going to do anything right there on the depot platform."

"That what you think?"

Fraser lifted his eyes from the fire. "Shouldn't it be?"

Cook took his time answering. "I think you *all* should be scared of me." Cook met Fraser's gaze. "Playing ball, they got to be scared of me. I liked that, used it to beat them. People who're scared don't think straight. They didn't like being scared of me, a colored boy, but dangerous all the same. Maybe more dangerous because he's colored. They thought maybe I was playing some different game than they were, that it mattered more to me, that I'd do something they wouldn't. They were right."

"What different game?"

"You know how you felt up on that bridge, swinging in the wind? Like you were trapped, nowhere to turn, nothing you can do, every move going to get you in worse trouble, even get you killed?"

Fraser nodded.

"That's being colored. Trapped. Nowhere to go. Can't afford to step wrong. Not once." Cook stared into the fire. "Throwing me out of baseball probably saved my life. I was going to start something, sooner or later, and I would've ended up dead. I didn't know it, but they knew."

"Must've been hard, giving up something you're really good at."

Cook fed the fire some wood he had split with the farmer's ax. "I was hot about it, but it was out of my hands. Every ballplayer knows it's coming one day, the day you're too slow, too weak. I wasn't there yet, but I could see it."

"I've been feeling that way about doctoring."

"Doctoring? No such thing as too slow for doctoring. That's something *old* men do."

Fraser smiled. "Not too slow, maybe, but losing the fire. Since my wife, Ginny, died, it feels different. Not as important. I still want to help people, get to know them. When they get sick, some people seem to become more who they really are, more than at any other time. It's like they're stripped bare. They don't have the energy to pretend. It's a privilege to know them that way." Cook was nodding. "But with Ginny gone, when things go bad, I can't let go of it. I could talk to her about those times and get out from under them. But not now. They weigh on me. I don't know if I can keep on with it."

"There's a big world out there, lots of things to do, 'specially for a large white man like yourself."

Fraser laughed. "Don't you ever stop thinking about race?"

"Nope, that'd be dangerous, dangerous for any colored. You might end up acting uppity, get sassy." They watched the fire flicker and pop. "So," Cook started, "when I was through feeling angry and sorry for myself, that's when I decided to start this newspaper."

"Have you ever done that kind of work?"

Cook smiled. "I've read a whole heap of newspapers and I've known lots of newspaper men. Doesn't look all that hard." His face grew stern. "I'm through with sitting around bellyaching while the world goes to hell in a handbasket. I've got a voice and an arm, and I can lift them both against all this injustice I've been swimming through my whole life. I've got something to say. It doesn't matter how much I get to say or how many days I get to say it. The Lord never lets you know how many days you'll have. But I've got to start."

"I envy your passion."

"Mrs. Cook says it doesn't make me easy to live with."

Fraser smiled. "I can see her point." He sat up straighter and stretched his spine. "Time to talk about Baltimore?" Cook said nothing, so Fraser pressed on. "The people there—the Surratts and Sam Arnold—they're not going to be eager to talk with the likes of us. I figure John Surratt is least likely to cooperate. He never did show any remorse, just stuck to his story that the Booth conspiracy was exactly that—the *Booth* conspiracy. So let's start with him. Why don't we run at him first?"

"He should be *last*," Cook said. "The others'll clam up as soon as John Surratt passes the word. He's the hard case. Think of it. He's the one who ran off to Europe and never looked back while they hanged his mother for his crimes. A man who turns his back on his own mother—he ain't about to make a spontaneous confession. Not ever."

Fraser offered a compromise. They could start by checking out John Surratt. He was the only one they knew where to find, courtesy of Townsend. Surratt might lead them to his sister, or to something else.

"No matter where we start," Cook said, "Stoneman'll be looking for us. And he'll send men who aren't just watchers. He'll send the doers next time."

The fire was down to embers. A half-moon gave the land a ghostly pall. A mule snorted and kicked the ground.

"You figure there's any chance we work this out," Cook said, "we actually get proof of what really happened? And that anyone will believe us if we do?"

Fraser lifted an eyebrow an inch. He shrugged even less.

Cook figured that was as good an answer as there was. Lying back on his blanket, he didn't expect to fall asleep, but he did right off.

Chapter 20

Cook didn't think Annie and Dusty would walk as far into Baltimore as they did. The mules' objections to traffic could no longer be ignored when two autos rumbled down a street at the same time, triggering a spasm of head shaking, shying, and even the beginnings of rising on back hooves. Cook persuaded Fraser to dismount and stable their steeds. They could manage the rest of the way on foot.

Baltimore didn't compare to New York as a city, but after four days on the road, Cook felt the lure of its conveniences. They found a rooming house with that bedraggled look he prized. Domestic thoughts washed over him: a hot bath, a kitchen-cooked meal, clean clothes from their trunks. He pushed those thoughts out of his mind.

According to Townsend's wire, Surratt worked for the Baltimore Steam Packet Company, which should be easy to find. It was bound to be a nest of former Confederates. "This," he declared, "is one Southern town. I'm telling you, it's no place to be colored."

"You say that about every city," Fraser pointed out.

"That don't make me wrong."

They split up, since they were so easy to pick out when together. Fraser went to claim their luggage from the train depot. Cook wanted to look over the shipping company.

He found its terminal on Light Street, facing the harbor. A steamer, the *Georgia,* sparkled in the sunshine. At the front of the vessel, white-jacketed staff guided passengers coming down the gangplank. At the rear, a Negro freight gang shouldered bales of cotton. After hoisting a bale, sometimes teetering briefly, each man would center himself for the tramp down to the pier and a waiting wagon. The sun was strong and the air thick with humidity. The men's dark skin shone with sweat and their shirts clung damply. Cook watched from a shady spot on the street.

During a lull in the stevedores' efforts, Cook fell in with a group of them as they drained pails of beer from a nearby tavern. He said he heard the company was hiring.

"Where'd you hear that?" The question came from a medium-sized man, older than the others.

Cook said he heard that a fellow by the name of Stoneman said so. A wordless buzz passed through the group. The silence was thick. The men finished their beers and began to move back to the ship.

Cook followed the man who had spoken to him. "What'd I say? Haven't had that kind of effect since I farted in church."

The man stopped and looked off into the middle distance. "If you're a man for Stoneman," he said, "then don't none of us need to be with you."

"I didn't know he had that reputation," Cook said. "What's he look like? Where's he usually found? Sounds like maybe I need to steer clear of him."

"Got a face," the man said, "like a clenched fist. He's big and broad and bald. He drinks up at the Skipjack, over on Charles Street." After starting toward the ship, he turned back. "It's your business, but I never heard of him hiring colored, not even a yellow one."

Before leaving, Cook resolved on one more gambit. He picked up a piece of paper from the street and folded it into a message-sized packet. He walked to the offices of the steam-ship line. The building was brick, its multipane windows flanked with black shutters. With his hand on the doorknob, he saw a small sign: "DELIVERIES IN THE REAR." A gravel walk led to a rear door. Cool air embraced him as he entered. He would gladly have spent the rest of the day there.

"Boy, what you want?" The question came from a thin young man wearing spectacles, vest and cravat, and sleeve garters.

Brandishing his fake message, Cook said, "Yes, sir. Have a message here for Mr. John Surratt."

"My uncle's gone for the day," the young man said. Reaching, he added, "I'll see that he gets it."

"I'm supposed to hand it to him direct. I couldn't find him at the Skipjack."

The young man *tsked* dismissively. "My uncle wouldn't set foot in that dump." He narrowed his eyes. "Who are you, boy? What's in that message? Give it here."

Cook bowed quickly and reached back for the doorknob. "I needs to check back with my boss, sir. Sorry to be a bother to y'all." He left quickly.

Three hours later, he laughed about it as he banged a crab with a wooden mallet at a waterfront saloon. His lips burned from the pepper the crabs were boiled in. "There I was, face-to-face with Anna Surratt's son, with a scrap of paper in my hand and no more plan what to do next than that spotted dog has right now." Cook nodded over at a skinny mongrel sitting near their table, hoping to get lucky. "I was glad to get back to the street."

"What'd he look like?" Fraser asked.

"Scrawny, medium high, one of those little mustaches that's the best some men can do." After wiping his hands on his trousers and taking a long pull on his beer, Cook leaned forward. "Thing is, I followed that boy most of the way home, up Charles Street." He tried to pick a piece of crabmeat from a corner of the shell. It was a lot of work for not much nourishment. "Asked a man on the street for the Surratt place. He said I meant the Tonry house, then pointed it out."

Fraser smiled. "That's first-rate. You found Anna Surratt in, what, six hours?"

"I think maybe I'm done with the Surratts. That boy at the steamship office, he's going to remember me. He looked at me real close."

They decided that Fraser would approach Anna Surratt Tonry at her home. She wasn't supposed to be quite right in the head, not since her mother was hanged all those years ago. Fraser was a doctor, so he could offer his services. Cook would take care of selling Annie and Dusty, then come up to the Tonrys' neighborhood to watch for Stoneman and his men.

"Remember," Cook said, looking up from his crab. "Call her 'Miss Anna.' You're in the South."

At ten the next morning, Fraser stood on the front stoop of a simple row house on East Twenty-Eighth Street. He told the young woman at the door that he was Dr. Robert Sanders here to see Miss Anna. He liked having another new name.

"What are you here for?"

"Her brother, Mr. Surratt, asked me to look in on Miss Anna. He thought perhaps I could assist her."

The young woman's brown hair was tucked into a practical bun. Her face was flushed from domestic chores. She looked uncertain. Fraser adjusted his suit coat to emphasize his respectability. He held his medical bag in front to project authority and trustworthiness. She stepped back.

"I'll show you the way," she said.

Miss Anna's bedroom was at the head of a narrow flight of stairs. "Ma," the young woman called out, "Ma, here's another doc Uncle John sent. He's going to make you better." Looking back over her shoulder, she whispered to Fraser, "She's been like this for more than a week."

Fraser confronted a white-haired woman whose age wasn't clear. She lay under a light coverlet that suggested she was long and slender. In her narrow, still-pretty face, the eyes looked wounded.

She paid little attention as he performed a rudimentary physical examination. He tried conversation. How was she feeling? She grunted. Was she sleeping well? Another grunt. Was there pain? A low moan. Headaches? No response at all. He asked if something was worrying her. No answer. He sat with her for another minute. The slap of wet clothes against a washboard came from the backyard.

He had read about such nervous disorders in females but had not seen one. It seemed unlikely he was going to learn from her about her brother's role in the Lincoln assassination. He wished he could help her. With a sigh, he decided to try aspirin. He mixed the powder with some water. She drank it dutifully. He left more powder with the daughter, who gave her name as Clara. He promised to return in a day.

Next morning, Miss Anna was sitting up when he crested the stairs. She smiled. When he asked if she was feeling better, she nodded. Fraser conducted the same examination and asked the same questions. Despite her better spirits, she was still taciturn. As Fraser prepared to leave, she spoke, her full voice startling him.

"You can't help me, can you? None of the others could."

"Your case is a confounding one."

She shook her head. "I despair of ever feeling well again, of waking up with strength in the morning."

Fraser found the conversation uncomfortable. Until now, he could tell himself he was seeing to her condition in good faith, even though he had another motive for seeing her. But he knew he shouldn't lie to his patient. This woman had nothing to do with killing Abraham Lincoln. Then again, she might know something useful. "I can find nothing wrong with you bodily. Certainly, though, your sentiments are preventing you from that enjoyment of life we all wish. I fear your health may be undermined by some personal loss you're harboring."

The woman looked away from him and appeared to think for a moment. "You want to know about my mother, don't you?"

"I know of her sad fate, of course, and have wondered if it's part of your melancholy. I hope you know that everything you tell your physician is held in the strictest confidence." When she didn't respond, he continued. "Is it, I wonder, that you miss your mother, even after all these years?"

"Of course, I do, but it's more than that."

"Indeed." Fraser's pulse began to race. He disciplined himself to be silent and wait.

"I feel as though I can trust you," she said. "You have a kind face. I slept well last night for the first time in ages."

All Fraser could think about was how he had deceived her, but he couldn't relent now. Not now. "That's welcome news," he said. "I will leave more of the aspirin."

"Please do, Dr. Sanders, but you are right that an unhappiness poisons my days. I'm burdened by the lies in my life, lies from my family. My brother, John, he's lied to me about so many things, but so did Mother. And I've realized that her fate was perhaps not the injustice I thought it. That's . . . crushing me."

"What is it," Fraser asked softly, "that's brought you to these conclusions?"

"The money." Fraser waited. "John's money. It keeps coming, like the rain. Oh, he's cautious. He tries not to draw attention to himself. But there's too much of it and there always has been. Money doesn't arrive for no reason."

"From where does it come?"

"New York. Some place called Spencer something or other."

Fraser's pulse was galloping. "Why couldn't it be money that your brother is properly entitled to?"

Miss Anna smiled. "You don't know my brother. He has a talent for spending money, especially on fine clothes, but not the least idea how to make it. He never has."

Fraser had to ask. "Forgive me if I pry. My question is not medical. You knew Booth?"

She nodded and seemed to relax her nervous vigilance.

"What was he like?"

"Wonderful. Graceful and handsome and kind. And thoughtful. Like the person we wish we could be."

"I understand he was appealing to the ladies."

"Oh, Doctor, he charmed every one of them, and the men, too, and the dogs and the chickens as well. But, you know, I think it was the ladies may have dragged him down."

"What do you mean?"

A cloud passed over her face. Her eyes drifted from him and the tension in her face returned. "Oh, it was such a long time ago." She sank back into her despond. No question from Fraser, no matter how gentle, could rouse her. He placed the aspirin mixture on her table and bade her farewell.

Walking toward North Charles Street, where he could catch the streetcar down to the harbor, Fraser's mind was ablaze. Anna Surratt Tonry would never deliver testimony in a courtroom, or even speak in public. Indeed, even when she was young and her mother's life was at stake, she had barely stumbled through the most rudimentary testimony, ending with an emotional breakdown that—to Fraser's eye—continued. Nevertheless, she described a new connection between John Surratt and Barstow. As Townsend predicted, it was the money that had left tracks, and was still leaving tracks. Barstow was the money man for Surratt now, just as he must have been for Surratt and Booth in 1865. Those payments in gold in Barstow's memo book for early 1865, those had to have been for Surratt and Booth.

And Barstow surely hadn't been operating on his own. He was a Confederate officer. Was it an official army effort? Or maybe he formed his own venture, a renegade operation dedicated to making millions with smuggled cotton? Barstow must have had allies in the North. Julius Spencer, his future partner, he was one. Who else?

Too late, Fraser noticed the man walking toward him, almost upon him. It must be Stoneman, approaching at a quick pace, with a face exactly like a clenched fist. Flight would be useless. His henchmen would be nearby. Fraser resolved to brazen it out. It was daytime on a city street. What could Stoneman do?

Making no eye contact with the powerfully built man, Fraser made to pass by. Then he couldn't breathe. Strong arms pinned his own arms to his sides. He was thrust into the dark of a wagon that smelled like a cigar store. He smelled ether.

Chapter 21

Watching from less than a block away, Cook could scarcely believe how Fraser walked right into it. The man didn't have the sense God gave an ant. He could have crossed to the other side of the street. He could have run. He could have shouted bloody murder. He even might have walloped Stoneman. Fraser didn't seem to appreciate that he was a big man and could hurt someone if he put his back into it. And he should have known that Cook was close by, able to help out. But instead, he tried just to stroll past Stoneman? That wasn't ever going to work. Now Cook had to find a way out of this mess.

Riding a bicycle he borrowed from outside a house, Cook shadowed Stoneman's wagon to the pier in front of the shipping terminal. There the wagon's contents—doubtless including Fraser—were loaded onto the *Georgia*. With luck, they might only beat the tar out of Fraser and dump him on some lonesome shore or island of the Chesapeake Bay. But Cook feared worse. Stoneman had to be losing patience. He would want a permanent solution to the problem of Fraser and Cook.

He stripped off his shirt and joined the line of stevedores carrying bundles of cured tobacco leaf up the ship's gangplank. Cook kept his head down and put the load on his right shoulder, screening his face from the boss. The other men said nothing. Hauling heavy loads in the heat didn't make men sociable.

He used his first trip to canvas the situation. They stacked their loads near a hatch. Others took them down a ladder into the hold. Cook had to get on to that duty. On his fourth trip up the gangplank, Cook noticed that the pile of tobacco next to the hatch was mounting. "Boss," he said to the foreman lounging against a railing, "how about I help clear some of this off?"

The man squinted through the smoke of his cigarette. "Why, you're just a coon Horatio Alger, ain't you?" Another stevedore dumped his load, then turned around.

Cook ducked his head. "Boss," was all he said.

After a long drag on his smoke, the foreman flipped the stub overboard. "Go get 'em, Horatio."

The descent into the hold was treacherous. Cook had to tilt his load at an awkward angle to clear the hatchway. At the bottom, he waited for his eyes to adjust to the murk. Three other stevedores were stacking the sheaves. Cook figured they were delaying their next trip up the steps as long as possible. One pointed where he should set his load down. Stretching his back, Cook took a good look around, then headed back up.

After three more trips, he had a plan. He found a spot at the front of the hold that had been left unfilled to allow a door to swing open. The door was locked, so Cook could hide there until the ship set sail. Then he would have to find a way into the rest of the ship.

By early afternoon, the cargo was loaded. Left alone in the hold for a moment, Cook stepped into the nook in the front. His muscles objected to crouching, but he held the position while the others finished the job, one grumbling that the old guy sure had made himself scarce. Cook winced when he heard the hatchway bolt slam shut from the top. He wasn't sure what he had gotten himself into.

The engines grumbled. Sensing the boat's motion, Cook ventured from his nest. The dark was near total. By memory and touch, he found the door handle and the lock underneath it. He pulled his picks out of his pocket—they were getting a lot of use—and went to work. He couldn't judge time in that black place, but it took a long while before he was slowly easing the door open. He entered a dimly lit passage that seemed to run next to the ship's boiler.

They probably stashed Fraser in an equipment room or a baggage room. If they put him in an empty passenger cabin, there was little hope. Cook couldn't wander the boat, shirtless, checking passenger cabins. So he stayed below and tried each door to an internal room. Luckily the locks were simple ones.

The third one was the charm. It housed pipes running from the engine room, coils of rope, and a few tools. It shimmered with heat from the engine. Fraser lay unconscious on the floor, off to the side, hands and feet bound. He didn't appear to be injured. Pulling his knife from a sheath strapped to his calf, Cook cut away Fraser's ropes. He couldn't revive him. Cook would never get him off the boat in that condition. More pressing, Stoneman was bound to check on his prisoner.

Cook pushed the inert man into a far corner, behind the pipes, then donned Fraser's jacket. It fit Cook well enough.

He assumed Fraser's former place on the floor. He placed his feet against a pipe to make it easier to rise quickly, then looped ropes around his wrists and ankles, and assumed a fetal position. He chose an angle that concealed his face and hands. His right hand gripped the knife. He waited in the roasting heat. His sweat made the knife handle slick. Baffles at the top and bottom of the door admitted a little light. It was better than the cargo hold.

Twice, steps passed by but didn't stop. Then two sets of feet paused and blocked the light at the lower baffles. The door opened and someone stepped in. A voice said, "Make sure he's still out."

Cook lunged, driving the knife deep into the midsection of the first man, who grunted. Cook stabbed again and pushed the knife up. It stuck in his chest; he couldn't pull it out. Cook desperately heaved the body away. There stood Stoneman, grinning, holding a long, evil-looking blade. With his heel, Stoneman kicked the door shut and stayed in front of it. Shifting his weight, he came forward, forcing Cook into a corner.

At the edge of his vision, Cook saw a short section of water pipe on the floor. But Stoneman was too close. To reach the pipe, Cook would have to expose himself to Stoneman's knife. The first man's blood was on the floor.

Cook dove for Stoneman's leg, the one opposite his knife hand, driving through the knee with his shoulder. It was like slamming into a tree trunk. Cook bounced to the side and down on the floor. The impact caused Stoneman's slash to be high. Arching his back to avoid the blade when Stoneman pulled it back, Cook scrambled to the pipe. He grabbed it and rolled back into Stoneman's legs as the man swung again. Stoneman came down with a crash.

Gasping, Cook spun onto his knees and swung the pipe down, two-handed, with all his strength. Stoneman grunted. Cook swung again, harder. He was angry that he couldn't reach the man's head. He swung again. And again. Stoneman wasn't moving, but he had a knife. Cook swung three more times. He was hitting mostly rib cage, stoving it in.

Still on his knees, Cook straightened and sank back on his heels. His hand was sticky with the first man's blood. No, the blood was warm. He was cut on the upper arm. Cook reached for the wound with his other hand. The cut was high, near the shoulder. Not an easy place for a tourniquet.

He ripped part of the shirt from the man he had stabbed.

Using his teeth to hold the fabric and his good arm to tear it, he came up with a strip. He tried to tie it around his arm, using his teeth again. Blood was everywhere.

The engine eased off; they must be nearing a port. Cook stumbled over to Fraser. He shook the man, then slapped his face. Fraser moaned and his eyelids fluttered. "Jamie," Cook hissed. "Come on!" He shook him. "Come on!" Fraser stirred. "You got to get up," Cook insisted. "Right now." Fraser rolled onto his hands and knees.

Cook stood. He had to find a way out. He grabbed a coil of rope and slowly moved into the passageway. He could hear Fraser lurching behind him. Cook tried a facing door. It was an empty office. He ran to the porthole, which was on the river side of the ship, facing the far shore. He tied the rope to a pipe in the room and went back for Fraser, who was on his feet, but shaky. His eyes weren't clear yet.

They lowered themselves to the water down the rope. Cook's left arm was no good. He could barely feel it. Fraser went into the river with a splash, but then came up again. Two colored fisherman watched them from a nearby dinghy. A white man without a coat. A Negro wearing a jacket but no shirt. The fishermen slowly rowed near where both men were trying to swim. Those fishermen held their fate.

"Get on the far side of the boat," said the man handling the oars. "Hang on there. We'll move down to where there's not so many people." Cook and Fraser did it. "Keep your heads down," the man said. They did that, too.

Chapter 22

Cook and Fraser drowsed in the narrow late-morning shade of the shed. The September sunshine unlocked sweet grass smells. The earth, soft with recent rain, yielded to their weight, which had grown over three days of rockfish, muskrat stew, and fresh corn. Women worked in the garden nearby. A breeze carried their voices, then dropped them. The men had left before sunrise to check crab traps and trail lines for rockfish or trout or bluefish. The children tried not to bother the two men staying in the shed.

Cook rested his bad arm on a wooden crate. Fraser had sewed the gash together with ordinary needle and thread. The wound was too deep to heal on its own. The stitching had to hurt, but Cook refused laudanum, insisting he couldn't afford to addle his wits any more. Fraser, whose own wits felt scrambled after being etherized, didn't insist.

They didn't provide much explanation to their saviors, Rafe Washington and his brother, Gabriel. Cook said they were on the run from some rough types, which Rafe and Gabriel surely knew already. They had only defended themselves, Cook added.

Fortunately, the Washington brothers were disposed to help folks in trouble, especially colored folks.

Sleeping in the shed was fine, though closer to the outhouse than ideal. Fraser tried to give Rafe some money, but Rafe wouldn't take it, so Fraser started doctoring the family. He drained a cyst for Gabriel's wife and prescribed quinine for Rafe's fever, which had come and gone for years. He wasn't sure quinine would help, but it shouldn't hurt.

Mostly, Cook and Fraser had lazed around the small farm on Pine Chip Road, across the river from Chestertown. They slept heavily at night and napped in the day. They worried there would be an investigation of the killings on board the *Georgia.* In town, Rafe reported, the talk was that no one knew who killed those two white men. He couldn't ask about it, though. It wouldn't do to seem too curious. Fraser offered to help on the farm, but Rafe made a face and told them to stay out of sight.

When Fraser tried to talk about what happened on the ship, Cook acted like Fraser hadn't spoken. Fraser had a jumbled memory of struggling, of grunts and heavy breathing, a blood-slick floor, sprawled bodies. A knife protruded from a chest. A face stared vacantly. Fraser knew what they had to mean, but he couldn't string them together, link cause and effect, and then the next cause and the next effect.

Fraser plucked a long stem of alfalfa with feathery white blooms at the top. He chewed one end. "Not sure I've ever seen so much trouble grow out of something that started out honest and true," he said. "We're trying to figure out a killing, not get people killed."

"Some people," Cook said, "need killing."

"You think God will hold those against us?"

Cook sighed and pulled his legs up at the knees. "You thinking I'm going to hell for that?"

"Not you, us. It was killing. It's on our heads."

"Not on mine. I *saved* a life—yours." He looked over at Fraser. "What d'you think hell is like? Big vat of boiling oil? Devils with tails and pitchforks poking you in the behind?"

"Yeah, when I was a boy. What else?"

"Well, we ain't kids now." When Fraser said nothing, Cook added, "So if there's some men need killing, who're going to kill a friend of mine, I ain't going to lose sleep over how those little demons with pitchforks'll think about it."

"I said thank you, more than once."

With his good hand, Cook clapped Fraser on the thigh and squeezed it. "You did. So we need to get out of here, let these people get on with their lives without desperadoes like us around their necks." Cook let a smile play on his face. "It's possible Stoneman had so many enemies they can't know who actually killed him."

"These people know it was us." The women were gathering up their tools, the tomatoes and squash they'd picked.

"They're country Negroes. Nobody thinks they know anything. If they say they don't know nothing, white folks believe it. It's the good part of having people think you're stupid. I've played stupid a time or two."

"Couldn't have been very convincing."

"Doesn't have to be. White folks just know I'm naturally stupid."

"Whoever was paying Stoneman's going to send someone else after us."

Cook shrugged, his gaze locked on the tall weeds that bent before the wind. "If coming after us involves getting killed, they may find it's getting harder to get good help." He turned his head to Fraser. "So, we going through with this whole business? I'm not feeling the fire coming off you, not like it used to. Getting too rough?"

"I took up this quest—" he smiled and shook his head.

"Maybe that's too dramatic. No, okay, I took up this quest because it seemed so important, and what I was doing had stopped seeming that way. This mattered. But now, it's turning out to be more than I bargained on, and I'm thinking about Eliza, too. She's changed how I think about things. We set out to solve a puzzle, not refight the Civil War, end up running from men trying to kill us."

"A man's got to choose what matters to him," Cook said. "I made my choice. This matters." He pointed with his thumb over his shoulder, behind him, toward the Washingtons' two-room house. "I went inside that house, here on this tired-out land. These folks've got nothing, or next to nothing, but you know the one framed picture on the wall? Abraham Lincoln, Father Abraham himself. He mattered. The people who took him away, they cheated a whole nation. That's what they meant to do, and they did it. But they especially cheated me, and Rafe Washington and his people, and all our people. That matters to my babies back in Steubenville, to the world they'll live in. And I aim to even that score." Cook stabbed the air with the index finger of his good hand, his voice low and intense. "So, Dr. Fraser, you need to choose. You in or you out?"

The silence stretched out. Fraser knew he should be weighing the pluses and minuses of his decision, gauging the risks against the likely benefits. Yet his mind felt empty. He felt the warm air on his face. He looked over at Cook, who had leaned his head back against the bleached wood of the shed. Fraser's eye followed a hawk gliding on the wind, turning circles in the high white sky.

"We know," Fraser said," that Barstow bankrolled John Surratt."

"Yeah? How we know that?"

Fraser described what Anna Surratt Tonry had told him. It meant, Fraser said, that Barstow paid for Booth, too. Cook objected. He was jumping past the evidence, that woman wasn't ever going to testify to anything, and they had missed their chance to talk to John Surratt.

This time Fraser objected. "He was never going to talk to us."

"Okay," Cook answered, "but what about Sam Arnold? Shouldn't we try him?"

Fraser didn't answer right away. "I guess so," he finally said. "We should."

But what Fraser wanted to talk about was Barstow's game. He'd been thinking about their dinner at Delmonico's. The old fox expressed real regret that George McClellan didn't become president, that the Union and Confederate armies hadn't conquered the rest of North America. Had that been the purpose of the Booth conspiracy, to reverse the results of the 1864 election, install McClellan as president and embark on continental conquest?

Cook wouldn't buy it. First, he pointed out, the last thing the United States needed right then was more territory. The Civil War started because of the argument over spreading slavery into new lands. More territory would have meant more arguments.

Fraser was ready for him. Canada would be non-slave, and Mexico would have slaves. It would be like all those compromises from before the war, with slavery south of some line and no slavery above it.

Cook grew exasperated. After three years of war, he insisted, the North wasn't going to give up on slavery, just let it keep on. Union troops already occupied Louisiana, much of Arkansas, Mississippi, and Tennessee. Slaves had been freed wherever the Union troops went. Lots of them made themselves free, just walked away. The Emancipation Proclamation took effect. No crazy foreign invasion was going to undo all that, certainly not one that involved killing Abraham Lincoln.

Cook gestured with his good arm. "Why would you believe anything Barstow said? When you and him were at that fancy restaurant, he had to know who you really were, what you were really about. He stuck you on top of that bridge just two days later. Why would he tell you the truth about anything?"

Fraser had no answer.

After sundown that night, Rafe joined them out behind the shed. Cook and Fraser explained that they would leave separately. They figured that some men would still be looking for a white man and a Negro, both large, traveling together. Rafe suggested that Fraser leave on one of the ferries that crossed the bay. With his beard growing out, he could put on some country clothes and pass for a laboring man, so long as he kept those soft hands in his pockets. Fraser should leave the Washingtons' place before dawn; Rafe would row him to the other side of the river and he could walk to the wharf.

They agreed that Cook should wait a couple more days to heal up. Cook didn't stand out so much on the farm. He could cross the bay on a boat with some of the Negro watermen, who would set him down in a quiet inlet. Rafe shook hands and went to join his family.

Fraser and Cook went back over their plans. Fraser would go to Sam Arnold's place in little Friendship, Maryland. That was where Townsend, the writer, said he lived.

"Now that man, Townsend, that's something we got to talk about," Cook said. "I've been thinking on him. There's a string of coincidences we're piling up." Cook had a serious tone. "Okay, so we go see him at that strange castle, whatever you want to call it, and you head off to Indiana, just like he says, right?"

Fraser nodded.

"And there's two rough customers there who beat you bad, right?"

"I was probably pretty conspicuous there," Fraser objected, "and I was going to see Weichmann every day."

"But why on earth was anyone looking for you there in that nowhere town? You think these people just watch whomever Weichmann talks to, every day of the year?" Cook didn't wait for an answer. "No, they were looking for *you*. Okay, then you get back home and decide to head back out, this time I'm along for the ride. What do you do first? Check in with Townsend about where that Creston Clarke is. And what's waiting at Lake Erie? That nigger-lover letter. We go on to New York, which Mr. Townsend knows, and we have us a high old time there, almost die in interesting ways. When we decide to leave, first we ask old Townsend how to find people in Maryland. Shoot, we weren't learning, were we? We met that fellow on the train, remember the one at the depot in Elizabeth, the one you thought I was mean to?

"So now, we're getting careful, even crafty. We get on those mules and ride through the country, dodging shadows, but we go straight to where Townsend knew we were going, to Mrs. Anna Surratt Tonry. And where does Stoneman find you? Two blocks from her house."

Fraser's mouth felt dry. "So," Fraser said, "you think he's been tipping them off, that he's in with Barstow and his Sons of Liberty? That would mean he was bought long before we ever turned up."

When Cook didn't answer, Fraser reminded him how Townsend's books and articles were completely devoted to the lone-madman theory. "If you're right, that means that those men who killed Lincoln not only remade history, but then they paid him to write them out of it. And they aim to *stay* out of it." Fraser shook his head. "We might as well have worn bells around our necks."

Cook nodded. "If we stop telling Townsend what we're up to, this business might get easier. Worth a try."

That night, as they settled on the straw in the shed, Fraser pulled out the banknotes in his money belt. He had dried them since dropping out of the *Georgia* into the Chester River. By lantern light, he counted out forty dollars to leave for Rafe. Cook said he'd leave it where Rafe's wife would find it. She'd have more sense and less pride about keeping it.

Fraser split the rest of the banknotes between them. Over the last two weeks, they'd made a pretty heavy dent in his funds. Fraser didn't regret that the money was going. That's what he meant to do with it.

Cook said he wouldn't linger in Chestertown any longer than he had to. He told Fraser to watch his step. "That Arnold may know you're coming, may know all about you. He, what, grew up with Booth?"

"Went to school with him."

Fraser planned to take a room at the National Hotel on Pennsylvania Avenue. That was a sentimental choice. John Wilkes Booth slept there on the night before he killed Lincoln. Cook said he'd find someplace less conspicuous.

In Washington, Fraser continued, they could talk to that Hale woman.

Cook smiled. "The one whose daddy was a senator, was supposed to be engaged with Booth?"

"Yes, she traveled with him in New England the week before the killing, then had breakfast with him on the morning of the assassination. He had her picture in his wallet."

"Didn't he have pictures of four other women, too?"

Fraser shrugged. "She was the only one he was supposed to marry. Also—" he reached into his jacket pocket and pulled out the leather frog book. He showed how the cover opened to the drawing of the frog, the outlines of which had blurred, but the other pages were wadded up, permanently stuck to each other. "When you wore my jacket into the river, this went in with you. It's dry now, but we're never going to get to read it again. Tried slicing the pages apart with a knife, but they just tear up."

"Why didn't you leave that in the luggage?"

"Had it in my pocket to study."

Fraser handed it over to Cook, who tried to thumb the pages apart. "Hell, we couldn't make any sense out of it before. No chance now. Might as well dump it, I guess."

"I don't know. It may be more important than we thought. Barstow and those Sons of Liberty knew we were on to the Booth and Lincoln business, but they didn't actually try to kill us. They only got really rough, with the bridge and the steamboat, after we got this frog book. I wish I knew what it was about."

Cook handed the book back to him and he put it back in his jacket pocket.

"You just be sure you get to Washington."

"Don't you worry. The Clarke theater company's going to be there, and I'm hoping to attend a performance or two."

Chapter 23

Employing a new level of caution, Fraser spent much of the day watching the Arnold farm from a grove about 200 yards downwind of it. The white-haired gentleman, wearing a battered hat, moved stiffly through his chores in a fenced yard. He finished them by the time the sun was in Fraser's eyes, about midafternoon. Small of stature, with a yellow-white beard that drifted well down his shirt, Sam Arnold had an elfin quality that belied his involvement in the crime of the century. His only company was a half-dozen dogs and a like number of cats. They seemed to regard Arnold as a peer.

The old man settled in a rocking chair on the front porch, a book in his hand and a jug next to him on the floor. One cat sat in his lap and another on the arm of his chair. The dogs arranged themselves at varying distances, rising to investigate the few passersby with unhurried curiosity and occasional woofs. No one stopped, and Arnold hailed no one.

Fraser slipped down to the road and walked to the village store three miles away. The storeowner led him to the back, where he produced a gallon jug of apple liquor. On his way back to the Arnold farm, the pink sunset streaked the sky. Fraser tried the liquor. It burned, then warmed, then began to dizzy. He should have bought something to eat. His plan for approaching Arnold was close to no plan at all. Perhaps the liquor would produce one.

The gate latch taxed him. It looked like a simple wire looped over the fence post, but a mechanism held it shut. It didn't spring free when Fraser lifted the lever. He took a step back. He looked at it. The gate hung at an angle. Fraser wedged his foot under the gate and lifted it, then freed the lever. The gate swung open. His sense of pride was way out of proportion to the accomplishment.

Some of the dogs greeted him, sniffing and circling. A brown mutt of medium size thrust her snout into his private parts. Fraser waited. She snorted and moved aside.

"Evening," Fraser called up to the porch. Arnold regarded him with a level gaze, then took a swallow from his jug and set it back down. Fraser walked slowly toward him. "Mind some company? I'm new around here." He stopped at the porch steps.

The old man seemed to lack the need to blink. "Anyone drinking Hansen's liquor is new around here."

Fraser grinned affably. "A mite rough, but it gets the job done."

"You weren't invited." It wasn't a question.

"No, sir, that's right. Just—"

"Dogs watched you in those trees all day. So you're either a thief or someone wants to pester me about John Wilkes Booth." Tilting his head slightly, Arnold added, "You look soft for thieving."

Pointing to the step to the porch, Fraser said, "Mind if I set down?"

"Some, but go ahead. You're welcome to waste your evening. I don't talk about the past."

Fraser took a swallow from his jug. The brown dog came back and settled near him. Arnold's gaze returned to his book. Fraser took another swallow and started describing his investigation. He realized he was scrambling things and started over, beginning with Mr. Bingham on his deathbed. Arnold looked up sharply at the sound of Bingham's name.

"Tell me that man's still dead. I read that he died."

"Yes, sir. He's dead."

Arnold shook his head. "That was the best news I'd had in many a year. That man ruined my life. Why, he presented nothing but lies in that trial. Once a lie is on the pages of history, you can't erase it. When I heard he'd passed, the world felt cleaner."

"He was my friend."

"He was my enemy. I was no part of any scheme to kill anyone. I told Booth the kidnapping idea was crazy. I was a hundred miles away when it happened. I wasn't there."

Fraser used his jug to stifle his response. It would do no good to remind this old man that he spent months smuggling weapons for Booth, planning Lincoln's abduction, and actually laid in ambush for the president. Or to mention the letter Arnold wrote to Booth two weeks before the assassination, the one where he urged Booth to consult with "R——d," linking the Confederacy and Booth. Arnold knew all that, and an argument wasn't going to help anything.

A new dog, a big bluetick with a solemn visage, limped up to the gate. Fraser went to let him in. The hound whimpered slightly and licked a front paw, looking sad. Fraser bent down to look him over. A nail on a front paw was torn, an angry-looking splinter wedged in his pad.

"Probably running after something, not looking where he was going," Arnold said, hovering over Fraser's shoulder. "Old Jasper, he's game, but not the smartest."

"I'm a doctor. Mind if I take a hand?"

"Go ahead. Seems he trusts you." Arnold produced tweezers and scissors, which Fraser heated to avoid infection. Arnold held the dog while he worked. The paw spurted blood when the splinter came out, but Fraser got it stopped and wrapped it tight in a bandage that wouldn't last more than sixty minutes. When he was done, Jasper lay down and started chewing off the dressing.

Arnold offered Fraser some supper, boiled eggs and dark bread. They sipped liquor and talked dogs until Arnold rose to turn in. He said Fraser could sleep in the barn. In the night, Jasper and two of the cats joined him.

Arnold was at his chores before Fraser awoke, somewhat the worse for the liquor. He decided he had to try two subjects with Arnold. He would start with the connections between Booth and the Confederacy. Arnold's letter to Booth was too important not to ask about. Also, he would ask about Michael O'Laughlen, another conspirator from Baltimore who was an old friend of Booth's. Arnold and O'Laughlen had lived to-gether for weeks in early 1865, preparing to kidnap Lincoln. Unlike Arnold, O'Laughlen was in Washington City on the night before the assassination. That night he attended a party at Secretary of War Stanton's house, a party that included General Grant. Next day, the day of the assassination, O'Laughlen was with Booth close to Ford's Theatre. Yet, O'Laughlen seemed to play no role in the attacks that night and then took his secrets to the grave, dying of fever in prison. Maybe Arnold knew those secrets.

When Fraser entered the house, the old man was setting out a bachelor's breakfast of cold biscuits and coffee. They ate in si-lence.

"Mr. Arnold," Fraser started, "I don't want to bother you about Booth and most of what went on with all that."

"No need to talk about it. I've written down everything that matters. Left a full record. When I'm called before the Lord's tribunal, which is the only place where I still might receive justice, my account will be released. It has been my sad misfortune to draw a black destiny, but I am not resentful. It is all God's will."

"I'm sure it will be many years before the world will have a chance to read that document."

"Doc, I don't tell myself those lies, so you don't need to either. I'm about played out, reaching my three score and ten. Lucky to get this far."

"Sir, a couple of small things." Arnold regarded Fraser without expression. "That letter that you wrote to Booth, before the night at Ford's Theatre—"

"Won't talk about that letter, Doc. I wrote to stop a madman from doing something crazy. Nothing more to it." Arnold spoke with little inflection, but he was talking.

"But the reference to Richmond—what did it mean?"

"It meant I was telling him anything I could to stop him. I couldn't believe any sensible person would approve his scheme. But Booth, he was part sorcerer, part serpent. He could talk the birds out of the trees, but no one ever talked him out of anything."

"But why Richmond? Had he been talking to men in Richmond, with the Confederacy?

"If he did, I knew nothing about it. I was writing whatever came into my head."

Although Arnold's tone remained even, his eye had a defiant look that discouraged further inquiry. This was the point on which Arnold was most vulnerable. Those two letters separated by blanks—not even an actual word, just "R——d"—had earned him four years of prison misery. It had been foolish to think Arnold would suddenly unburden himself of all guilty knowledge. Arnold stood to leave the room.

"The other thing," Fraser said quickly, "was Michael O'Laughlen."

"Yes, Mike. He was a gay companion."

"You must have gotten to know him pretty well when you lived together."

"The way men know each other when they're young, their blood's high, and their thinking's cloudy. We saw one vast sea of pleasure before us, and we swam in it happily."

"And you were together at the prison, down at Fort Jefferson."

"That place wore him out. Mike wasn't as strong as he seemed."

"Here's what I'm wondering. Mike comes back to Washington City just before that night, the night at Ford's Theatre, and he's seeing Booth, but he doesn't seem to *do* anything for Booth that night. If he wasn't going to be part of what they were doing, why did he go to Washington?"

"I wasn't there."

"I know, Mr. Arnold. But I wondered if maybe Mike said anything about it, while you were in prison, maybe when he got the fever. You and Dr. Mudd were right there with him, you'd known him from before, it just seemed he might talk about it. Like a regret that he came back to Washington at all."

"He did regret that. He regretted that, for sure."

Arnold stopped talking and looked down at the rough wooden table in the kitchen. Fraser watched the old man. Small emotions flitted across his face like swallows at dusk, disappearing as quickly as they arrived. His eyes looked to grow heavy.

"Mr. Arnold?" The old man looked up at Fraser. "Was Mike supposed to attack Stanton that night, or General Grant? I can't figure out any other reason for him to be there."

"I wasn't there."

"I know, sir. But did he say anything like that?"

"Nope, never said that."

"What did he say?"

Arnold gripped the back of a chair. "Mike said it was lucky General Grant left town that day, lucky for both of them. But it didn't turn out that lucky for Mike."

"That's what he said?"

"Half crazy with fever when he said it, but yes, sir, that's what he said."

"So that means he was supposed to kill Grant, but then had nothing to do when Grant left Washington that afternoon, right?" Arnold didn't answer. "What do you think?"

"I think you'd better leave."

Chapter 24

For almost an hour, Fraser idled against a building that faced the Surratt house on H Street. He thought he was inconspicuous, looking like any city man who preferred loafing to working. He had acquired a four-button suit from Zimmerman's haberdashery. It featured a checked pattern that Fraser wouldn't wear in Cadiz. A hot bath and a shave at the National Hotel had left him feeling sleek and smart, finally shed of the terrors of the *Georgia,* no longer sleeping outdoors or in barns.

The sky was overcast, but the clouds weren't serious about rain. In front of the house, carriages flowed back and forth. Gaudy yellow streetcars rocked by. The traffic paid no heed to the evil that had been hatched behind the walls of that house. Washington was placid. It lacked the urgency and self-confidence of New York, and also lacked the swagger and sweat of Baltimore. Like a middle-aged matron, it was unhurried, secure in the tax revenues that poured in from the rest of the country. It might never be great, but it would never want.

To Fraser, the Surratt house looked oddly normal, squatting on an ordinary street. Painted white with dark shutters. A flight of stairs led sideways up to the formal entrance; a low door granted entry on the level below. A mansard roof with two gabled windows crowned three levels of double windows. How could those conspirators have fit into that plain house? John Surratt, his mother, Mary, and sister, Anna. Louis Weichmann, young and flighty, fresh from seminary. Two other female boarders. The magnificent Booth, radiant with destiny. The terrifying Lewis Paine, huge and blandly malevolent, stood at that door after mutilating William Henry Seward. The sniveling Atzerodt, who could not even face his target, Vice President Johnson, lurked in those shadows. They had all been there.

He walked east to the end of the block, crossed and walked back in front of the house. He wanted to rap on the door, lift his new homburg, and begin scouring the premises for clues. He scanned every brick and window pane but kept moving. Detectives and souvenir seekers, not to mention later owners, had long since grabbed or trampled anything that might be evidence. He kept walking, then turned down Seventh Street. He was supposed to meet Cook.

When Cook arrived in Washington, he moved into a boarding house up near New York Avenue. It was safer for them to be apart, and Cook also valued some privacy after weeks of being together on the road. He could think better with a space of his own.

He had wired for their luggage to be shipped from Baltimore, but he received a jolt when he rummaged through his trunk for Barstow's memorandum book. He wanted to reexamine some of the entries from early 1865, but the book wasn't there. After more frantic searching, he had to face the fact. The memo book was gone, as was the dictionary for cracking the cipher. The Sons of Liberty rifled through their belongings.

Fraser still had the frog book, but its condition meant that it, too, was yielding up no secrets.

Fraser stopped by Cook's room in a state of high excitement over what Sam Arnold said, but his spirits deflated quickly when he learned that Barstow's memo book was gone.

"That means they watched us in Baltimore," Cook said, "and after that business on the ship, they're looking hard for us now. And now our proof's gone. What Sam Arnold told you ain't proof either. All we got is what's stored up in our heads. Say, for example, I print in my newspaper that O'Laughlen was going to kill Grant. That man Arnold's just going to say it's all a lie, and then where are we?"

"Of course," Fraser agreed. "He's going to say that no matter what. That doesn't mean we shouldn't get the truth out. What he told me is important. They meant to kill Grant, too. Lincoln, Johnson, Seward, *and* Grant. A clean sweep. Is that something dreamed up by some hysterical actor in love with the romance of the Old South?" Cook was working a toothpick on the lower left side of his mouth. "Someone wanted Lafayette Foster to be president," Fraser continued. "No doubt about that. But the goal wasn't conquering Canada and Mexico, like Barstow was talking about. He said that to send us off on a wild goose chase, make us look like fools."

Cook grunted in agreement.

"One funny thing," Fraser said, "is how they sent only one killer to each target. Booth to kill Lincoln. Atzerodt to kill Johnson. Paine to kill Seward. And O'Laughlen to murder Grant. But when Grant leaves town, they don't switch O'Laughlen over to help Atzerodt even though Atzerodt sure needed some help, which even Booth should've realized."

Cook threw his toothpick at the wastebasket, but missed. "They weren't your top-notch squad of killers."

"Talking to Arnold's got me wondering what Booth and O'Laughlen talked about that morning, you know, April 14th."

Fraser stood up and walked to the window. "They talked right over on Seventh Street." He shook his head. "Maybe Booth was trying to give O'Laughlen some other assignment, but he wouldn't do it. Maybe O'Laughlen was proposing an alternative and Booth rejected it. Damn, what I would give to know."

"Wishing ain't going to make it so." When Fraser made no reply, Cook stretched his long arms and arched his back. "Let's go over what we're supposed to get from your old ladies."

"You know about Lucy Hale Chandler, you know, Bessie Hale," Fraser began.

"Booth's fiancée."

"Right. And then there's Mrs. Lafayette Foster. Her connection's pretty obvious."

"I already have a line on her."

"Really? That fast?"

"The *National Tribune* had a piece just today, she was at some society party. It's incredible what's news when white folks do it. Drinking tea, that's news."

"Did it give any clues how to find her?"

"Rich white lady, a bit long in the tooth—not that many places for her kind to be. I'll find her."

"And then there's Mrs. Grant, the general's widow. I think she lives with her daughter, or travels with her."

"She'll be easy. She's somebody, someone people talk about after they see her. If I met her, I'd probably talk about it." Cook tilted his head to one side. "So, while I'm nosing around the city, you're going off sparking with your lady friend?"

"Just patronizing the theatrical arts." Fraser smiled.

"Give my regards to Miss Eliza."

They agreed to meet for breakfast in the morning.

The marquee above the entrance to the Columbia Theatre proclaimed that the Creston Clarke company would be appearing for three weeks, into early October. Wall posters exclaimed over their featured productions and invited the public to attend them all.

Entering the dark lobby, Fraser's heart rose at the sight of Eliza speaking with two men in workmen's garb. Standing at a distance so he wouldn't overhear the conversation, which was animated, he tried not to betray his anticipation. He had thought of her often since New York, remembering her as lovely in every respect. Memory, however, had been a cheat. She was far lovelier. Her beauty unnerved him; her hazel eyes conveyed an intelligence and sympathy he longed to share.

She greeted him as "Dr. Fraser," a formality that sank his feelings momentarily, but they revived with her smile. She had much to do, she explained, but invited him to watch the current rehearsal. She could dine with him. He should call for her at 7:30 at her hotel. He recognized this storm of emotions. He was in her grip. With an inner squirm, he knew that meant he was no longer in Ginny's. But he wasn't.

The actors were mounting a scene from *Macbeth*. It began with a hungover servant whose cavorting was downright comical. Fraser, who thought of Shakespeare as serious business, was delighted. Sitting in the back of the theater, he laughed at the servant's speech on the influence of liquor on lechery—that liquor provokes it and unprovokes it, makes it stand to and not stand to. It was a lot funnier on the stage than when he read it.

Armored lords stomped onstage. At their center stood Creston Clarke with a brooding countenance. The murdered king was discovered in the wings. "Horror, horror, horror," an actor howled. Drawn into the drama, Fraser's mood swung to dread. He could not stop looking at Clarke. Portraying Macbeth the murderer, his face contained both guilt and a suppressed gloating.

"Enough!" Clarke called out. Clearing his face of emotion, he began to chide an actor for a clumsy entrance. Fraser found

Clarke's transformation unsettling. Moments before, the actor's face had shown the heart of murder. Now its expression was peevish. Did this hopelessly vain actor have such an intimate yet blithe knowledge of murder? Had his uncle, John Wilkes Booth, enjoyed the same easy familiarity with assassination—first acquired through pretense, then implemented in brutal reality?

What, Fraser found himself thinking, did it do to a man to kill another? Cook had killed just a few days ago, then said those men needed killing. That was Cook's way of thinking. How many men walking the streets of Washington had killed someone? Many of the old soldiers, to be sure. Thousands, maybe. Hundreds, at least. He was surrounded by killers. Could he be one?

Fraser left the theater and bought an *Evening Times* from a newsboy. He felt an uncharacteristic desire for whiskey but remembered the servant's homily about standing to and not standing to. Whiskey was not the way to prepare for his evening with Eliza. After skimming the headlines, he ambled along the streets with a detached regard.

Fraser paused in front of the White House. According to the headlines, McKinley had just arrived from Ohio, but the president wasn't visible from the sidewalk. A lone policeman nodded to Fraser from the end of the semicircular drive. Two carriages stood near the mansion's entrance, their drivers chatting away the time.

Fraser wondered how McKinley's reelection campaign was going. In pursuit of Booth's ghost, he had lost track of events in his own time. Settling at a tavern on G Street, Fraser drank a beer while the newspaper informed him of recent catastrophes. A hurricane had devastated the Texas coast. Pennsylvania coal miners were striking. Fraser thought of one-legged Lew Evans in Adena. If he were a coal miner, Fraser thought, he surely would be tempted to strike.

Then his eye fell on a story from New York. The presidential campaign there was growing spirited. The Democrats were relying on the Tammany Hall machine to roll up a big margin that would carry the state for William Jennings Bryan, but the Tammany Tiger was struggling that year. Then he read the name of the Tammany boss: Boss Croker. The connection jumped into his mind. Croker. Croaker. The frog book.

Fraser uttered an oath under his breath. He and Cook were such rubes, a couple of dopes from Ohio. Barstow was paying off the Tammany boss. That was how you built a giant bridge across the East River. And that's what Barstow had meticulously recorded in the frog book. Which was why, after Cook burglarized the office of Spencer, Barstow, the Sons of Liberty graduated from merely dangerous to outright murderous. Cook and Fraser had posed some kind of threat as they excavated around the Booth conspiracy, but how much real evidence could they come upon thirty-five years later? But this bridge payoff scheme could tilt the outcome of this year's presidential election—now, that was worth spilling some blood over.

But they never had made any sense of the entries in the frog book, and the book itself now was a ruin. Fraser tore out the newspaper article and stuffed it into his jacket pocket. He had to talk to Cook about it.

When Eliza swept into the hotel lobby to meet him, Fraser decided Boss Croker could wait. She was winsome in a pale blue dress. He thrilled at the thought that every male eye in the room was trained upon her.

The restaurant, less than a block from the Willard, was quiet and refined. After oysters—a disgusting food that Fraser learned to tolerate while hiding in Chestertown—he could not contain himself. "I have," he said, "been unable to get you out of my mind."

"Dr. Fraser," she said with a quizzical look, "what exactly are you saying?"

"I seem to have fallen in love with you." Terror surged through his brain. What had he done? Even one beer had been too much. But then came a rush of elation, a surge of energy released by the plain fact that there was no turning back, nothing to do but charge upon the citadel at full speed and devil take the hindmost. He had lost his head entirely, and wasn't sorry for it. "I hope that doesn't seem hasty. I assure you I'm not a hasty man. I've made that declaration to only one other woman in my life, and I married her. And I hope to marry you."

Eliza's eyes were alight. She dabbed at the corner of her mouth with her napkin. At least she wasn't angry or offended. "I confess," she said with rather a merry smile, "that some might think this conversation a bit premature, and most would think this a public location for it. But I do give you free license to return to it on some occasion that seems more fitting." She softened her smile and looked directly into his eyes. Fraser felt like he had scaled the Matterhorn in his bare feet.

Before his inability to speak became too embarrassing, Eliza shifted her utensils on the table and asked if he had noticed how quiet the city seemed. "Congress isn't in session, you know," she said, "so the city grows a bit dull. I have feared that our attendance will suffer as a result, but this was the best time for us to pass through on this southern tour. It's difficult to balance everything when making up our schedule."

Fraser could form no response. He was still agog over his temerity in professing love and proposing marriage, not to mention the warmth with which she received it. After awarding him another smile and an unguarded view into those bewitch-

204 David O. Stewart

ing eyes, she surprised him by asking if they had made any progress on the Lincoln assassination.

He cleared his throat. "Yes, yes, I suppose we have. That possible connection to smuggled cotton seems now to be quite sound. We also have some substantial evidence that the conspirators intended to kill General Grant, too, which would have left the government quite adrift, permitting all sorts of mischief. I think the assassination really was an act of state by the Southern government."

"But," Eliza objected, "Wilkes wrote in his diary that the decision to kill Lincoln was his alone, that it was designed to preserve slavery and defend the Confederacy."

"Those were desperate days, difficult ones to imagine. The Confederacy was dying, the world turning upside down. Booth need not have known the true motives of those who conceived and paid for his effort. Or perhaps his notebook, or that entry in it, was created by the people who arranged his killing. He was, I am sure, merely the pawn in the gambit. Like all pawns, he was readily sacrificed."

"I've always believed that much." Eliza's eyes shone with a vehemence he hadn't seen before. "It's been a curse for the Booth family all these years, you can have no idea. It is no small matter to be a close relative of a man supposed to be a great villain, indeed, the greatest. I spoke with you that first time because I hoped it might be a balm to the family to know that Wilkes was manipulated, that bad men took advantage of his passionate nature."

A waiter approached with plates of roast squab, a specialty of the house.

When the waiter had withdrawn, Eliza touched Fraser's arm and looked up at him. "Forgive me. I know that Wilkes's crime cannot be condoned, and I don't, but it's hard to watch it wear down those you love, year after year."

Fraser assured her that there was nothing to forgive, that her generosity of spirit toward the Booths only made her more dear to him. And, he added, he had thought of a way in which she might be able to assist his inquiry, if she were willing.

"Of course." She waited with a steady calm.

"I would like," he said, "to speak with three ladies of standing in this city, and of somewhat advanced years."

"Whatever for?" Eliza directed her attention to her squab, which was so delicate as to defy easy consumption. Fraser longed to pick his up with his fingers and be done with it.

"They may know something important about the Booth conspiracy. They are Mrs. Martha Foster, Mrs. Julia Grant, and Mrs. Lucy Chandler."

Eliza placed her knife and fork on her plate and sat back. "My," she said, "you are aiming high. Wasn't Mrs. Chandler engaged to marry Wilkes, she was Bessie Hale then?"

"Indeed. She traveled with him in New England in the week before the assassination. She even had breakfast with him on April 14th here in Washington. He carried her photo."

Eliza gave him an admonishing look. "Along with photos of four other women." As Fraser hacked ineffectually at the bird before him, she added, "Why don't you just wait for the steak, Jamie? It will yield far more easily to your desires."

With a shrug, he abandoned the effort. Her smile again warmed him. He wondered if her remark meant something more.

"Perhaps something can be arranged," she said. "You know our premiere is the day after tomorrow. We usually have a supper party afterward to allow Creston to burn off his high spirits. We could include your ladies on the guest list."

Fraser agreed that the occasion might suit his needs.

Fraser admired the lobby of the National Hotel. Oversized leather chairs and couches remembered former splendor but did not cling to it, their arms worn to the cross-hatched softness of chamois cloth. Sprawling chandeliers burned under a light coat of dust, providing the sort of indirect light favored by aging courtesans. It was a large space, but still provided intimate corners suitable for conversations that might later be denied.

Passing through in the morning, on his way to breakfast with Cook, Fraser heard a deep voice call, "Doctor! Doctor!" Knowing no one in the city who would match that voice—actually, knowing no one in Washington at all save for Speed Cook and the Clarke troupe—Fraser kept walking. He had registered under a false name, as Cook insisted, so no one should know he was a doctor. Movement to his left drew his eye. It proved to be the rotund form of George Townsend, bearing down upon him. The writer sported a walking stick, bowler hat, and broad smile. Fraser was not pleased.

After perfunctory greetings, Townsend drew Fraser aside. He asked, sotto voce, about Fraser's progress with his "inquiries" into that "matter of mutual interest."

"I recall no matter of mutual interest," Fraser said. He turned to walk away.

Townsend placed a restraining hand on his arm. "That would be a mistake."

"One of many, no doubt." Fraser felt a glow of righteousness as he turned on his heel and continued to the hotel newsstand.

He walked north and then west, ending up at a simple restaurant where the downtown district petered out. The proprietor waved him toward a table that still bore the clutter of an earlier meal. Fraser pushed the dishes aside and sat down. After a few minutes, Cook sat across from him. "If they followed you," he said, "I didn't see it."

As the proprietor cleared the dishes, Fraser recounted his exchange with Townsend. Maddeningly, Cook said that he should have talked to the writer.

"But," Fraser objected, "you're the one who persuaded me not to trust him."

"Don't trust him, sure. But this ain't no accident, him showing up in this hotel lobby. He's Jed Stoneman in a less violent form. I'm hoping that after the business on the boat, they're deciding not to send any more tough guys after us. Townsend's not the type to pull out any ether on you, so talk to the man."

"But I can't tell him what we really think about the assassination."

"Look, this man knows more about the Lincoln business than he's ever written. Plus, he's in Barstow's pocket. So you need to play him, just like a bass. Don't you ever fish?"

Fraser remained silent.

"Tell him he was right about everything, but we're at a dead end, what can he tell us?"

"He's not going to tell us the truth," Fraser said.

"Okay, but we can learn from his lies. He tells us something to throw us off the track, we know not to look in that direction. You remember telling me something just like that?"

"Yeah, right before I went to dangle off the top of a bridge."

"Maybe we're closer than we know. If they sent Townsend to us, if they're ransacking our luggage, it means the game's still on. You don't always win with a brilliant play. Lots of times you just hang on until the other guy does something boneheaded. Here's a chance for them to be boneheaded, just in case your tea party with the old ladies doesn't solve everything."

"So I stride up to him and announce, 'Mr. Townsend, I was wrong earlier. I really want to have a nice long chat with you.' "

"Those are *just* the words, though you want to work on your tone of voice. He'll be waiting on you. You talk with him a while; then I can follow him. Maybe we can learn who's pulling his strings."

"We know. It's Barstow."

"Who else? Where are they? Let's see what we find out, okay?"

After they ordered breakfast, Fraser pulled out the newspaper article about Boss Croker. Cook laughed out loud as he read it. "Oh my," he said. "Seems like we weren't even playing the same game as these people."

"If only that frog book wasn't ruined."

Cook was quiet for a moment. "They don't know that, do they? All they know is that they didn't find it, so we still have it. One more reason to talk to Townsend."

"Listen, Speed. I don't care at all about Croker and Tammany. We're investigating Booth."

"As the editor of an Ohio newspaper, I'm interested in everything."

It turned out to be as easy as Cook predicted. Townsend was planted in one of the overstuffed chairs at the side of the hotel lobby. Late in the morning, Fraser marched up to him, apologized for his earlier rudeness, and proposed they share a drink. Townsend, the soul of courtesy, insisted on paying. Fraser had little experience with whiskey before noon, so he resolved to nurse his shot of rye.

Fraser offered Townsend an edited version of their "inquiries" on the "matter of mutual interest." He left out the violence and dangling off the bridge tower. He didn't mention Anna Surratt Tonry or Sam Arnold. He said he was increasingly convinced that Booth's efforts were paid for by other people, and that he had an idea who might have handled the payments. He claimed to be flummoxed over who was behind it all, which was true enough.

After listening impassively, Townsend said, "Sir, I applaud your industry. You have made a capital effort, capital indeed. Tell me, is that darky still working with you?"

"No," Fraser said, "he didn't prove reliable. We separated in New York. You may recall that he was out of sorts when we visited at your home?"

Townsend nodded, so Fraser continued. "I'm grateful for your help until now." The words, worked out with Cook ahead of time, felt leaden in his mouth. "And I wonder if you might be able to provide some additional guidance?"

"Only too happy," Townsend said. "There is one thing that occurs to me. I would propose that you join me in visiting another man who could cast some light on the matter."

"What other man? Have you told him of my activities?"

"You must trust me on this. What do you say to tomorrow afternoon at four?"

Fraser was ready. "I have a commitment then with, ah, a lady. You wouldn't expect me to break a commitment to a lady. Perhaps we could meet on the following afternoon at the same time?"

Townsend said he would try to meet Fraser's schedule. He would leave a message with the hotel desk, in Fraser's assumed name. As the writer levered himself upright and headed for the door, Fraser had the feeling that this bass might be playing him.

Townsend didn't walk very fast. The side-to-side motion in his stride reminded Cook of a duck as he watched the potbellied writer start up Sixth Street. Cook loitered a distance behind, confident he could keep Townsend in view.

In front of a jewelry shop, a carriage drawn by a striking pair of matched bays slowed. The writer climbed aboard smoothly, unexpectedly nimble for his age and girth. As the bays sped up the street and turned left onto E Street, Cook attempted to flag a hack to follow. Three passed him by, either occupied or uninterested in stopping for a colored man. Cook tried to follow on foot. When he rounded the corner of E Street, the bays were nowhere in sight.

Cook choked down his annoyance. Even failure taught its lessons. Townsend was definitely not working alone. He was part of a well-managed organization, Barstow's.

Cook strolled over to a store selling neckwear. He cast his eye up and down the street, looking for anyone who might be watching him.

Chapter 25

⤮

Dinner-jacketed men mingled with jewel-bedecked women in Clarke's suite at the Willard. Fraser struck up a conversation with a likely looking couple, but met only a tepid response. Their eyes wandered as they mouthed pleasantries, then smoothly disengaged and set off in pursuit of more significant companions.

Fraser had not enjoyed the performance of *Richelieu*, though Eliza said the play was one of Clarke's favorites. The drama seemed awkwardly constructed, meandering episodically through plots and murders, all pulled together in an artificially wise closing speech delivered by Clarke as Cardinal Richelieu. Watching in the darkened theater, Fraser again reflected that for a family like the Booths, who aped bloody and conspiratorial tragedies on a nightly basis, real-life assassination might feel familiar. The theater as a school for assassins.

As Fraser looked for somewhere to place his empty champagne glass, Eliza caught his eye. She was speaking with a tall woman, sturdily built, whose severe features suggested judgments being drawn. Her silver gown looked as though it had been worn many times.

"This is Dr. Fraser, about whom I was telling you," Eliza said as he approached. "Jamie, may I present Mrs. Chandler?" They shook hands. "I was reminding Mrs. Chandler that we met in Boston some years ago when I played Portia in Edwin Booth's company, but she remembers only Edwin's Shylock."

"Oh, dear," the older lady insisted, "I am sure you were wonderful, Mrs. Scott, but Mr. Booth, well! He was divine."

"Jamie," Eliza said. "Mrs. Chandler and you might talk in the next room?" She led them into a small dressing room.

"My dear," the older lady said, reaching for Eliza's hand, "I just now see it. It's a remarkable resemblance. But I have not thought of him in so long. I am pleased to know you."

When Eliza closed the door behind her, Fraser and Mrs. Chandler faced each other in narrow chairs. He dove into the tale, explaining that his study of the Booth conspiracy had unearthed no record of her statements on the assassination. He hoped she could recount any memories she had of the days leading up to it.

"I fear I will disappoint you as much as I did the detectives back then," she said. "My father arranged for my statements never to be made public, but they would have revealed nothing. Wilkes never breathed a word to me of his plans. He had so many secrets. Though I was appalled by his crime, I do believe the secrets appealed to my romantic side.

"You must realize," she added with a flutter that included a blush on her papery cheeks, "I was totally besotted. A day with Wilkes was worth a lifetime with most men. He was electric. As a young woman I had been rather sheltered, so I found him a revelation. I suppose he took advantage of me, but I didn't care then and I certainly don't now. It took me ten years to stop comparing every man I met, quite unfavorably, to Wilkes."

Fraser pressed, asking about her time with Booth in Newport and Boston in the week before the assassination, and her breakfast with Booth on the fateful day. Mrs. Chandler waved her hand dismissively. "I must seem like some pathetic dodo bird, but I noticed nothing. He seemed just as he always did. I was not then the best observer of character."

"While you were with Booth, did you have any contact with a man named Samuel Barstow, or Julius Spencer?"

She looked over his shoulder, then said yes, Spencer sounded familiar. "I think I'm quite sure. Mr. Spencer—perhaps a businessman? He met Wilkes in Newport, when we arrived on the packet boat from New York. Wilkes described him as a business associate, but Wilkes had no more head for business than does a six-week-old puppy. I suppose Mr. Spencer gave him money, because Wilkes became quite cheerful and resumed spending lavishly, much to my delight. Wilkes was like that. If he had money, he spent it, and he had not had much in the days immediately before. Mr. Spencer must have brought a good deal because Wilkes was still spending when we had breakfast in Washington on the next Friday, that terrible day."

As they passed back into the main party, Mrs. Chandler gave Fraser a stern look. "I trust," she said, "you will do nothing to burden that fine young woman, Mrs. Scott."

Fraser had no time to puzzle over the remark, for that very Mrs. Scott was bearing down on him with a round-faced woman in tow. Introduced to Mrs. Ulysses Grant, Fraser was momentarily speechless, a response that seemed to give Mrs. Grant satisfaction. He gestured for her to enter the side room. It felt like escorting a patient into his examination room.

When seated, Fraser surprised himself. "My father," he began, "served under your husband in the Vicksburg campaign. He was a captain in the Ohio volunteers. It's a matter of pride in my family."

"Is your father still with us?" she asked.

"No, he died a few years after the war. I was still small."

Mrs. Grant sighed and reached for his hand. "So many sad stories." Her sympathy seemed genuine, but her eyes didn't look directly at him. They focused somewhere to his left. He began to wonder if the absence of direct eye contact was a condition brought on by the Washington climate.

When he asked her about the day of the assassination, he needed only to sit back and listen. From the avalanche of information that tumbled from her, two incidents stood out. The first was vivid in her mind thirty-five years later.

"I was lunching with a friend," she said, "and we each had a child with us. It was all quite domestic. During the meal, I became convinced that a man at a nearby table was attempting to overhear us. The general, of course, was recognized everywhere, but I was not yet used to being watched in public. The man was dark, yet pale of complexion, handsome yet peculiar. He pretended to eat his soup, raising a spoon to his lips but never tasting it. Very peculiar. He sat with three other men but paid them no mind, listening only to us.

"Well, in the afternoon, the general and I left by carriage for the depot. We were going to the New Jersey shore. And this very same man rode by us at a pounding gallop, then stopped, wheeled his horse with a great show, and rode back past us again. Each time he swept by, he glared at the general. Let me tell you, the general immediately marked him out as a dangerous man and observed that he did not care for his looks.

"And, of course, we learned very soon that that man"—she nodded her head with finality—"was John Wilkes Booth."

"He didn't speak with you or General Grant?"

"Not a word."

"Did the men with him at lunch prove to be part of his conspiracy?"

"I don't know. He was the one I noticed. Those moments, my dear doctor, are seared upon my soul."

"So you are convinced that Booth intended to attack General Grant as well."

"I have no doubt of it. The newspapers had reported that the general and I would view the play at Ford's Theatre that evening with the Lincolns. When Booth saw us leaving for the depot, he had to know his plan was disrupted."

Yet Mrs. Grant's second incident suggested that Booth adjusted his scheme to the Grants' plans. On the morning after the assassination, General Grant left to take a special train from New Jersey back to Washington. After he left, Mrs. Grant opened a letter addressed to the general. Though unsigned, it stated—she recited this breathlessly, with her vibrating eyes fixed on the ceiling—*"I thank God you still live. Your life fell to my lot and I was on the cars following you. You escaped me only because your car door was locked. Thank God!"*

"So, someone followed you on the train?"

"So the letter said."

"And intended to kill the general."

"So the letter said."

"And desisted because the door was locked?"

"I suppose he feared that breaking down the door would alert my husband and others. The general was a fighting man."

Fraser decided to try one other line of questions. What, he asked, was the general's attitude toward those who wished to import Southern cotton for northern mills?

Mrs. Grant made a face. "That's quite simple. He thought they should be hung, starting with his own father. That was the one thing, at least the one thing I knew about, where he disagreed with Mr. Lincoln, but the general never trimmed his view on it. Why, you know"—she dropped her voice, though no one else was with them—"he refused to honor licenses to ship cotton that the president himself had signed. It was war! 'In war,' he always said, 'you do not do business with the enemy.' "

Returning to the party, Fraser felt pleased with his evening. A figure at the entrance, leaving the party, caught his eye. From the back, it looked like Townsend. But that wasn't possible. Fraser heard Eliza's voice.

"Jamie," she said, drawing close to him. How dear she seemed, her face alive with feeling. "I fear you just missed Mrs. Foster. She's gone down to her carriage. Perhaps you could catch her? She's small, white-haired, in a silver gown."

Fraser left quickly. He took the steps two at a time to the hotel lobby. At the curb, he strained to pick out a figure matching the description of Mrs. Foster. There, at the corner, a small woman wearing a mantilla over her hair was reaching for a carriage door. He trotted to her side.

"Mrs. Foster?" he asked, cupping her elbow. Two bright blue eyes looked up at him and caught the glow from the streetlight. "Forgive me for intruding," Fraser rushed on, "but Mrs. Scott suggested I make sure you get home safely, and I failed to see you leave until this very moment."

"That's very kind of Mrs. Scott," the lady said, "but I will be quite all right, thank you very much."

Fraser kept his grip on her elbow and guided her up to the carriage seat. "Truly, Mrs. Foster, I would value the opportunity to spend a moment in conversation, and if it's not too late, perhaps we could talk as you ride."

"Oh, I suppose that would be all right."

Fraser hurried to the other side and climbed in. When the driver pulled away from the curb, he introduced himself. He had worried about this conversation. The widow of Lafayette Foster could hardly welcome the suggestion that Abraham Lincoln was killed in order to place her husband in the White House.

"Mrs. Foster," he began, "I have recently been in New York

and visited with a quite impressive gentleman there, Samuel Barstow. Do you know him?"

"I don't believe so." Her expression was mild, her manner decorous. Fraser was not eager to distress Mrs. Foster.

"I believe his former business partner, Julius Spencer, may have had business connections in Connecticut. Perhaps you or your husband encountered him? The firm name is Spencer, Barstow and Company."

"Julius?" The old lady smiled as the carriage swayed through quiet streets. "Dear Julius. My husband's cousin. Something of a black sheep."

"He was a cotton broker? It's the same man?"

"Oh, certainly. A very charming man, as only a rogue can be."

Fraser saw a way to press the matter. "Mr. Barstow," he said, "was boasting that this Spencer fellow used his connections with your husband to get licenses to ship cotton from the South. I doubted him very much, but he was adamant."

"That's not something I could know about, could I—what this other man might say about what Julius Spencer said? But you should know that Senator Foster was quite wary of his cousin, although he believed that the Union war effort was actually strengthened by supplying our New England mills with Southern cotton. How else were we to clothe ourselves? President Lincoln entirely agreed with Senator Foster on that point, despite"—she whispered in a conspiratorial manner—"the views of the great Ulysses."

"I resented the remarks of this Barstow," Fraser volunteered, "implying some . . . I don't know, collaboration between your husband and these Southern cotton types."

"Senator Foster stood by the Union always, though his type of Republican—wishing only brotherly relations with the South—did not fare well after the war."

"Did he and his cousin, this Mr. Spencer, patch things up then, after the war?"

"Why, yes, of course. They had never really broken off, I think. Lafayette just was very careful about being seen with Julius. Julius was a bit bullheaded about political matters, if you know what I mean."

"I shall certainly put Barstow straight about Senator Foster next time I see him."

After depositing Mrs. Foster at her home, Fraser walked back to the hotel, his mind overflowing with new information. He found Eliza bidding farewell to the final guests of the evening. When they were gone, he took her hand. "The night is almost as lovely as you," he said. "Will you look at it with me?"

"Just for a short time," she said. "It's been a long day."

When they began to walk up Fourteenth Street, Fraser said he had heard a good deal that surprised him that night. "For example, I had no idea you were an actress." He feared his tone was more chiding than he intended. He had accepted the idea that she was part of the racy world of the theater, but to have been an *actress*—that carried further implications.

"Oh, that was ages ago."

"How long ago?"

"Years and years."

"Still and all, that's rather a rich life to imagine for a man from Cadiz. What else," he asked, "might I expect to find out about you?"

She did not answer right away, then sighed. "Oh, Jamie, I have omitted much of my history from our relations. It's not a splendid history, but you've been kind to me, and I have—not intentionally, mind you—placed you in an awkward position, so I suppose I must tell you. I have waited far too long to do so. And then we will part."

"We will have no conversation that ends with parting." He placed his free hand over hers.

"You will say different when I've finished." They had reached a stretch of large homes. She paused and perched on a low wall at the corner of H Street and Fifteenth Street. He chose to stand facing her. The moonlight fell lightly on her fine features. "You may recall the name Ella Turner, or Nelly Starr."

"Of course. She was Booth's . . . companion. She tried to kill herself after the assassination."

"My mother. And Wilkes was my father." Fraser inclined his head forward to conceal his features. "My mother was overcome with despair when she learned what he had done, but she soon regained her balance and set off on a difficult path. My Aunt Asia, Creston's mother, learned of my existence some years after and sent funds to help us. A former . . . companion . . . to a great villain does not have very excellent prospects. And those prospects are not enhanced by having a child out of wedlock."

Eliza's voice had become soft. Fraser felt his face go slack with disbelief. Could this be true? He sat heavily next to her.

"She claimed," Eliza said, "to be the widow of a soldier, which was a common thing then. Still, my mother was always afraid of being exposed. We moved often. She instructed me that this was a secret few people would be grateful to know. I was twelve when Mother died of a fever. Before she died, she gave me Aunt Asia's address and told me she was a kind woman who might help. Aunt Asia took me into her home as a sort of servant, but soon I was one of the family. Creston and his brother became my brothers. And in that family, my family, everyone takes a turn on stage. I was not a bad actress, or so some said. Perhaps I did inherit that from my father. My husband, though, preferred that I abandon the stage, so I did."

When she fell silent, he groped for words. "I do understand why this was difficult to talk about." His hands felt glued to the insides of his pockets. "It is, though, a good bit to digest."

"My husband and I—he knew all this—we had a quiet, happy life until I lost him, too, to a streetcar accident. A preposterous way to lose a husband. Creston tried to bring me back to the stage, but I had no more passion for it. To be truthful, I became subject to a paralyzing stage fright. So I've been the company's business manager."

"And then I came along."

"Yes, a dear, earnest man came to me from Ohio and seemed determined to prove my father not quite so black a monster, perhaps the dupe of blacker ones. Someday I hope you'll forgive me, and I hope I've not compromised your effort." She turned her head and looked up at him with glistening eyes. "I meant you no harm. I didn't expect for us to become such good friends."

"Eliza, for me it is so much more than that!"

"I know, Jamie. And I'm to blame for that, too." She placed a hand on his arm. "Please, walk me back to the hotel."

They passed down Fifteenth Street in silence, glimpsing the White House to the west as they neared the classical immensity of the Treasury building. In the quiet hotel lobby, Eliza said a quick good-bye. He stood for at least a minute, perhaps more, unable to order his thoughts.

What in heaven's name had he gotten himself into? How could he be in love with the bastard child of John Wilkes Booth? It would be like marrying into the Borgias or the family of Jack the Ripper. She had deceived him entirely, never breathing a word of it—like any experienced actress, wise to the debauched ways of the theater. Was she just feigning that she cared for him so he would persist in this investigation and somehow rehabilitate her unforgivable father? And yet how could he be thinking this way about her? He had taken the measure of her character and looked deep into her eyes. He knew in his heart that she was true. She couldn't counterfeit the feelings she showed for him. It couldn't all be the artifice of the trained performer.

Could it?

He was in far over his depth.

When he reached the sidewalk, he shrugged out of the rented dinner jacket and flexed his shoulders. Somewhere in this rotten town he should be able to find some whiskey. He set off to do so.

Chapter 26

"So, are you going to curl up and die on me?" Cook placed his face a few inches from Fraser's. "We don't have time for this mooncalf business."

Fraser, unshaven, was in his underwear. He'd spent the night in an armchair before the window, staring into the alley behind the hotel. He cradled an empty bourbon bottle. He had drunk it all without ever feeling drunk. The hammering in his head felt like a hangover, or just fatigue. He might have slept part of the night, but he couldn't remember it.

Cook shook his head. "I figured you for someone who'd back out when things got rugged. This isn't even the rugged part, and there you go."

Fraser could not sort through his stew of feelings—a carousel of betrayal, longing, outrage, and simple shock. He wished Cook would stop yammering. Finish their investigation of Booth? Wasn't he quite the investigator—falling in love with John Wilkes Booth's daughter? Correction: Booth's illegitimate daughter. Merely thinking it felt like treason. He was supposed to solve historical puzzles, not become part of one. He should never have left Cadiz.

All through the night, as his mind cycled through his problems, he felt certain about only one thing. He loved Eliza Scott, or whatever her name should be. He had no idea, however, what to do about it. He was aware of Cook pacing behind him, the man's suppressed rage penetrated even Fraser's miasmic mood. Fraser cleared his throat.

"You actually going to talk?" Cook continued to pace.

"Simmer down. Sit there on the bed. I'll tell you."

He started with Eliza. No point talking about anything else. Even if it was Eliza's secret, Cook was entitled to know. Fraser drew a perverse satisfaction from Cook's stunned silence. But it didn't last long.

"C'mon, Jamie. Who knows whose daddy is whose in this world? 'Specially when your mother, well, knows a lot of men."

Fraser lunged at Cook, grabbing him around the shoulders and jamming him back on the bed. He reared back and cocked a fist. Before he could throw a punch, Cook gripped his hand. Even lying on his back, the man was powerful. Fraser lunged again, leaning all his weight on Cook's uplifted arm, driving it down, but he couldn't free his hand. Cook hugged him close with his other arm. Fraser twisted and pushed with all his strength. His legs pawed the floor for traction, then pushed off a chair, tipping it over with a crash.

"Whoa, whoa, big man," Cook said, his voice strained by effort, not anger. "Dumb thing to say. Didn't mean anything. Miss Eliza's a fine woman."

Suddenly, Fraser was exhausted. He didn't want to fight. He didn't want to think. He didn't want to remember where he was or what he knew. He went limp, then rolled off the bed.

"You need some sleep, son," Cook said. Fraser lay down on his own bed with a whump.

"Rise and shine." Cook put some melody into the greeting. He had waited as long as he could, but it was noon. He had to get Fraser sobered up, fed, cleaned, and halfway making sense by four o'clock, when he was supposed to meet Townsend. That meeting could be dangerous. Those Sons of Liberty were bound to be close by. Fraser had to cover some ground before he'd be fit to deal with Barstow's thugs.

With cajoling, threats, sympathy, and ridicule, Cook stirred Fraser to a mostly functional condition. When Fraser's hands began to shake, Cook took over shaving him, leaning over from behind so the strokes would be like the ones he used to shave himself. By the end of an hour, Cook was unwrapping two large sandwiches he had purchased at a nearby shop. He set one before Fraser. Fraser ate only the bread and drank glass after glass of water. Cook decided that was good enough, under the circumstances.

Fraser scowled. "Speed, that stuff before—"

"We need to stay on the problem before us. Tell me about your old ladies' party. And about what you're going to do with Townsend."

"Right." Fraser bit off some bread and chewed it deliberately. He swallowed with equal care. He sipped water and cleared his throat.

When he finished relating his conversations with the old ladies, he said that he considered two points to be established. First, General Grant definitely was a target of the conspiracy, though they couldn't be sure how the conspirators intended. They might have meant to kill him but gave up when he left Washington. Or perhaps one of them—O'Laughlen or even John Surratt—followed him on his train and meant to kill him there but lost heart.

"Don't see how that was what Mrs. Surratt told John Bingham," Cook said. "Trying to kill Grant wasn't any secret; Bingham accused O'Laughlen of it during the trial. And news of a failed attempt to kill Grant wouldn't have hurt the republic. Would've made Grant more popular."

"I agree," Fraser said. "It also would make Mrs. Surratt and her friends more guilty. In fact, it might even point to her own darling boy, John." After a pause, Fraser started again. "I also think the cotton traders, beginning with Julius Spencer and Samuel Barstow, were behind Booth. They must have planned to move a mountain of cotton to Northern and English mills as soon as Lafayette Foster became president. They funded Booth. They must have given him his plans."

"Mrs. Surratt could have told Mr. Bingham about Julius Spencer," Cook said. "He was kin to Lafayette Foster, the man that Spencer and Barstow were trying to make the next president. She could have heard from Booth or her son about that Foster business, about Spencer backing Booth. Both of them passed through New York, probably met with Spencer. And Bingham thought this threatened the republic because those cotton men knew who they were acting for. It could've been any number of Democrats, even General McClellan."

"Wait a minute. By disclosing this secret to Mr. Bingham," Fraser said, "wasn't Mrs. Surratt taking the chance that he would prosecute all of those Northerners who were supporting the South?"

"That's exactly it. Don't you see?" Cook grew more animated. "That's what she wanted. Mr. Bingham was a real firebrand. Townsend called him a zealot. You've read the transcript. Every day of the trial, he was putting Jefferson Davis at the center of the conspiracy. Mr. Bingham's the one you'd expect to be most enraged that Northerners like Spencer were involved in killing the president. In the moment of victory, she wanted to set the victors to tearing at each other's throats. She was aiming to be like Samson pulling the temple down on herself and on her enemies, too."

"But Mr. Bingham didn't fall for it." Fraser took a bit of bread.

"You know," Cook started, "something started eating at me after you left Chestertown and while I was coming over here. We've put a whole lot of stock in what Bingham said while he was dying, about what happened thirty-five years before then. Well, what if he got it scrambled up when he talked to you? Maybe it was Stanton who told *him* something about Mrs. Surratt. Maybe Lewis Paine told him something about John Surratt. The man may have been delirious, or just not remembering too good, being old and sick and all."

"I was there," Fraser said. "He was in his right mind."

"I figured you'd say that. What if he was just wrong back in 1865? What if he made the wrong decision? What if it made no difference to the republic whether he revealed or didn't reveal what Mary Surratt told him? The man wasn't perfect, we know that. He put those perjured witnesses on the stand. We could be running around risking our necks for nothing."

"I don't think so." Fraser took a second. "Look, I've had those thoughts, too. And if you want out of this thing, I understand. But I know the man he was and I know what he said."

Cook nodded his head. "Okay, okay, at least we know what you want from the meeting with Townsend."

"What?"

"Proof. Something I can write in the *Ohio Eagle* that will get the attention of everyone in America."

"You can write what we know. We've learned a lot. And we've got Barstow's memorandum book—well, we had it."

"Sure, I can write it, but I can't say where I found it all out. That I stole Barstow's book? He'll deny it was his, and now it's gone, a pile of ash somewhere. That you interviewed three old ladies? Talking to you at a party's one thing, but that Chandler woman's not looking to remind everyone that she loved John Wilkes Booth. Mrs. Foster? If she knows what we're up to, she'll never say anything to dirty her husband's memory. The world will think I'm as crazy as the ones who say it was the Pope. No, thank you. You need to get us some proof."

Fraser made no answer. He looked lost in his own thoughts. Cook kept on. "And another thing. We can tie Booth to Barstow and Spencer. Fine. But we're still weak on who was behind them. You don't think a couple of cotton hustlers were really the root of this whole thing, do you? In 1865, Barstow wasn't any tycoon. He was a young officer in a losing army. Spencer was a cotton man at a time when the cotton business was nearly dead. Those weren't men with big money or the connections to make this all happen. No, sir, there was someone back of them. So for both of those things—for proof, and for who was back of Barstow and Spencer—that's what we need Townsend for. And he's just the ticket for both."

"Or maybe he's my ticket out of this world."

"That's why we need to plan out how this thing's going to work. Let's talk about Townsend."

"That's another thing. It was only for a second, but I could swear it was him at that party last night. How could he have gotten there?"

"I've got no idea," Cook said, "but I think I know where Townsend's going to take you this afternoon." He had visited the pricier stables in the city's central district, asking about the fine pair of matched bays that pulled Townsend's carriage. Cook had claimed that his boss wanted to purchase the horses. It wasn't long before he found a stableman who knew and admired that team. Cook traced them to a house on the far side of the White House, on I Street past Seventeenth. The house, Cook reported, was owned by James "Pete" Longstreet, Robert E. Lee's corps commander.

"Well, I'll be," Fraser said. "After all those denials, every one of them saying the Confederacy had nothing to do with the killing of President Lincoln. And where does this trail lead to but to Longstreet, who sat at the top of the Southern army."

"Sure, but why," Cook asked for what felt like the hundredth time, "did Bingham think that news about Spencer and Barstow would threaten the nation? The way I see it, that man Stanton's at the center of it. He's the one who Bingham goes to after Mrs. Surratt makes her confession, and he's the one who persuades Bingham to keep it a secret. Maybe Stanton did it to keep himself in office, like Townsend said."

Fraser frowned. "Why would we believe what Townsend said? Also, that would mean Stanton either hoodwinked Mr. Bingham into keeping mum or Mr. Bingham was in on it. He was too smart to be hoodwinked and too honest to cover something up for Stanton."

"So," Cook said, "I've been trying this one out. Say it was to preserve the peace by protecting someone, someone like Robert E. Lee. Lee's no hero in my eyes. The man slaughtered a few hundred thousand men to preserve slavery, but he did surrender all his troops when he finally got beat for real and true. He didn't take to the hills and keep the war going on and on, didn't keep on solely to bleed the North to death. Maybe Bingham and Stanton were afraid that something that implicated Lee would undermine the peace. Lee was like a god to Southerners. Still is."

Fraser shook his head. "You talked me out of that one months ago. Mr. Bingham was giving speeches that summer that Jefferson Davis planned the whole thing. He wasn't afraid to accuse the rebels of killing Lincoln."

Cook made a face. "Another thing. This connection between Townsend and Longstreet? I went up to the library at Howard University to check out Longstreet. After the war, he turned into a big Republican. He supported Reconstruction in the South. Still is a Republican. He's Commissioner of Railroads now, in the McKinley Administration. Because of that, even though he should be a hero to Southerners—got all shot up, led armies all over and into Pennsylvania—his name's poison down there. Some even blame him for losing the war."

"Okay," Fraser said. "So?"

"So why's Longstreet working with Townsend? We know Townsend's been shilling for Sam Barstow and the Sons of Liberty. Longstreet and Barstow were in the same army for four years, fighting for the noble cause of preserving slavery, but times've changed. They've been on opposite sides ever since the war. Doesn't fit."

"I'm getting confused."

"I know. It's just the longer we work on this thing, the less anything is the way it seems. I'm starting to appreciate one thing." Cook pointed his finger at Fraser. "They should still be worried about us. They still got lots to hide. After all, we know they're killers. They beat you up once, threatened you once, and tried to kill you twice. And they're not quite sure how much we know. And we've still got the frog book."

Fraser smiled and patted his pocket. "So how do we use it?"

"I'm not sure yet, but hang on to it. Now, let's think about this Townsend thing."

Chapter 27

Fraser arrived in the hotel lobby ten minutes late, just as he and Cook planned it. Townsend sat near the door, patiently looking at a newspaper.

"Doctor," he called out, "good evening. Our carriage is at the curb." In a quieter voice, he added, "Perhaps your colored friend could join us, which would save him the trouble of following us, and would save us the trouble of bringing him along."

"I don't know what you mean," Fraser said.

"My dear doctor, our business will go more smoothly if we are candid with each other. I come in peace."

"I have no colored friend in the vicinity to invite along."

Townsend shook his head. "Hairsplitting is a poor way to begin. Nevertheless, come along. We'll find him soon enough."

Sunshine poured from the sky on a brilliant afternoon. Cook held the reins of a gig in front of the red brick station of the Baltimore & Potomac Railroad. To elude the Sons of Liberty, he had ducked through alleys and back streets to the stable where he rented the gig.

He had an unobstructed view up Sixth Street to the squared-off, five-story National Hotel. The carriage with matched bays stood at the curb. Fraser, shading his eyes, was following Townsend into the rear seat. Cook couldn't see the driver.

With traffic thin, Cook intended to hang about a half-block behind them. He was barely past the hotel when a carriage swung in front of him, then slowed down. Looking to pull around it, Cook found another on his left. A large man in the right-hand seat smiled at him. He lifted his hat and pointed to the curb, evidently instructing Cook to stop. Sons of Liberty, Cook muttered.

Cook whipped his horse and hauled it to the right. Whacking the horse's rump again, he got it up the curb despite a whinny of protest and a high bounce off the carriage seat. Tree branches swiped at his face. Cook shouted to pedestrians to clear away. Two stumbled in their rush to escape the carriage and sprawled on the ground. The horse, thoroughly frightened, picked up his pace as Cook yanked him back into the street, banging off the curb with a second crash. After pausing in confusion over Cook's swerving path, the two other carriages pursued him at speed.

Pulling hard on the reins, Cook turned left onto E Street. The gig leaned heavily on its two outer wheels, then righted itself as the horse careened down the street. Cook had no idea where the carriage with Fraser and Townsend had gone. He couldn't worry about them.

Though Cook's gig had only one horse while pairs hauled the pursuing carriages, his rig was lighter and his horse more than willing. He flew through the first three intersections with a combination of timing and luck. From the clatter and shouts behind him, he knew his pursuers were not so fortunate. His luck held at the next one also.

Cook thought he might pull away, but then a streetcar stopped in the middle of the intersection with Tenth Street, discharging and taking on riders. Worse, a motor car idled there, belching black smoke. Several horses pulling nearby carriages looked jittery. From half a block away, Cook could see the intersection promised only collisions and mayhem. He scanned the sidewalks. Too narrow. An alley opened to the right. He yanked on the reins to slow the horse, then leapt out before the gig came to a full stop.

Cook ran down the alley and around a shabby building. He ducked into a doorway that stood steps down from a crossing with another alley. He crouched there, trying to control his breathing and listening for Barstow's men. He fingered the revolver in his jacket pocket. The knife lodged in his boot would be the better weapon, silent in its deployment. But if he faced all four, he would have to use the gun. They would come after him. Someone was bound to have seen him run down the alley.

Little street noise penetrated to Cook's hiding place. He heard no voices. Then, there it was. A step at the alley's entrance. Maybe another. And another. Cook shifted his weight. He could try to slip down the alley to the east, away from the building, but he would have to cross twenty feet of open ground. The risk was too great. Carefully, Cook tried the knob on the door into the building. It gave to his pressure. He pushed the door in.

He stood in a warehouse, a jumble of wooden tables and overstuffed chairs, wooden shelving tipped at odd angles. The air was damp. A single bulb dangled from the ceiling near the entrance stairs. It cast a weak light, more shadows than illumination. Cook could search out a place to hide within this wreck of a building, a spot where no one could sneak up on him from behind, where he could at least be sure to defend himself. That would mean another fight. Barstow's men didn't discourage easily.

Or he could work his way to another exit from the warehouse and hurry over to where he thought Townsend and Fraser were going. He had to follow Fraser.

Cook reached a staircase at the building's front and crept up it. Halfway up, he saw a glint of light back on the lower level. It was the sort of flash that would come from opening the alley door. If he kept them behind him, he might get out in one piece.

He took his bearings on the first-floor landing. Another pale bulb pushed thin streaks of light into the gloom. He strained his ears but heard only blood pounding in them. Wait. That was a voice, at the back. Maybe it was the building's caretaker. Barstow's boys wouldn't be talking. Cook looked longingly at the front door leading to the street. It was too obvious. They would post someone there, probably two men. He needed a side exit to a side passage. That, too, might be a trap. Emerging into another alley and then into the street, he would be a sitting duck. The roof was his best bet. From the roof he could cross to another building, maybe even another one next to it, then flee.

He continued to climb. The second floor was stuffed with more crates of paper records. It had to be a government warehouse. This much paper meant tax records, or maybe veteran pensions. The second level was only a half-floor. It opened out to a view of an old theater stage, which also was piled high with boxes and crates. Of course. It was Ford's Theatre. A cold wind passed through Cook's heart. He turned his head to the right. He could just make out a theater box overhanging the stage, where Booth shot Lincoln.

There was a noise from below. Lincoln's bad luck was no reason for Speed Cook to come to a bad end here. He started up the stairs again.

The third level presented more forests of forgotten records. The light seemed even thinner. He needed a way out. He felt his way down an aisle, stumbling over spilled papers. Overhead, he could make out a drop ladder up to attic space. That had to be it. The way out.

When he pulled the steps down, they neither squealed nor screeched. He sprang up them. At the top, the light was better. His spirit sagged. No way out. The ceiling was elevated well above the floor. The only exit points were skylights at the crest of a peaked roof. They were at least fifteen feet overhead, beyond his reach. There was nothing to stand on to get that high.

He ran down the drop stairs. Hearing steps from the level below, he leaned back into a side row. Two men passed under the light at the top of the stairs. One was the man in the carriage who had doffed his hat. Their movements were lithe, sure. When they reached the drop stairs, they began to ascend. If two were inside the building, then two were waiting outside, probably one at the front and one at the back. Cook still had to leave through another building. He could think of only one way to do that.

He moved to the front window at the left corner of the building. It had a six-inch ledge, plenty of room. He slowly lifted the window, climbed out, and pushed the window down behind him. There he met an unhappy sight. It was at least four feet to the corner of the theater. The roof of the adjacent building was a couple of feet higher than the ledge he stood on. Not easy, but he had no alternative. He gauged the distance for a few more seconds, then moved. He half-reached and half-jumped to the corner of the building, fingers desperately gripping the raised brick edge on each side of the corner. He used his momentum to swing his feet high up to the adjacent roof. For a moment, he hung horizontally in place, straining every muscle to lever his hips up on the roof and push his body weight after them. With a final heave, he was there.

The pitch of this roof was gentle. Kneeling, he could see that the closest window below him was open. Holding the edge of the roof, he lowered his legs through the window. When he entered, he confronted a young Negro boy who rose from a clerk's table, pen in hand and astonished look on his face. Cook grinned and held a finger to his lips. "Just passing through," he said in a low voice. "You have a fine day now."

Cook sped down two flights of stairs and reached the front door. He took a breath. He decided to turn left out the door, away from the theater, then hail a hack as soon as he reached the cross street.

He pulled the door and stepped through it. Big as life, square in front of him, stood a stout older gentleman.

"Mr. Barstow," Cook called out. When the man turned, the color drained from his face. Cook stepped next to him, his hand in his coat pocket pressing the muzzle of a revolver against Barstow's soft middle. "You and I are going for a walk." Cook nodded to the closest corner and nudged the man in that direction. He came along quietly.

"You," Barstow said in a voice that was surprisingly friendly, "are one acrobatic individual. You ought to be in the circus."

Chapter 28

As the matched bays pranced through Washington's leafy streets, Townsend became avuncular. For Fraser's benefit, he pointed out the homes of the prominent. He recalled the debutante party during the Civil War for young Blanche Butler, when her family's mansion on Fifteenth Street was festooned with thousands of white camellias. The fortress-like home of the Secretary of State, John Hay, loomed next to the equally monumental mansion of Henry Adams, scion of the Adamses of Massachusetts.

As Cook had predicted, the carriage pulled onto the gravel drive of a brick home at the corner of Seventeenth and Rhode Island Avenue, the home of General Longstreet. Tulip poplars, their leaves yellowing with the season, rose far above the three-story house. Townsend led the way up the front steps and opened the door. Confident that Cook was watching them from some concealed perch, Fraser followed.

Two burly men, somewhat past their best years, nearly filled the bright entrance hall. They advanced on Fraser.

"Doctor," Townsend said as he placed his hat on a table,

"these gentlemen will be glad to care for any weapons you may have."

Flanked by the intimidating reception committee, Fraser replied, "This is hardly the way to welcome a gentleman."

"Of course, you're right," Townsend said, "but it is entirely appropriate in these circumstances, Dr. Fraser—or is it McIntire?" Fraser made a small show of reluctance as he reached into his pocket and pulled out a revolver. He handed it over, relieved to be rid of it.

Fraser followed Townsend into a parlor. The shades were drawn against the sunlight. The keepers of his revolver remained outside.

Fraser's eyes adjusted slowly in the darkened room. A single electric lamp glowed at the far end. Five empty armchairs formed a conversational group. Following the lead of his host, Fraser sat. He selected the chair closest to the hallway.

"Who else is coming?" Fraser asked.

"Patience, my dear doctor. All will be revealed."

After a minute, Fraser asked again.

"Won't be long," Townsend said.

More minutes eased by. Fraser yawned, pleased that he could seem unconcerned even as anxiety ate at his insides. Something was amiss on Townsend's side. Was there a problem with Cook? Townsend stood and walked to the front hall. On his return, he nodded to Fraser but said nothing.

A door on the far side of the room burst open and Barstow stumbled in. "Sam," Townsend called out, standing up. Cook stepped through the same door, keeping a gun aimed at Barstow.

Two of the burlies from the hall piled into the room with guns drawn, but Barstow stopped them with an outstretched hand. "Afternoon, gents," Cook said in a strong voice. "Sorry to be late, but your friend here threw me off schedule. If you make one move toward me, I will shoot this nigger-hating son of a bitch."

"Go on," Barstow said to his men. "Get out." They backed out slowly.

With the gun, Cook waved Barstow into a chair next to Townsend. "Mr. Barstow," he said, "you've been treating Dr. Fraser very poorly, when all he has done is exercise his American right to ask questions. However, he is a large-minded man, and more interested in the answers to his questions than in repaying your bad manners. So why don't you start telling us what this soiree's all about?" Cook sat across from Barstow and Townsend, who exchanged glances. "Now," Cook said, "would be an excellent time to start talking."

"Doctor," Barstow said to Fraser, "you've gone to a great deal of trouble, and caused a great deal of trouble, to get to this conversation. Mr. Townsend here has persuaded me that I have been following a poor policy, attempting to prevent you from learning that which you have no reason to know. He insists that a better policy is to tell you what you want to know and rely on your good sense to understand that no one else should. For now, and under the current circumstances . . ." Barstow paused meaningfully. "I've decided to follow Mr. Townsend's recommendation. We will shortly be joined by someone who, I hope, will persuade you of the folly of your effort."

Cook smiled slowly. "That's good, Sam, but just remember that even if you can't see the gun, it's pointed at you."

Townsend cleared his throat. "With your permission," he said to Cook, "I'll invite our guest?" Cook nodded.

Townsend walked to a door that led to the rear of the house. After a moment, an old man limped through it. Sporting extravagant white side whiskers, he leaned heavily on a cane of dark wood. His right arm hung limply. His cheeks had a translucent quality, revealing an inner terrain of blue blood vessels. He sat with elaborate care. Grunting with relief as he leaned back, he looked a greeting at each man in turn.

"General Longstreet," Fraser said, happy to demonstrate his knowledge of the man's identity.

Longstreet placed his good hand on top of the cane before him and answered in a hoarse whisper. "I know who you are, and I propose to proceed directly to business. Is that agreeable?" Pausing for only a second, he began again. "I'm informed that you have contrived an interest in the activities and connections of John Wilkes Booth. That's so?"

"Yes, sir."

"Major Barstow's asked me to speak with you, with both of you." He nodded to Cook. "Though long in the habit of distrusting Major Barstow, I have agreed, for my own reasons, to his request."

Townsend interrupted in a loud voice. "Perhaps I should provide some preface. I have told both of these gentlemen"—he indicated Longstreet and Barstow—"about John Bingham's statement on his deathbed, which you shared with me in the spring, including his statements about Mrs. Surratt's confession. So they know why you're interested in this subject. Of course, I cannot know exactly what Mrs. Surratt told Mr. Bingham, but I have a fair idea of what Mr. Bingham might have concluded from what she said. And I have a fair idea of what you have been able to unearth. You've been most resourceful. That's why I proposed to Major Barstow and General Longstreet that we arrange this conversation."

He nodded to Longstreet, who made to speak. Instead, the old man coughed lightly. He coughed again, then erupted in a hacking paroxysm that turned his face bright red. He spat into a large handkerchief produced from a jacket pocket. As the flush faded from his cheeks, he jammed the linen back in his pocket.

"I never met that young fool Booth, but I can tell you certain things that may put your minds at ease about the current state

of our republic. Or perhaps not. That will be up to you."
Longstreet moved his gaze slowly from Fraser to Cook and
back. "But I'm one of the few left who can tell you much of
anything. There's always Major Barstow, of course, but I've
never known him to tell the truth. Townsend describes you as
men of sense, so I assume you wouldn't accept his word, or
Townsend's, about anything."

"General," Fraser broke in, "we know that Booth had money
from the Confederacy, and was actively working with agents of
the Confederacy, but we think more were involved—"

Longstreet had reached down next to his chair with his good
hand and lifted a shiny ear trumpet to his left ear. After a few
moments, he dropped the device in his lap and raised a restraining hand. "I will do this my way," he said in his urgent, raspy
whisper, "or not at all. You can ask questions when I'm done. I
may answer them. Or you're welcome to leave and meet whatever fate Major Barstow might have in mind for you."

Cook smiled with some malice. "Or the major may meet the
fate we have in mind for him."

"That may be," General Longstreet said quietly, "but the
major, among his other qualities, is undeniably persistent. That
is a quality you should respect."

Fraser leaned forward to cut off the exchange. "We'll listen,
General, then we'll decide what to do," he said.

"Probably ought to start near the end of 1864," the old man
said. "By then, we knew—those of us in the army knew—that
we were going to lose the war. If George McClellan had been
elected president in November, an honorable peace between
two American nations was possible. But that hope died with
Lincoln's reelection. He wasn't going to end the war that way."

Longstreet started coughing. Again, the coughing built in intensity until he appeared ready to burst. With a long, unsteady
breath, he regained his composure.

In the silence, Cook asked, "What you mean is, McClellan would have agreed to one country with slavery forever?"

Longstreet looked over at him. "Yes, I suppose that was the idea. My service to my country during the war was also service to slavery. I have tried to atone for that ever since, and God will judge whether I have. That atonement, I fear, is the principal reason why I am increasingly denounced by my countrymen for most of the defeats suffered by the Confederacy."

After the 1864 election, the old man continued, the Confederates contrived ever more desperate plans. One group proposed tunneling under the end of the White House that held Lincoln's office and blowing it up. "Lunatics," Longstreet said. "Pure lunatics."

Booth and others worked on the equally fanciful plan to kidnap Lincoln and hold him hostage, perhaps trade him for peace, or at least for Confederate prisoners of war who could rejoin the army and restore Southern military fortunes. The times, Longstreet repeated several times, were desperate.

"You see," he went on. "The war changed wherever Sam Grant took over. He understood that he had to break our spirit, not just our armies. So he sent Sherman marching to the sea. He proved we couldn't protect our homes or our old people, or our wives or our children. And on the battlefield he showed us in the bloodiest way possible that we didn't have enough soldiers or bullets. I had loved Sam Grant like a brother since when we were at West Point together. He married my cousin, you know. But in war he was the very angel of death." Longstreet shook his head ruefully.

"We always had spies and agents. They were supposed to find out where the other side's armies were, where they were going, how many of them there were. Then, as our affairs grew more perilous, the spies proposed to win the war for us. They were going to mount an invasion from Canada, to free our soldiers in Northern prison camps and open a new battlefront in the north." Longstreet drew a long, uncertain breath. "It was crazy, every bit of it. One of the scarcest commodities during war is sense, and in an army that's losing, it's nowhere to be found.

"Major Barstow," Longstreet said with a nod to the silver-haired man across from him, "came forward in the final days of the Petersburg siege. Bitter days. The men were starving. General Lee had decided, and I agreed, to break the siege and run to North Carolina. There we could hook up with Joe Johnston and his army and fight Billy Sherman. We'd had enough of Sam Grant. Major Barstow laid out a plot. He proposed to lop off the Union command: Lincoln, Grant, Edwin Stanton, even Andy Johnson. The next president would be weak, he told us, and would have no real legitimacy.

"None of us," Longstreet breathed, "had ever heard of the man who was supposed to become president then. I still couldn't tell you his name. We knew that Billy Sherman would be the strongest man left standing, and some of us felt he had some sympathies with our side. He hated niggers the way only a northern man can. Major Barstow's plan involved bringing George McClellan back from Europe, making him president or grand high pooh-bah, and then everything would be peaches and cream. We'd make an honorable peace with the Copperhead Democrats of the North, one that would allow the Southern people to hold their heads high and live as they always had. He claimed this scheme had support all through the North— senators and congressmen, governors and mayors, bankers and railroad men. And cotton men."

Longstreet stared at Barstow. "Just crazy, all of it," he said. "But General Lee didn't object. I don't know that he thought about it very much. He was fighting a war, one that was going poorly, and that takes a right smart amount of energy and attention. But he didn't tell Barstow not to do it. Lee wanted to strike any blow against the enemy that he could. So Major Barstow went off to Richmond and presented his plan to President Davis. And with his customary genius, Jeff Davis thought it was a capital idea."

After another coughing jag, Longstreet started again. "You gentlemen know how this ends. Major Barstow sent that pretty-boy actor to do the job with the damnedest bunch of defectives that's ever been collected in one place. No one had the gumption even to raise a hand against Sam Grant. I hear you've talked to Julia, his widow, about that, and so have I. They took one look at Sam and changed their minds, which was pretty smart, since Sam would have ate them for breakfast. The man they sent after Johnson ran away, too, and the one they sent after Stanton was so dumb he cut up Seward instead, the wrong damned man!" Longstreet allowed himself a rueful smile.

"Why, with Lincoln gone, Seward would have been a pushover for peace. Stanton was the strong man. But that idiot carves up Seward, most of his family, but doesn't even manage to kill him! It was fools as far as the eye could see. But one of them kept his head and did his job, and that was the pretty-boy actor. The only thing done right in that whole operation was to make sure he didn't live to tell who sent him."

"Also," Cook said in a flat tone, "the part about killing President Lincoln."

"Yes, sir," Longstreet nodded. "That, too." He shrugged with his good shoulder. "Of course, I've always assumed that the confusion of the assassination allowed Major Barstow to complete a few more cotton and tobacco deals with his Northern friends. Just to ease himself back into peacetime." Barstow did not react to Longstreet's remark.

Fraser took care to speak in a loud voice so Longstreet could hear him. "If you thought Barstow's plan was so crazy, why didn't you try to stop him?"

Longstreet gazed at him, then cleared his throat violently.

"Abe Lincoln was a soldier, just like I was and just like even Barstow here. You see what the war did to me." He gestured at his useless right arm. "Soldiers get killed, ruined. Townsend says your daddy paid his price, too. We knew what war meant. More than half a million died, at least that many went home less than whole. Do you have any idea how many men I ordered to their deaths? Or how many were killed by my soldiers on my orders? At the end of the war, one more killing could hardly get my attention. Was Abe Lincoln's life worth more than any one of the boys who fought for me? Or your father's?"

After another silence, Fraser asked, "How many people know this secret?"

"Fewer every year," Longstreet whispered. "Other than you, Townsend here's the only one figured it out on his own. Which is pretty damned remarkable. Doesn't actually seem that hard to figure out. It's like the whole country decided not to notice something sitting right in the middle of the road."

Cook shook his head. "Don't count on it being a secret much longer. We're going to tell this story when we get out of here. The world needs to know the evil you people did."

Longstreet shook his head and scratched his abundant side whiskers with his good hand. He sighed.

"You maybe should think about that," Barstow said. "First off, we'll all deny it just like we have for thirty-five years. That's worked pretty good so far. In fact, we'll wonder how you ever came up with such outlandish ideas. Second, you're late, extremely late, with this news."

"It's never too late for the truth," Cook said.

Barstow smiled. "I disagree. You'll be one more crank with a new theory. You'll never dislodge the story of John Wilkes Booth as the sole author of the conspiracy to kill Lincoln. No one wants to believe anything else."

"But it's not true," Fraser said.

"Doctor." Barstow turned to face him. "I thought you'd be smarter than that." Returning his gaze to Cook, he said, "Third, you're a black man. How could you possibly know such a thing? And you," Barstow faced Fraser, "are a well-meaning country doctor who has fallen under the spell of John Wilkes Booth's illegitimate spawn."

Fraser couldn't conceal his anger. "You wouldn't dare make such an accusation."

Barstow smiled. "We wouldn't? But it's even true. Don't you think the newspapers of Mr. Hearst and Mr. Pulitzer would find that considerably more interesting than some crackpot theory about an assassination that was solved two generations ago and is settled in the pages of history? Now, Booth's bastard child—*that* would sell newspapers!"

They fell silent when Longstreet held up his good hand. He began again. "Those are Major Barstow's reasons. And to his credit, he hasn't yet presented reasons that would involve pain and injury to you. He can favor very crude methods. As you say, that sort of tactic hasn't worked so far with you gentlemen, but Major Barstow is a determined individual who, it should be clear, is not limited by good sense and judgment."

Longstreet paused. "I suspect that all of his reasons are odious to you. But allow me to offer one that should not be. It's the one that worked with Mr. Townsend."

Townsend inclined his head in acknowledgment.

"John Bingham wouldn't want you to reveal these matters. Old Bingham took his secret to the grave with him because he thought that was the best thing. He was glad to accuse Jeff Davis of the crime—even without the evidence to prove it. But when he heard the true story, that Northerners also were behind the killing of Abe Lincoln, he knew it would threaten the Union and the peace. And he knew that nothing was going to bring Abe Lincoln back. That's why I've been silent these past thirty-five years. Through all those years I've been trying to reconcile North and South so we can rebuild a great nation. And that's why you, too, should remain silent. Because Bingham was right."

After only a moment, Longstreet hauled himself up from his chair. He made his painful way to the door that led to the rear of the house. He left the ear trumpet in the chair.

"What kind of a writer are you?" Cook said to Townsend. "You learn the truth and then hide it, let the culprits get away clean? Instead, you write a bunch of nonsense that you know isn't true. Which side are you on?"

"Bingham's side."

Barstow stood abruptly. "My men will not molest you on your return to your hotel, or on your departure from this city. But, please, do not doubt that the Sons of Liberty will be watching you, and that we're prepared to do what's necessary to preserve the integrity of history."

"On the subject of what you might be prepared to do," Fraser said, not rising from his chair, "you should understand that we are in possession of a small leather book with a fetching image of a frog on its first page. You know what I am describing?"

"Go on," Barstow said quietly.

"That book, and our interpretation of it, are in a safe place. A very safe place. And it will reside there unless something happens to one of us." He pointed at Cook and then at himself. "In that event, well, that frog book would immediately be released to the public, along with everything we know about it. You don't want that to happen, Mr. Barstow."

"I don't know what you're on about," the older man said, "and I don't think you do, either."

"I'm on about the boss frog of New York City and his good friends."

"You can't mean it!" Cook was pacing across the small hotel room, covering it in three strides and turning back.

Fraser sat in the lone straight-back chair. He shook his head. "I can. Longstreet made sense. Even Barstow made sense. No one's going to believe us. They'll all deny it. We don't have any hard proof, not even the memorandum book anymore, not to mention the frog book being a wreck. Thank God we can use it as a bluff. What would it gain us to make accusations we can't back up?"

"It's the truth!"

"Keep your voice down. We'll get thrown out of the hotel."

"That'd be a good start. Then we ought to burn this place down." Cook stalked to the window and stood with his hands on his hips. "I knew it. I knew you didn't have the gizzard to see this all the way through. Well, I do."

"Speed, you do what you think is best, but you need to consider what Longstreet said. He's right about what Mr. Bingham wanted. Think about the sacrifice he made. Mrs. Surratt gave him the evidence to prove he'd been right all along, that the Confederacy had planned the assassination, but he suppressed that evidence his whole life. Lots of people conceal facts that prove them wrong. Not many conceal facts that prove them right."

"I've had it up to here with the saintly Mr. Bingham. He did what he thought was right. Fine. This is thirty-five years later. We have to make up our own minds." He pointed at Fraser. "I know what's making you turn tail and run. It's what Barstow said."

"I haven't backed down from Barstow and his men."

"Not that part. I mean the part about your lady friend. You're going to conceal the biggest crime in our history just so you can sweeten up that woman, so you keep her secret. I've got news for you—there's lots of women out there."

Fraser ran a hand through his hair. "I still think Longstreet's right. We can't go ahead with this. Anyway, I can't."

"I can."

Chapter 29

When a cold October wind whipped through the plaza in front of the Harrison County Courthouse, several thousand people shivered as one. It was eighteen months since the last such gathering, when John Bingham died. It seemed a lifetime ago. The old gentleman had brought out this crowd as well, or at least his memory had. This time Mr. Bingham was present only as a bronze likeness. Another endless ceremony dulled the crowd's vitality. This one was to dedicate his statue, which towered in front of the courthouse.

It was Fraser's second time in Cadiz since the meeting with General Longstreet. He came back during the winter to pack up his things and arrange to sell his remaining property. In three short weeks he had helped four Cadiz babies into the world, starting with the Gable family. He greeted each birth with unmixed joy, one more sign that his soul had grown lighter. Eliza did that. She changed a great deal more for him. He would be a country doctor no more.

On the dais, Senator Spriggs was working through some

standard pieties about Mr. Bingham. He assured the crowd that Bingham would be a household word long after each in the audience had ceased to be, and after what they had done had crumbled and decayed. After spending half a year chasing Mr. Bingham's secret, Fraser had no confidence in history's memory. Would anyone remember Mr. Bingham one hundred years from now? Would what they remembered be even remotely true?

Fraser took Eliza's gloved hand and gave it a small squeeze. She was the prize from the race that he and Cook had run. She had taken persuading to marry, but she wanted to be persuaded. Marrying her meant he would leave Cadiz. She was too bold a bloom for Harrison County, and Fraser found that New York suited him. There he could improve his medical knowledge and skills, drinking in the advances of new research. And Eliza's theater world remained magical to him. Her generous skirt concealed her current condition, only three months along, and he hoped to be luckier this time. Poor Ginny. He and Eliza laid flowers on her grave that morning. He felt sad about Ginny, but also grateful to her. She had brought him joy. Now he was blessed with a second chance at love, one he could not claim to deserve, but he intended to make the most of it.

Cadiz was doing itself proud for this ceremony. The speakers numbered not only a United States senator, but also a Japanese diplomat and now, after the singing of the hymn, Reverend Wolf stepped forward. The pastor of the A.M.E. church proudly recited the achievements of Harrison County's colored people. They had acquired property, founded schools, started farms and businesses. They were, he said, the best testament to Mr. Bingham's wisdom in fighting for their rights. His voice rising, he proclaimed that they had redeemed the man's sacrifice.

When the program was over, many seemed reluctant to leave. The town band continued to play, showing an unfortunate enthusiasm for the marches of Mr. Sousa. Men and women admired the Bingham statue, exclaimed over the current harvest, and expressed hopes that the new president, young Roosevelt, would be equal to the task of succeeding McKinley, shot down by an assassin only a month before. At least there was no mystery about that assassination.

Fraser and Eliza greeted his old friends, asked about their lives and told about life in New York. After some time, Fraser spied a large figure some distance away. He excused himself.

"Speed!" he called out.

"Dr. Fraser."

"I hoped to see you." Fraser stretched out his hand. When Cook took it, Fraser used a two-handed grip.

"I came to pay my respects." Cook nodded at the statute.

Fraser grinned, releasing his friend. "I'm glad you did. Can we talk?" They fell into step and circled the crowd. "You printed it after all. I saw the edition you put out about the assassination."

"Ah," Cook said, "fat lot of good it did. We ran off our usual thousand copies, and another thousand for posterity. I mailed it to every American newspaper I could find an address for. Do you think even one of them picked it up? Even one? They probably all laughed themselves sick over the gullibility of that poor colored man down in Steubenville, he must be crazy stupid. More evidence of the power of the lie."

"But you did it. You were true to yourself."

"I also mailed that edition to every library I could think of, hoping they'll save it, maybe the time will come, maybe fifty years from now, maybe a hundred, when someone will look back at that and say, damn, that man was on to something." After a second, he looked over at Fraser. "Is Mrs. Fraser angry about it?"

"I tried to explain it to her, but I can't say she sees your point of view. Not entirely."

"How about Dr. Fraser, my investor?"

"I think I know why you did it. Maybe I would have, too, in your place. But I've got to say I'm just as glad no one else picked it up. I'm sorry I couldn't join you in writing it."

"You're not the first man's done the wrong thing for a woman. But it shouldn't matter that you wouldn't write it with me. *I* wrote it, wrote it all up just so. I shouldn't need a white man to say what I wrote is all right."

After a few more strides, Fraser said, "The articles you're doing on Jim Crow have been terrific. Are you getting any re-action—any threats?"

Cook stopped and glared at Fraser. "Threats? Threats are my breakfast. It's the rocks through the windows that make me jumpy. You tell me, how can I live in this country, where I'm supposed to sit down and shut up, just because I'm colored?" He resumed walking. Cook fell into that passionate form of declamation that Fraser had come to know during their jour-ney together. America was getting worse, Cook said. Segrega-tion was spreading, lynchings every week. Freedom from slavery wasn't enough. Equality was what colored people needed, and they were getting less of it, not more. Colored people, he said, had no future here. They needed to go to Africa, where they could live their lives proud and hold their heads up high. When they were chasing Mr. Bingham's secret, Cook couldn't go to places where Fraser went, do things that Fraser did. Cook didn't know that he could take that anymore.

They kept walking, now on their third orbit of the plaza.

"It didn't feel right," Cook said, "using your money to print all that about Miss Eliza's daddy."

"I knew what you were going to do. And I think I wanted you to try. You were entitled to that." Fraser stopped and smiled. "You know, I've trusted my life to one man in my life, and that man took care of me."

Cook shook his head. "You always were the sentimental one. So now I'm supposed to say the same thing about you?"

Fraser grinned and put his arm around Cook's shoulder. "Come on, now. You feeling brave enough to say hello to my wife?"

Author's Note

The opening scene in this novel—the deathbed statement of John Bingham about the mysterious midtrial disclosure of Mrs. Mary Surratt—is drawn from *Bingham of the Hills,* a largely unread 1989 biography of Bingham by Erving E. Beauregard. Beauregard describes the scene in a single paragraph and attributes it to a family story related to him by the grandson of Bingham's physician. I came upon the passage while researching a book about the Andrew Johnson impeachment trial (*Impeached*); it stuck in my mind for several years and would not be dislodged. I read widely about the Booth conspiracy and became dissatisfied with the standard portrayal of Booth as the crazed, vindictive assassin. The conspiracy was too big to fit in that frame. Because the provenance for Bingham's deathbed scene is by no means sturdy, and because Bingham never disclosed what Mrs. Surratt told him, a fictional treatment allowed me the freedom to explore the Booth conspiracy in the speculative fashion warranted by the known facts.

The character of Jamie Fraser is inspired by the physician who attended John Bingham but is an entirely fictional charac-

256 David O. Stewart

ter. Speed Cook also is inspired by an actual person: Moses Fleetwood Walker, who came from Steubenville, Ohio, and was the last black man to play in the big leagues until Jackie Robinson officially broke the color barrier. More about Walker is in David Zang's book, *Fleet Walker's Divided Heart: The Life of Baseball's First Black Major Leaguer.* The various Surratts and Booths portrayed in the book, along with Bessie Hale and the widows of Lafayette Foster and Ulysses Grant, all were alive in 1900, when Cook and Fraser set off to unravel the secrets of the Booth conspiracy—all, that is, but the fetching Eliza, John Wilkes Booth's illegitimate daughter. Although it is entirely plausible that Booth sired a child out of wedlock, and although a courtesan named Nelly Starr did attempt to kill herself after the Lincoln assassination, Eliza is an entirely fictional character. Also, Lafayette Foster *was* second in line for the presidency in April 1865, a fact that seems to have interested virtually no one over the years. Until now, that is.

I am grateful to a number of people for helping this novel along, beginning with my extraordinary agent, Will Lippincott, who supported me on this departure from my previously beaten path. I am most fortunate that John Scognamiglio, my editor at Kensington, saw some potential in this book and has been an insightful reader. I also thank the early readers who have helped improve all of my books, and did so again: Solveig Eggerz, Joye Shepperd, Catherine Flanagan, Phil Harvey, Robert Gibson, Frank Joseph, Kathy Lorr, Leslie Rollins, Susan Clark, Tom Glenn, Alice Leaderman, and Linda Morefield.

I have heard it said that when a man writes a book, his principal purpose is usually to impress some woman. For me, it's always the same woman—my wife, Nancy. She says she likes this one. I hope so.

Please turn the page for a very special Q&A
with David Stewart!

Why did you want to write about one of the worst crimes in American history, the assassination of Abraham Lincoln?

That's exactly the reason. The assassination denied America the leadership of its greatest president at the beginning of perhaps his greatest challenge—rebuilding a nation torn apart by civil war and somehow integrating the freed slaves into American life. And there are still so many unanswered questions about the crime.

What are those unanswered questions?

This was not just a lone gunman, some crazed lunatic. Booth had assembled a team of assassins, though not all were terribly impressive human beings. They targeted anywhere from three to five top officials of the Union government—not just President Lincoln, but also his vice president, his Secretary of State, and very likely his Secretary of War and the General-in-Chief of the Union Army. As the lead character in the novel realizes, it was not an assassination so much as an attempted coup d'état. Could this one unemployed actor plan all of that by himself? Hard to imagine.

Who was John Bingham?

Bingham was the lead prosecutor of the Booth conspirators in the summer of 1865, and as a congressman went on to write the guarantees of "due process" and "equal protection" in the Fourteenth Amendment. On his deathbed in 1900, Bingham confided to his doctor that Mrs. Mary Surratt—one of the Booth conspirators who was hanged—had told him a secret that could destroy the republic. The secret, he said, would die with him, and so it did. This book tries to imagine the terrible secret that Mr. Bingham took to his grave.

What evidence leads you to conclude that the Booth conspiracy was wider than generally thought?

Really, five broad points:

It was a giant conspiracy that targeted the top leaders in the North; as noted above, more of a coup d'état than an assassination. Not the plan of a lone crackpot.

Booth and several of his coconspirators lived without resources for many months before the assassination; someone was paying for them. ("Follow the money!")

Booth and John Surratt both were agents of the Confederate secret service.

Booth's escape route led him repeatedly to Confederate spies as he successfully evaded thousands of Union soldiers who were searching for him; not something a lone evil genius could have achieved.

Mr. Bingham's deathbed statement: What else could he have learned from Mary Surratt that would have threatened to destroy the republic?

Your two lead characters are very different—a white doctor from small-town Ohio and an African-American ex-ballplayer. How could they become friends in America in 1900?

That relationship was one of the challenging elements of the writing process, and the short answer is that it's a very rocky partnership—as you would expect. They are united in their need to find out the truth about the Lincoln assassination, but race and experience keep pushing them apart. America was a very racist place in 1900; the Jim Crow segregation laws were spreading, and it was fascinating and infuriating to imagine the feelings of an educated and sophisticated African-American like Speed Cook. The bond between the two men becomes real and powerful through the story, but I felt that a racial divide would always be there. And so it is, right to the end.

One of your main characters, Speed Cook, is an African-American crusader for racial justice who was the last man of his race to be driven out of professional baseball. Did you just make him up?

Cook is an entirely fictional character, but he was inspired by a very real man, Moses Fleetwood ("Fleet") Walker, who came from Steubenville, Ohio. Walker was, in fact, the last African-American to play in the big leagues between 1888 and 1947, had attended Oberlin College and the University of Michigan, and was a fighter for the rights of black people. He wrote a remarkable pamphlet after the turn of the century arguing that black people should return to Africa because they would never be treated fairly in America. For a multi-talented man like Fleet Walker, being a black man in America in 1900 had to be a special form of torture.

Why move from writing non-fiction—you have had three successful books on American history—to a novel?

It was all about this particular story. I first read about Mr. Bingham's deathbed statements when I was researching my second book, *Impeached,* about the impeachment trial of President Andrew Johnson (Mr. Bingham was the lead prosecutor in that trial, too!). The account of Mr. Bingham's deathbed statement appears in a very obscure biography and has never been explored by anyone. I walked around with it in my head for three years, trying to figure out what I could do with it. I read as much as I could about the Lincoln assassination and finally decided that only a fictionalized account would allow me the freedom to explore what Mr. Bingham said and what it might have meant.

Why set the story in 1900, thirty-five years after the assassination, when the trail of the Booth conspirators would already have been quite cold?

The most obvious reason is that Mr. Bingham told no one about his secret until 1900 and I wanted to be faithful to that fact. There's a saying about historical fiction that you can make up a lot, but Abraham Lincoln has to be tall; that is, you should be faithful to facts when they're known. Also, sometimes an investigation can be more successful many years later, when passions have cooled; some people may be more likely to talk when they are facing the prospect of taking their secrets to the grave. Finally, I have always loved Josephine Tey's novel, *The Daughter of Time*, in which a twentieth-century detective attempts to investigate the strangling of the little princes in the Tower of London almost five hundred years earlier. I hoped to work some of that same magic with the Booth story.